GHOST HOUSE

This is only a dream, she told herself. *Please dear Lord make it a dream*!

She sank to her knees and began to cry in her terror. She wanted Gary.

Suddenly she felt strong arms around her. She bent her head to bury it in Gary's shoulder, trembling in the darkness.

A bright light caught her eyes just then, and she squinted to see one of the policemen standing behind it. "I'm all right," Melanie mumbled, edging closer to Gary.

Then she turned to look at Gary. There was no one there at all . . .

About the Author

CLARE McNALLY attended the Fashion Institute of Technology in New York City where she studied advertising and communications. She has worked on a children's wear magazine, freelanced as an advertising copywriter and edited a technical magazine. She has written two sequels to *Ghost House, Ghost House Revenge* and *Ghost Light* and has recently completed her fourth novel, *The Prey*. She lives on Long Island.

Ghost House

Clare McNally

CORGI BOOKS

GHOST HOUSE

A CORGI BOOK 0 552 11652 1

Originally published in Great Britain by Bantam Books Inc.

PRINTING HISTORY
Bantam Books edition published 1979
Corgi edition published 1980
Corgi edition reissued 1983

This book is set in 10/11 English Times

Corgi Books are published by
Transworld Publishers Ltd.,
Century House, 61–63 Uxbridge Road,
Ealing, London W5 5SA

Made and printed in Great Britain by
Hunt Barnard Printing Ltd., Aylesbury, Bucks

For Michael, for believing

Acknowledgements

Thanks to Mike and John Pastore, and July Althoff

Ghost House

Prologue

September 10, 1797

The execution was over.

The fires had died down, emitting now only snakes of gray smoke. Sparks of orange flashed sporadically from the bits of charred wood, lying in a soft mound that the salt wind of the bay would soon sweep away.

As appalling as it was, as unjust as it seemed, the scene had been repeated so often that the onlookers were only mildly affected by it. They had seen it before, the girl, screaming of her innocence. The priest, praying softly and not really caring what happened to the girl's soul.

And the executioner—his face a mask as he brought the torch down to her feet.

When it was over, the women gathered their children and the men set about returning to work. Soon, they would forget the scene. Soon, when they were busy with their daily tasks, no one would guess that they had cried so viciously for such young blood.

One man remained behind today. His tall, caped figure cast a long shadow over the smoldering pile. He dropped to his knees before the blackened skeleton, reaching his hand out to wrap his fingers around what had once been a soft, pink hand. He had held that hand. . . .

When the town constable walked up behind the

man, the constable heard a faint snapping sound, like the breaking of a twig. But when he tapped the man on the shoulder, the constable did not notice how tight the man's fist was when he rose. Or that the skeleton was no longer whole. The man held a treasure in his fist, and he brought it home to wrap it forever in a cloth of blue and gold.

1

Gary VanBuren turned his station wagon into the gravel driveway of his new home and pulled up to the front door. He sat there for a moment, taking in the property around him and the house that loomed enormously in the center of it. Even though he had seen it a dozen times before, slamming doors and kicking radiators before signing the contract, he was so awed by the size and beauty of something he could now call his own that he was barely conscious of his hand twisting the key from the ignition. He felt very good about this place, as he had from the first time the real estate people took him on a tour of it. How could he resist it, with its old-fashioned charm? And best of all, a good deal of the old furniture was miraculously still intact. Gary, a lover of antiques, had bargained with the realtors to buy the pieces. Without them, the house would have lacked something. It certainly didn't lack dust, but a good cleaning would make it a wonderful place to live. Or so Gary thought.

It was just magnificent. A leaf-lined porch stretched across the front, broken at the center by four steps, leading to carved double doors. There were bay windows on either side, and an old-fashioned swing hung from the wooden board ceiling.

He raised his eyes to see a window of amber stained glass in the center of two larger windows. At the peak of the roof, a weather vane turned lazily, as if it couldn't decide which way the wind was blowing. The original Colonial mansion was largely hidden by Victorian additions.

Gary turned around to ask the children what they thought of the place, but the seat behind him was empty. As soon as the car stopped, his wife Melanie and their three children jumped out to explore their new home. Gary smiled, imagining the children's reactions. This mansion on Starbine Court Road, in the Long Island town of Belle Bay, was a far cry from their six-room apartment on East 79th Street in Manhattan. They had lived in the apartment since the birth of their oldest child, twelve-year-old Gina, and it was about time the kids had a back yard to play in.

Gary went to find them, stepping carefully on the slate stones so that his footsteps would not crush the thick grass of the front lawn. Gary respected its clipped and trimmed beauty, even though the lawn had long before turned to the beige of early October.

Around the side of the house, he caught sight of Melanie, holding hands with their son. Kyle was eight years old, and the very image of his mother. He had her small nose and her freckles, and a mouth that seemed to take up his whole face when he smiled. His only resemblance to Gary was his curls, and even then he got their blond color from Melanie. Gary's own hair was dark and tightly curled, as if he had just stepped out of a pool.

Kyle was rambling on in an animated way, waving his arms and jumping up and down.

"It's so big!" Kyle cried, making a sweeping gesture that took in the entire grounds. "Do we really own it right down to the beach?"

"Halfway into the woods," Gary said. He looked at the trees that bordered two sides of the hill on which the white mansion sat. "But we can use the beach any time we want. Now, how about helping me carry some things inside?"

Kyle followed his father back to the car, still holding Melanie's hand. He climbed into the back and pulled at a lamp. With a grunt, he jumped down.

"Kyle, isn't that too heavy for you?"

"No, Mom," Kyle insisted. He took one arm away and bounced it on his hip as proof. "See? It's not heavy at all."

Melanie sighed. "You're right, honey. I guess I was just being an old nag."

"You're not a nag," Gary said distantly.

"Gary?" Melanie asked, a surprised lilt in her voice.

Gary didn't answer her. He rarely spoke to her at all these days—ever since he had found out she'd had an affair with another man. It was too hard to talk to her. It was hard to even *look* at her. When he did, all he could think was that her lips had kissed another man's, that those slender legs had felt another's against them. He had hoped the excitement of moving would change his attitude toward her, but the wounds were still fresh enough to resist the remedy of even this major change in their life-style. He had to admit it was a blow to his ego, but he made no apology.

He looked up at Melanie, briefly, and felt something jump inside him. My God, she was beautiful. Her hair was the color of golden honey, falling thickly over her shoulders in soft waves. That face, with its blue eyes and delicate nose, could have been carved by a great master. And her smile . . .

Melanie caught his look and started to say something. But just then, their two daughters appeared at one of the bay windows, giggling and waving. Framed by the white curtains, they were a sweet picture, and the artist in Melanie saw a portrait in the scene. Gina, with her long hair falling in dark waves over her shoulders, was a night-and-day contrast to five-year-old Nancy's fair-skinned, golden-curled looks.

"It's the most beautiful place I've ever seen!" Gina gasped, her eyes bright with the enthusiasm of a twelve-year-old experiencing something very new.

"I knew you'd like it," Gary said. "Wait till you see your room."

"First help me carry some things inside," Melanie said.

For the next half hour, the family moved the few odds and ends they had brought with them in the car.

Gary and Melanie had spent the previous weekend at the house setting up all the furniture and belongings that the moving van had brought out from the city.

"Ready for a tour?" Gary asked.

His two older children agreed in unison. They walked to the end of the hall, Kyle counting the doors as he passed them. At the end, some six feet above the floor, was a stained-glass window. The sun was shining through its amber panes, and the elongated shadows cast by the stairway's carved posts were almost grotesque. As Gary led the children up the steps, Kyle rubbed his fingers up and down the double twists of the railings.

"Oh, Daddy, look!" Gina cried, pointing to the brass sphinx that decorated the post at the top.

"I know what that is!" Kyle cried. "We learned about them in history. It's a finks."

"*Sphinx,* you nutty kid!" Gary said with a laugh.

"It's from Egyptian stories, isn't it?" Gina said. "Half-woman, half-lion. But there's really no such thing."

"I know that," Kyle said, with a twist to his lips.

Gina and Kyle each took one of Gary's hands, and the three of them walked down the long hallway. Halfway down, it was branched by two smaller halls, each of which was decorated at the end by an amber window similar to the one downstairs. Each hall had doors spaced in military rows.

"There's so many doors!" Kyle cried.

"Some are closets," Gary said. "Here, this is going to be your mom's art studio."

He took them into a huge, brightly lit room. Its windows stretched from just a foot above the floor to nearly touch the ceiling. Gary knew they would take some cleaning, but once the film of dirt was removed, the sunlight would shine in beautifully. The room was empty except for a single, worn-out couch and a pile of cardboard boxes.

"There are closets just like this one in all the bedrooms," Gary said, opening a door. "These shelves are good and strong."

He pounded his fist against one of the four shelves. Kyle stepped in beside him and imitated his actions.

"I hate to use a cliché, but they don't make these like they used to."

"What's a cliché?"

"A sentence people use so many times it gets to be a drag," Gary told his son. "C'mon, get out of there."

"Can we see our bedrooms?" Kyle asked.

"Gina's is right across the hall," Gary said.

The little girl gasped in amazement when Gary opened the door, her eyes immediately focusing on the bed. It was a huge, canopied thing. Melanie had discovered a beautiful white quilt in the attic and had had it cleaned for her daughter's new room. It was a perfect match for the heavy velvet curtains that hung around the bed. They had been drawn back with new gold tassels to reveal posts carved in the same spiral design as that on the staircase.

"Oh, I love it!" Gina squealed, throwing her arms around Gary's neck.

"Take a look at the other furniture," Gary said, hugging her.

There were two tall bureaus, each covered with antique lace. Though the lace had faded to yellow, it was still delicate. Gina touched it, very lightly, as if it were a magnificent piece of art. She then moved across the room to find a desk, carved with intricate scrollwork. The two glass doors of the desk were etched with a simple boat design. On one door, the boat was initialed with the letter *L*, on the other, with the letter *B*.

"L.B.," Gina read. "That must be the lady who first owned this."

"I'd guess so, honey," Gary said. He bent down to open a few of the little drawers. "You can keep lots of treasures in here. And the bottom drawer has a lock that still works!"

"I just love it so much," Gina said, shaking her head in disbelief.

"Hey, when are we gonna see my room?" Kyle demanded.

"Right now," Gary told him.

Kyle's bedroom didn't come near the splendor of Gina's, but it didn't bother him. He was delighted that his bed was high enough to require a step.

"Do you think the guy who lived here was a sailor, Dad?" he asked, staring up at a painting of an eighteenth-century ship. Similar paintings hung on the walls of every room they had inspected.

"I suppose," Gary said. "In fact, there's a post in my study that I think might have had a telescope on it once. Come on, I'll show you."

Both children gasped at the huge, faded map that completely covered one wall. Kyle followed the paths of arrows that had been inked on it, moving his finger from Long Island to Wales. Gary showed them the telescope stand, its brass fittings green with age. There was a stone fireplace in the room with nautical designs carved in it, and a huge painting of a storm at sea hung above it, remnants of the early days of the house. Gary wondered how all these antiques and paintings had survived during the years the house had remained empty. Especially recently when the prices on antiques had skyrocketed, the house must have been a tempting target for burglars. "Why should I try to solve the mystery?" Gary thought. "Whatever the reason, I've got a house full of antiques. And at a good price."

"Can we see the downstairs now?" Gina asked.

"Later today," Gary promised. "We have some chores to take care of after lunch."

"Ooohhh," the children groaned together.

"Never mind 'ooohhh,' " Gary said. "Everything needs a good cleaning, and we still have to unpack!"

The children babbled among themselves at lunch, barely tasting the food in their excitement. The kitchen, bright in the late afternoon sun, was an anachronism, with its polished Formica counters and modern stove and refrigerator. When they stepped from it into the adjacent dining room with its heavy oak furniture, it was like walking through a time tunnel.

The downstairs had the same nautical, dark-wood decor as the upstairs. There was a bay window in the dining room, just like the ones at the front of the house, and an enormous fireplace. Gina stayed in there with her mother and Nancy, folding tablecloths and napkins to put them in the hutch. Melanie found a box marked *dining room* and pulled out plates and glasses, rearranging them on the hutch shelves. She unpacked various knickknacks and stood looking around the room. She had rearranged them a dozen times before deciding everything was in its proper place.

Kyle and Gary had taken charge of the living room. Gary had brought a rug from the apartment and wanted to cover the bare wooden floor with it. He and Kyle pushed it as far as it would go, then Gary held up pieces of furniture as Kyle kicked it along with his foot.

"Oof!" he groaned. "This is heavy, Dad."

"Don't wear yourself out, son," Gary said. "We've got other things to do." Kyle worked busily, whistling along with Gary; father and son were delighted with their new home.

After a day of hard work, everyone was ravenous at suppertime. When Gary realized that no one had remembered to pack salt and pepper, Gina started to giggle and soon everyone joined in her laughter, unaware that a pair of hungering eyes were staring through the bay window, fixed on Melanie.

2

Melanie drove Kyle and Gina to school that Monday to introduce them to their new teachers. St. Christopher's was on the other side of town, and the three of them had a chance to get a good look at their new neighborhood. Belle Bay was a peaceful little place, its one main road lined with small shops. Melanie made a note to tell Gary about the antique stores she had spotted.

People were walking along the road, browsing in front of store windows even at this early hour. An occasional group of children skipped down the sidewalk, and a big black dog laced its way through the few parked cars.

Gina's teacher was an elderly nun, a very kind woman with a bright smile. She sat down and talked to her new pupil, including Melanie in the chat. Watercolor paintings by budding Renoirs decorated the walls of the classroom, and the names of the winners of the previous day's spelling bee were displayed in the corner of one blackboard. Melanie was brought back to her own grammar-school days, some two and a half decades ago.

"Where do you live?" the nun asked.

"Starbine Court Road," said Gina. "On top of a big hill."

The nun's smile faded, then returned quickly, but not so quickly that Melanie didn't detect the change.

Gina, on the other hand, was too interested in hearing about her new class to pay attention. At last, the nun stood up and walked Melanie out into the hall.

"Do you like your house?" she asked.

"It's lovely," said Melanie. "But it needs a bit of fixing up."

"Well," said the nun, "best of luck in it. God bless those who live there."

She reentered her classroom before Melanie could ask what she knew of the house.

* * *

The rolltop desk Gary had ordered for his study finally arrived after a ten-day wait. He followed the movers up the stairs, guiding them so that they didn't scratch the walls or the desk. He tipped the two husky men and then set about arranging his papers in the new desk. The paperwork he brought home from the office every night gave Gary a good feeling. To his mind, the volume of work to be handled was proof that he and his partner, Warren Lee, had a thriving legal practice.

Gary had found an antique lamp in the city that week. Removing it from the box, he carried it across the room to the desk, its long cord dangling.

Then, suddenly, the cord became taut—as if someone had stepped on it. Gary tripped and went flying forward. His body struck the window with a loud thud, then fell back to the floor. Dazed, he stared up at the panes of the window, watching them vibrate in almost perfect unison with the beating of his heart. It set his head spinning. Around him the dark walls of the room swirled, until the paintings on them seemed a blur. Gary touched his head and drew back a finger spotted with blood.

"What in the hell?" he asked himself. But the blood was not quite so frightening as the realization of just how hard he had smashed against the window.

Just a little more force, he thought, and I would have gone right through the damned thing.

He tried to stand up, to see if the lamp plug had snagged on anything. That would explain how he had tripped. But dizziness overcame him, and he sank back down to the floor. Sitting Indian-style, he rubbed his arms, fighting off a sudden chill.

"Leave her!"

Gary looked around when he heard the voice. Across the room, the lamp sat upright, its cord lying innocently along the floor. The room was quiet except for the hum of the radiator. Gary told himself he was hearing things. He thought he heard a faint shuffling noise, like footsteps, and called, "Kyle, are you hiding in here?"

No voice answered. There were no giggles to give his son away. The children weren't up here at all. Gary pulled himself to his feet and walked slowly out of the room. He heard someone on the stairs and met his wife at the door to the bathroom. She stood watching him as he popped two aspirin in his mouth.

"I heard something fall up here," she said. "Are you all right?"

"Fine," Gary said. "I just stumbled."

He was glad the side of his head that had been cut was turned away from her.

"Gary, we're in a new home," Melanie said carefully. "Can't we talk about starting a new life?"

"Later," Gary said, heading back to the study.

Before Melanie could answer him, he disappeared into his room.

Infuriated, Melanie called after him, "Stop being so stubborn! I've forgotten Terry! Can't you?"

But Gary wasn't listening. Melanie repeated the words again, softly to herself. She really had pushed Terry Hayward from her mind. He meant nothing to her now. But two months ago, he had been a very important part of her life. By God, it was nice to have a man open doors for you and toast the color of your eyes.

They had met in March. Melanie had been shopping that day. Absorbed in finding a sophisticated dress for the opening of her first one-woman art show, she hadn't been watching Nancy. Bored, the little girl had wandered off in search of more interesting pastimes. When she couldn't find her daughter, Melanie had panicked. Soon she had all the salesgirls helping in the search. Then a young man appeared; Nancy was clutching his hand and chattering away to her new friend. As Melanie threw her arms around Nancy, alternately scolding and kissing her, Terry stood by patiently until Melanie remembered to look up and thank him. Terry looked like something off the cover of an old-fashioned romance novel. His face was deeply tanned and his hair was coal black and curly.

As they waited for an elevator, they exchanged social pleasantries.

"Tell me what you do," Terry asked.

"I'm an artist," Melanie said. "In fact, I'm having a show up at the Merkin Gallery. On West 54th. Will you come to the opening party? It's the least I can do to thank you."

"You can bet on it," Terry promised.

He did show up that day, and every day during the show's week-long run. Melanie brought Nancy a few times, and the little girl was always delighted to see Terry. To her, he was "Uncle" Terry, who brought her little toys and played games. Melanie loved to see her child so well entertained—it was rare that she or Gary found the time to play make-believe and other preschool games. Watching the two together, Melanie began to form a strong feeling for this handsome young man. So when he asked her to lunch, she accepted—telling herself it was as a friend. But when the meal was over, she knew it was more than that, and it frightened her. She tried to convince herself that only Gary mattered, but Terry made it so difficult when he brought her roses and candy—something Gary hadn't done in years.

After their fifth lunch, Terry kissed her warmly before they went their separate ways in front of the restaurant. The warmth of his lips forced her to open her eyes—somehow she had fallen in love with Terry Hayward.

In the cab ride back to her apartment, Melanie said to herself over and over that the kiss was meant to be Platonic. But every denial of Terry's affection was contradicted by the knowledge that she truly liked his attentions. And the feeling was strengthened even more when she walked into the apartment to find Gary so busy with his papers that he barely gave her a "hello," let alone a kiss.

She stayed awake most of the night, feeling a delicious sense of anticipation when she thought of Terry, and yet feeling a tug of warmth and love to see Gary lying next to her. She would stop this. Tomorrow she'd tell Terry that everything was over. My God, she thought, she'd been seeing him for two months now! It was time to end whatever it was that was happening between them.

And so she attempted to tell him her feelings at lunch the next day, when they sat on the steps of the 42nd Street library. Terry took her hand in his, but she pulled it away.

"Please, I know people in this city," she said.

"So what would they do? Tell your husband?"

"He'd kill me."

"That isn't the first time you've said that," Terry said, taking her hand again and holding it more firmly. "What kind of man is he?"

"He's just wonderful," Melanie said. "The sweetest man on earth."

"You still love him?"

"I do," Melanie insisted. "That's why I don't think we should see each other any more. Terry, let's stand up right now and go our separate ways—before we do anything more than hold hands."

"Off into the sunset," Terry joked. "C'mon, let's go for a walk. We can talk about this."

Somehow, the walk led down into the IRT subway, and Melanie found herself riding with him to his Greenwich Village apartment. She didn't say a word to him, but fixed her eyes on an ad for a secretarial school. Three people riding on a pencil into the future. Melanie thought it looked silly, but still she stared at it.

Terry brought her upstairs to his apartment. Even though he was always neatly attired, his rooms were in disarray. He had thrown his suits over the back of a chair when they came back from the cleaners, and they still had their plastic bags on. Shirts and socks hung from every available doorknob or covered the floor. In the bathroom, where Melanie had immediately retreated, wet towels slopped over the floor. Looking for a glass for water, she was surprised to discover a dozen bottles of pills in the medicine cabinet. Was her handsome lover sick?

"That's his business," she said, closing the door softly.

Melanie trembled throughout their lovemaking, at first from guilt, and then from a strong passion that this beautiful man brought out in her. He was so terribly gentle that she found herself sinking in ecstasy—forgetting Gary, forgetting the children. And it was just like that every time they came here for the months after that, just one or two days a week, when Melanie could get a sitter to stay with Nancy. Melanie thought heaven would last forever.

Their dates were only marred by Terry's occasional irrational outbursts of temper, usually at slow waitresses or reckless cab drivers. Once he'd even gotten into a fist fight with a burly man on the subway. But, as Melanie tried to tell herself, "no man is perfect."

The end came on a warm day in Central Park.

Terry and Melanie were sitting on a bench, while Nancy played nearby. Nancy came over and put her head in Terry's lap.

"Can I have fifty cents for ice cream, Uncle Terry?"

"It's too close to your dinner time, Nancy," Melanie said.

"Please? Oh, please?"

"Here, kiddo," Terry said, pulling out two quarters.

"Damn it," Melanie said after Nancy had left, "I told her she couldn't have it and you deliberately defied me!"

"Look, what's the big deal?"

Just then the sun came from behind a cloud and shone brightly in Terry's face. For the first time during the hour they had spent together, Melanie got a good look at his eyes. They were glassy and distant, not Terry's eyes at all. Melanie recalled the bottles of pills at his apartment and asked, "Are you taking some medication?"

"Just some pills to keep me going at work," Terry said. "It's getting really bad there."

"I'm sorry," Melanie said. A moment later, she added, "I thought you said you jogged to keep yourself in shape. What happened?"

"Jesus friggin' Christ!" Terry yelled, standing abruptly. "Since when are you my damned mother?"

The very first thought Melanie had when he stormed away was that she had really known very little about this man. She should have sensed something was wrong with him. But he had always managed to be kind and considerate toward her—at least until today. Melanie shivered, and not from the cool wind.

Nancy came back and climbed upon the bench. She wrapped her arms around Melanie's neck. Her mother's hair blew forward and brushed over the soft ice cream. Melanie didn't move to clean it.

"How come you're crying, Mommy?"

"I'm not crying, honey."

"Yes, you are!" Nancy cried, pointing to her mother's red-rimmed eyes. "Where's Uncle Terry?"

"He's gone," Melanie told her. She stopped short and knelt down to her daughter's level. "Nancy, Uncle Terry was a bad, bad man and I don't want to hear you talk about him ever again."

They didn't say a word to each other for the entire subway ride, and when they got home Melanie told Gary she was sick and went straight to bed. Gary, unable to talk to his wife, immediately questioned the children about her behavior. Nancy, wanting only to help, told Gary all about Melanie's fight with her Uncle Terry.

Gary listened incredulously. Later, alone in their bedroom, Melanie confessed everything, hoping Gary would forgive her. But he was too shocked to do anything but move his pillow and blanket to the living-room couch, where he would sleep for the rest of their stay in the apartment.

Melanie cried herself to sleep that night, her emotions a mixture of guilt, self-pity, and horror. But when morning came, so did her strength, and she steeled herself to go down to Terry's apartment. When he opened the door to her, she couldn't stop her hand from flying to her face in horror. He was dressed in the same outfit he had worn the day before, although now it was soaked wet. He hadn't shaved yet. His hair, usually combed so neatly, hung in his eyes. Those eyes were glazed.

"Come in," he said, pulling her arm when she hesitated.

"I only came to tell you goodbye," Melanie said, trying to keep her eyes fixed on his. She shuddered.

Suddenly, Terry grabbed her by the flesh of her upper arms and shook her. This wasn't the polite gentleman who had rescued Nancy; this wasn't the handsome lover who bought her roses and paid her compliments. Melanie could smell liquor on his breath. She struggled to break away from him, crying out.

"I will have you again," he seethed, pushing her against the wall, "if I have to kill you first."

Melanie reached up and scratched him with her long fingernails, drawing blood. When he let her go, she ran from the apartment on numb legs. Somehow, she managed to reach the street before he started after her, and miraculously, a taxi pulled up to the door. She jumped inside just as Terry raced out of the building. Her heart pounded loudly, and she shook with nausea. She tried to calm herself by thinking that Gary would be waiting for her at the apartment with forgiving, open arms. But when she walked in the door, Gary didn't even look up at her. For a week, he refused to speak to her, not even to ask her to pass something at the dinner table.

"Gary, please?" she asked plaintively.

"Don't 'Gary, please' me," her husband said coldly. "It's your own fault. Don't talk to me, damn you!"

The children cast sidelong glances at each other and picked nervously at their food. They watched their mother's eyes widen, then close with tears as she jumped from her seat to run to the bedroom. Her sobs filled the apartment. Except for that, the rooms were so completely silent that the sound of the phone ringing made Gary jump. He sent Gina to answer it.

"Hello?"

Heavy breathing. Gina frowned and repeated her greeting.

"Hello? Is anyone there?"

"Hello, kiddo!" someone with a loud, bright voice said. "I'm coming to your place tonight to have fun! Ha! Ha!"

"Who's this?"

"Gina, hang up," Gary ordered.

But the little girl was too nervous. From the other end, the laughing man whispered a string of obscenities, naming parts of the body that Gina didn't yet know about. But she was bright enough to know this man was no friend and that his words were wrong and filthy. She began to cry, until Gary wrenched the phone from her.

"Listen to me, you mealy-mouthed faggot," Gary snapped. "Don't call here again!"

He slammed the receiver. "It's okay, Gina, just a stupid crank. It won't happen again."

But it did happen again, the next night, and the next, and the next, until they were afraid even to lift the receiver. When they brought their problem to the police, they were told to get an unlisted number.

They didn't have to. A week later, Gary found the house in Belle Bay, and they began to make preparations to move. By late September, after three months of listening to the crank calls, they were out of the apartment and far away from Terry Hayward. Everything was safe and easy now.

* * *

It was late. Melanie rolled onto her side and stared at the spot of light that filtered through the lampshade. The lamp cord hung in a series of tiny metal beads and ended in a sculptured lily. Gary used to bring me flowers, she thought.

She picked up a paperback novel and threw it with all her might. It struck the door with a loud bang.

Melanie held her breath, waiting for the steps that would come running to see what had happened. But the steady tick of the grandfather clock down the hall was the only sound in the sleeping house. Melanie drew aside her covers and put on her robe and slippers; maybe a strong cup of coffee would help.

The yellowing bulb of the kitchen chandelier gave the room the peacefulness of an empty church. Melanie felt herself relaxing. She set the pot on the stove and leaned against the counter to wait for the water to boil, ready to catch it before the whistle woke up everyone in the house. Then she made herself a cup of instant coffee and took it to the table. She drank it black tonight, not because she liked it that way, but because she was too tired to care. She sipped at the coffee, feeling the warmth rush into her chest. Soon her entire body eased. She looked straight ahead through downswept lashes as she drank. In the light of the chandelier she saw something on the counter that she hadn't noticed before. It was a tiny package.

Melanie lifted the parcel in her hands, examining it, feeling like a child who shakes a Christmas box to guess its contents. It was wrapped in a blue and gold brocade cloth and tied with a strip of the same fabric. She untied the ribbon. When the fabric fell away, she found a pearl ring in her hand.

"Oh, Gary," she whispered, slipping the ring over her trembling finger. She held it to the light and bit her lip, tasting a mixture of coffee and salt tears. For the first time since their fight, Gary had given her a sign of his love. This proved she still meant something to him!

"I love you, Gary," she whispered, leaning her head back against the cupboard. She sighed. She wanted him now, more desperately than ever before. She needed to be with him.

She dumped the rest of the coffee into the sink, watching the brown liquid wash over the porcelain. The tail of the cat-clock swung rhythmically, its luminous eyes watching now the door, now the window. It was 3:42 A.M.

Melanie walked up the stairs and gave the sphinx

a pat. It stared hard at her. She half-walked, half-skipped down the hall, trying to keep herself from whistling. She stopped at the door to Gary's room—to her husband's room, she thought with a grin—and knocked softly. When no answer came, she leaned closer to the door and called softly. Silence.

She wrapped her fingers around the knob, but it turned only a fraction before jamming against the lock. Melanie's elation drained away to confusion. Why had Gary locked the door? Didn't this ring mean he wanted her tonight? Melanie raised a fist to her mouth and bit hard on her knuckles. She ran to her room, her slippered feet scraping softly on the floor.

Her foot caught on a string of worn carpeting, and she stumbled forward in the darkness. Oh God, she thought. Can't I feel rotten in peace?

There were voices coming from somewhere. Melanie looked around, blinded by the pitch darkness. It sounded so like a crowd, like people were talking just outside the house. Or just inside.

Melanie chided herself. "Voices! That's the radiator hissing! You're just tired, Melanie. So damned tired. . . ."

She let her head drop back down on the rug and began to slam her fist against it. Her tears had turned to sobs, and she buried her face in her robe to muffle them. Her body heaved up and down in furious spasms and she growled in her anger.

Then she felt a touch on her back. She quieted herself, but she didn't turn around. The touch stayed with her. She mumbled, "Gary?"

The voice that replied was sensuous, edged by the slightest accent. Accent? Had she really forgotten what Gary's whispers were like?

"I want to be with you now," he said.

"Oh, yes," Melanie sighed.

She let him lift her in his arms and carry her back to the bedroom. He laid her down softly and climbed in next to her, stroking her blonde hair with large fingers. His hand slid down her neck and over her shoulder, then pulled at the tie to her nightgown.

His fingers followed every contour of her body,

moving slowly over her breasts and down to her hips. He let them linger there, making odd spiraling patterns. Melanie began to notice how cold his fingers were. She put her hand over them and squeezed tightly. She loved this gentle way he was approaching her. It was so unlike their usual rough-and-tumble scenes.

He stopped massaging her and crawled down the bed to kneel over her. Again, he remained in the same position, until Melanie pulled him down to her and sought his lips in the darkness. They were full and passionate, but he kept them tightly closed. This strange way of kissing bothered her, but she didn't stop him. Strong arms encircled her, squeezing her. For a split second, Melanie thought of Terry Hayward, for this was almost exactly the way he had treated her during their lovemaking. But when she heard her lover's voice, Terry passed from her mind.

"You're here again," he said, kissing her neck.

"I always was," Melanie whispered.

"Don't leave again," he begged.

"Never," Melanie promised, stroking his hair.

She didn't notice when he left the room that night, for she fell into a deep sleep soon after their brief exchange of words. When she woke up the next morning, she lay with her eyes closed, thinking of the beautiful night they had had. Everything was going to be fine, she knew it now.

But if she had known that Gary had slept soundly throughout the entire night, in his own bed, and that it wasn't he who had locked the door, the beauty she remembered would have rotted away to horror.

3

Melanie was in such a giddy state that morning that she hardly paid attention to the food she was cooking. She absentmindedly poked her long fork at the bacon, humming to herself.

"It smells so good," Gina said. "Daddy, how come we can't have bacon every morning?"

"Don't they teach you about health in school?" Gary asked. "It isn't good to eat bacon that much."

"Mommy, I don't want my sunny eggs to run all over," Kyle said.

Melanie didn't answer him. She was thinking dreamily of the night she had spent with Gary.

"Mommy, my eggs!" Kyle said, louder now.

"Huh?" Melanie asked, waking up to the real world. "Oh, yes—no runny eggs for Kyle."

Gina reached over the table and tugged at her father's sleeve.

"I'm going to be in a play at school, Daddy!"

"Really? What kind of play?"

"All about Halloween," Gina said. "I get the lead role 'cause I'm the tallest in my class. I'll be a witch!"

"Oh, you're too pretty to be a witch," Gary said.

"No, I'm going to wear a pointy hat and a black gown. And I'm going to be real mean!"

"That'll take some acting," Gary said. "How many lines do you have?"

"Twenty-two, Daddy!" Gina answered, as if that were the most magnificent thing in the whole world.

"Well, you've only got two weeks to practice," Gary said. "If you want, I'll help cue you."

"Okay!"

Melanie came over to the table and set the plates down. Kyle stared at the yolk that oozed all over his plate, then looked up at his mother with a screwed-up nose.

"They're all runny," he complained.

"Oh, Kyle," Gary said, switching plates. "Take mine instead. Melanie, do we have any salt?"

"I think Mommy's got something nice on her mind," Gina said when Melanie didn't answer.

"Melanie," Gary said again. "How about some salt?"

"The world for you," Melanie said, laughingly handing him the shaker.

"Thanks," Gary said, shaking his head at her.

"Daddy, I'm going to be home late from school today," Kyle said then, around a mouthful of eggs and bacon.

"You're not in trouble, are you?"

"No," Kyle answered. "I'm gonna play football with some of my friends."

"You made lots of new ones?"

"Uh-huh, Billy, Kevin, Roger, Brian," Kyle said with a nod.

"Hey, we're gonna be late if you don't move it," Gina said.

"Kyle, finish your eggs," Gary told his son. "There's only a few bites left."

Kyle stuffed everything he could into his mouth.

"Oh, gross!" Gina cried.

"Kyle, sometimes . . ."

"You said to hurry, Dad," Kyle reminded him.

"Well, get your coats on," Gary said. He accepted goodbye kisses from his two older children.

"Mom, where's my lunch?" Gina asked. "MOM!"

Melanie responded to her name only after Gina had called it three times. She made a weak comment about not being awake yet, rising from her seat. Lunch bags were put in small hands, and her two oldest children were ushered out the door.

Melanie watched them through the glass door of the kitchen until they stopped down the hill to wait for the bus. Kyle pointed to a squirrel and said something that sent his sister into waves of laughter. We're lucky, Melanie thought. We never had that proverbial attack of sibling rivalry. If only Gary and I could be like the kids!

"Soon," she said out loud.

"Did you say something?" Gary asked, folding down his paper.

"No," Melanie answered, waving her hand as if to prove the air was free of her words. "How are you this morning?"

"Just fine," Gary said, frowning.

Melanie turned to fill the sink with breakfast dishes, smiling to herself. Behind her, she heard the scrape of Gary's chair against the floor and the click of his briefcase as he locked it.

Had this been just a day earlier, she would have also listened for the door to shut when he left the house. But after last night, she wasn't about to let him get away without kissing her goodbye.

"Gary," she said quietly. He turned around and took a step backward when she moved to kiss him. But she caught him squarely on the lips and held hers against them for a long moment.

"I'll see you tonight," she said, drawing away.

"Yeah, sure," Gary said. He turned his head and walked from the house, wondering why Melanie was behaving so strangely.

Melanie went back upstairs, humming the current disco hit. She wanted to paint now, even though the restless night had somewhat fatigued her. The studio was icy, and she pulled the drawstring on her robe until it wrapped her like the shroud of a mummy. She looked at herself in a mirror and was pleased with her figure. No one would guess she was thirty-eight, and today she *felt* younger.

She set out her paints and turned to the easel that held her current masterpiece. It was the portrait of Nancy and Gina that she had envisioned the first day they had arrived at the house. Gina was a blur of blues and greens and browns, while Nancy remained a penciled sketch. The two girls were waving and Gina had a knee up on the window seat. Melanie dabbed her brush into white paint and began to highlight the folds of her daughter's jeans.

"I want you!"

At the sound of the voice, Melanie's brush dropped to the floor, leaving a streak of sticky whiteness where it rolled over the boards. She could feel her heart beating, knowing Gary had pulled away from the driveway. She had seen him pass the bus stop!

The voice cried out again, so very near the door. It didn't sound like Gary, but it was similar to the whispers she had heard the night before. That strange accent—English?

"What are you saying?" Melanie asked herself. "Of course it's him! He sounded just like that last night!"

But logic was fighting against her. Gary hadn't had enough time to get back to the house. And if he had somehow managed that, surely she would have heard him. . . .

"Gary?"

Nobody answered her. There was a rustling along the rug outside her door, and Melanie watched for the knob to turn with her breath caught in her throat.

She could stand there all day, watching that doorknob, expecting it to turn, as if this were one of those silly old haunted-house movies. Doorknobs always turned in haunted-house movies, heralding knife-bearing prowlers. And a young woman would watch and wait, ready to let out a piercing scream as the camera lens zoomed down her throat.

In a quick, now-or-never motion, Melanie reached out and jerked open the door.

There stood Nancy, a sleepy-eyed cherub in a pink nightgown. Melanie closed her eyes in relief and laughed at her fears. Today was the day Nancy started afternoon kindergarten! She had been so busy that morning that she had forgotten the note she had tacked to the refrigerator with a pineapple-shaped magnet: *Nancy: PM Kinder Monday.*

"Melanie," she said softly, "you're a romantic turkey. Prowlers!"

"Prowlers?"

"Forget it, honey," she said.

She noticed her daughter wasn't carrying her favorite toy this morning. Instead, Nancy clutched at a large package wrapped in the same brocade material as the ring had been.

"What's that you've got?" she asked.

Nancy handed the package to her mother. She brought one of her thumbs to her mouth, then the other, and sucked at both noisily. Melanie turned the package in her hands, ignoring her daughter's bad habit for once.

"Did Daddy give you this for me?"

"It was on the rug," Nancy said around her thumbs.

"On the rug?"

"In the hall on the rug," the child explained, with a yawn that stretched her mouth into a tiny oval. She rubbed at her cheeks, flushed pink where the chill of morning fought with the warmth of her skin.

"Well, why don't we see what it is?"

"Yeah!" Nancy cried eagerly.

Melanie tugged at the ribbon, which was tied in a fancy knot. She wasn't sure where Gary had learned to tie a bow like that. Melanie let the fabric drop to the floor and held up a beautiful gown that seemed to be made of pure silk. It was yellowed with age, with sleeves that were tight to the midarm, then belled in rows of lace. It had a low-cut neckline and was delicately embroidered over the bodice.

"It must have cost him a fortune!" she gasped, wondering what antique shop he had found it in.

He hadn't mentioned the ring that morning. Most likely, he wouldn't mention this either. It was all part of a game they had played long ago, when they would leave little gifts around the house for each other. No thank-yous would be exchanged, but good-night kisses would be longer and warmer.

Let's play that again, Gary, she thought to herself, almost praying it.

She stooped down and hugged Nancy. This was proof Gary had finally forgiven her. And would she make him glad he had!

She lifted her daughter and carried her toward the stairs, singing. Nancy giggled. And a lonely being watched them, unseen, loving Melanie, needing her, and cursing the child who had come between them that morning.

* * *

Gary watched the man across his desk with eyes that barely took in his features. He only heard what the man was saying because it was second nature for him to pay close attention to his clients. That was what made him a good lawyer, he told himself. It kept all these high-paying people knocking at his door. Divorce Headache Number 297, he thought sourly.

Number 297 was making accusations about a wife who didn't understand him. Gary nodded and *hmm'd* where it seemed necessary. But today his thoughts wavered between his client's lamentations and Melanie's unexpected display of affection that morning.

Gary raised his hand to his mouth. He ran a finger over his lips, as if to prove to himself that Melanie had really kissed him. Even though she had surprised him, he liked it. Since the day he had met her fifteen years ago, Melanie's kisses had been something to write home about. Gary, momentarily forgetting his client, recalled the afternoon he had walked into a store that sold prints, intending to buy one for his newly opened law office. Melanie was standing behind the counter, her blonde hair pulled up in a high ponytail and her eyes made up with the heavy liner of the sixties. Gary recalled that she was wearing a miniskirt. She had looked much younger than 23, but when she spoke to him, it was with an impressive maturity. He had walked out of the store with five prints and the promise of a date the next Saturday night. Six months later, they were married.

Gary felt himself trembling inside to remember all the good times they had had together, all down the drain because of one stupid mistake. But he could have them back again, just by bringing flowers to her that night. He wanted them back again! Damn it. He missed her in bed. It had been so long. He started to smile, but his lips froze at the sound of his client's voice.

"You'll get me my fair share, won't you?" Number 297 was asking.

Gary nodded. The man eyed him suspiciously, guessing his lawyer wasn't paying much attention to him. But before he could say anything, the buzzer sounded. Gary punched the lit button and found himself talking to a frantic Melanie. Nancy had been hurt that morning and Melanie couldn't calm her down. Could he *please* come home?

"I'm on my way," Gary said, letting the receiver drop.

When he stepped out of the office, Warren Lee looked at him with questioning eyes, and Gary quickly explained what little he knew from talking to Melanie.

"Let me know if she's all right!" Warren called as Gary left.

Gary was into the elevator before he got both arms through his coat sleeves. At the parking lot, the attendant didn't seem to care that he was in a hurry. And, of course, Gary's car was on the top concourse. Gary tapped his foot impatiently, and when he saw the car ease down the ramp, he felt a surge of anger. The attendant was purposefully taking his sweet-loving time! Lazy bastard . . .

He shoved a bill into the man's hand and climbed behind the wheel. The station wagon slid back onto 50th Street and turned onto Madison Avenue. For ten or twelve blocks, it seemed everything would go smoothly. And then the traffic lights began to torment him. Each turned on its brilliant red just as he approached, making him wait on edge for endless seconds.

By the time he made it to Long Island, Gary was shaking with nervousness. Visions of Nancy bandaged from head to toe passed through his mind. What was it Melanie had said? That Nancy had somehow spilled hot water all over herself? (What a thing to happen to a five-year-old!) At last, he pulled up the hill to the house. He jumped from the car and ran inside, calling for Melanie.

Melanie was waiting for him in the kitchen, her eyes red from crying. Gary pulled off his coat and tossed it over the back of a chair, then sat down beside her. As gently as he could, he asked what had happened that morning.

"I just don't know," Melanie blubbered. "I had brought her down to breakfast—she had waffles. Then I had been upstairs working for just a few minutes when I heard her screaming! She somehow spilled boiling water all over herself from that teakettle."

Gary looked to where she pointed and saw the kettle on the floor by the stove. He went to it and picked it up, turning it in his hands. His reflection blurred where the metal had been dented. The mark was two inches long and so deep that only a tremendous strength could have bent it. Gary shook his head.

"We didn't even use that this morning," Melanie said. "I just don't understand. . . ."

"Is Nancy upstairs?"

"She's been resting since I brought her home from the hospital," Melanie said. "Gary, you should have seen her little legs! I can't imagine how much it hurt her!"

"What did the doctor say?" Gary asked.

"Just to keep her quiet," Melanie told him, "and that the real danger is infection. We have to keep her clean, and let it heal on its own. He says it probably won't hurt after today. He even gave her some pills to calm her down."

"I want to see her," Gary said.

She followed her husband up the stairs to the child's room. The little girl was curled up around her pillow, clutching it to her stomach. Her mouth moved steadily, chewing at her tiny thumbs.

Gary was stunned to see those tiny legs swaddled in bandages, hiding the ugliness of the skin beneath. He had seen burns before, and tried to fight a vision of redness and blisters that formed in his mind. He closed his eyes and swore silently. Then he walked closer and leaned over her.

Gary greeted her softly. At the sound of his voice, she threw her covers over her head and began to scream.

"MMMMOOOOOMMMMMEEEEE! ! ! !"

"I'm here, baby!" Melanie cried.

Nancy tightened her blanket protectively, terrified that the masculine voice she had heard belonged to the man who had hurt her that morning. Gary, not understanding that his daughter was afraid of him, tried to pull the blankets away to show her who he was. He gently touched her cheek where the blanket didn't cover it, then brought his finger away with a cry of his own. She had bitten him.

"What is *wrong* with her?" he demanded.

"I don't know, Gary," Melanie said over the child's loud sobs. "She keeps saying something about a *man* hurting her. But we were alone all morning!"

Melanie bent over her daughter and put her arms around her. Nancy was crying so hard that she wouldn't listen when her mother tried to tell her that Daddy was here. But Gary had had enough. He pulled Melanie gently away and sat down with Nancy. He couldn't help her if she wouldn't tell him who hurt her, he said. Daddy had to know who it was before he could make him not do it again.

It took some effort, but at last Nancy calmed down. She stared up at him with soft, bloodshot eyes.

"Daddy," she said softly.

"It's me, sweetheart," Gary said. "Want to tell me why you screamed like that?"

"A mean man hurt me, Daddy," the child told him. "I thought *you* were the mean man!"

"A man hurt you?" Gary said. "But Mommy says there wasn't any man here. Maybe you should tell me what he looked like."

"Make him go 'way, okay?" Nancy pleaded.

"I'll do that," Gary promised. He thought for a moment, then said, "Nancy, he wasn't your Uncle Terry, was he?"

Melanie gasped.

"No, Daddy," Nancy insisted. "He wears his hair like Mommy, in a 'tail. And he's big and tall."

She stretched herself up to show his height. Gary formed a picture in his mind of a latter-day hippie and asked Nancy if she remembered the man coming into the house. Nancy shook her head. She closed her eyes for a moment, seeing him in her mind. She told her daddy how the man was wearing a blue cloak and funny blue pants. His mouth was turned down in a scowl. He reached for the teakettle. . . .

"I'm scared, Daddy," she said, turning to bury her face in Gary's coat. Gary kissed her head and laid her back down on the pillow.

"Try to sleep now, baby," he said. "Mommy and I will stay here until you do."

"Don't let the mean man come back again," Nancy said sleepily.

Melanie and Gary stood by their daughter's bed until they were sure she was asleep. Then they quietly left the room and went back downstairs to the kitchen.

"Gary, you don't think I had Terry Hayward here, do you?" Melanie asked.

"Not on purpose," Gary said. "But he was threatening you for a long time."

"But he doesn't know where we live!"

"He could have found out easily enough."

"Nancy said it wasn't him," Melanie reminded him.

"She was frightened and upset," Gary answered. He sighed. "Well, okay. Maybe it was a delivery man."

"We didn't get any packages," Melanie said.

"Did you check to be sure the kitchen door was locked?"

"It was," Melanie said. "When I took Nancy to the hospital, I remember having to unlock it. But that's not the only mystery. Gary, I'll swear on my life we didn't use that teakettle this morning!"

"It might have been left on overnight," Gary suggested.

"Great way to set the house on fire," Melanie replied. "Oh, Gary! I'm so upset!"

"Do you suppose you'd feel better if you helped me move your things into my room?"

Melanie's smile was all the answer he needed.

4

The next morning, Kyle and Gina were waiting at the bus stop at the bottom of the hill. Kyle grabbed the signpost and spun around it, then went to pick up a rock to throw at the metal.

"Cut it out, Kyle," Gina said. "You're making too much noise!"

"Who's gonna hear?"

"Maybe the old lady," Gina suggested.

Kyle looked at the big gray house that sat a few hundred feet back from the road. All the lights but one were out, and in the square glow he saw an old woman staring out at them. He waved. The old woman smiled and waved back.

"She's awake," he said. "She won't care about the noise."

"Why do you suppose she stares like that?" Gina asked. "Every day she's up at that window!"

"I don't know," Kyle said. "But she sure gives me the creeps."

He hoisted himself up onto the low stone fence that wound around the old woman's property and started to walk along it. Gina walked beside him.

"I hope Nancy feels better when we get home," she said.

"Yeah, she sure hurt herself!"

"Someone hurt her," Gina told him. "I heard Mommy and Daddy talking about it."

"You were eavesdropping!" Kyle gasped. "I'm gonna tell!"

"If I tell you everything I heard, will you keep the secret?" Gina bribed.

"Well, okay," Kyle said, stopping to sit on the fence.

"Daddy says that someone threw hot water on her," Gina began. "And he thinks it might be that weird guy who used to call us up at the apartment all the time."

"He scared me," Kyle admitted. "I hope he doesn't know where we live! What else did they say?"

"Nothing," Gina said. "I had to move away 'cause I heard someone coming toward the door."

"Are you scared, too, Gina?"

"A little," his sister said. "But Daddy'll take care of everything. Hey, here's the bus!"

Kyle hopped onto the bus and took a seat beside Gina. The driver pulled away, and he looked out his window to see the old woman, just as he had seen her every day since he had started picking up the VanBuren kids. Probably a lonely old soul, the bus driver thought as he turned off the road.

* * *

The VanBurens' only neighbor on Starbine Court Road was an elderly woman named Helen Jennings. After bringing her through 85 years of life, fate had rewarded her by refusing her a family with whom she could spend her last years. She lived alone in her big gray house, with only a cat for company.

But Helen didn't suffer in her loneliness. Her life had a purpose—and that purpose was followed to the point of obsession. For Helen had made herself the unofficial guardian of the VanBuren family.

It was an obsession that had begun some eighty years earlier, on a day in her childhood, just a few months before her fifth birthday. It was a day made for children, with blue skies and sunshine beckoning them to climb trees and chase kites. Helen found her own little niche on a swing that hung from her favorite tree.

She stretched her bloomer-clad legs taut as she swung high, tucking them under the seat as she drew back again. At the height of each arc, she could catch a brief glimpse of the white house on the hill. It was empty—it had been for as long as she could remember. Mama said it was because the place was evil and people were afraid.

Up went the swing, almost as if it wanted to throw her over the hill, only to pull her back again at a teasing, dizzying speed. Each time she went up, she saw the house and its empty grounds.

Then, on one trip up, she saw something else. Moving as softly as the wind blowing through Helen's hair, a young man walked from the house to the stables. Helen, surprised, let her legs relax and scuffed her feet along the ground to stop the swing. She was curious—had someone new moved into the house? Perhaps he had a little girl she could be friends with!

She walked behind the swing to climb up the tree. Without effort, her feet found each knob and hole until she had reached a thick branch some six feet above the ground. Wrapping her arms around it, she snuggled against the wet bark and watched the strange scene.

The man, moving as unhurriedly as before, came out of the barn again. He was shaking his head at something, running his fingers through his thick black hair. Helen watched him, fascinated, as he paced across the path. But when her young eyes adjusted to their focus, she saw something that caused her to let out a startled cry.

She wanted to climb down, but something had frozen her to the limb. If the scene she watched was unreal, Helen, at an age when fantasy becomes reality, was much too young to know it. For when the man passed the rock fence, his legs did not obscure it! Helen could still see the stones—right through him.

And then, as if he had heard the thumping of her heart, he turned around and stared hard at her with cold, dark eyes. With a scream, Helen fell from her perch, landing on the ground with a bang. She turned her swimming head and breathed in the sweet, strong smell of . . .

. . . carpeting.

Helen opened her eyes and looked at the arm that had flung itself over the grass. The hand, a moment ago pink and chubby, was stretched thin now, spotted brown. She put it on the couch for support and pulled herself to a sitting position. She had been dreaming again.

* * *

Helen let herself return to complete consciousness, sitting on the carpet with her eyes closed. Then she pulled herself up onto the couch from which she had fallen and reached for her walker. She had long since learned to use it without assistance, and she had become so adept with it that she could even manage the stairs up to her bedroom.

Helen had thought once of calling someone to come move her things to the first level—at 85, stairs were an encumbrance—but when she realized that her bedroom window offered the best view of the house on the hill, she decided to stay put. Helen needed to watch the house. It had been her one obsession since that first day she had seen the man walking past the stone fence.

She had, after her first glimpse of him, told her family what she had seen. That was when the comments began, starting with her father, who patted her on the head and called her "daft." Her brothers and sisters called her a liar, but Mama didn't say a word.

Helen was undaunted. When no one was looking, she would sneak up to her sister's bedroom (later her own) and watch the house through the big bay window. On very rare occasions, she would see him. But he never appeared when someone else was there to witness the scene with her.

Until she was ten years old, the house stood empty. Then one day, as she was watching it, she saw a carriage pull up the hill. A man and his wife stepped out, followed by their daughter. But Helen never met the girl—never knew her name. Within a month, the man had packed his family's belongings and taken them away. In a brief conversation with Helen's father, he had said the house made his daughter nervous.

Another forty years passed, and though Helen's hair had begun to fleck with gray, the man who walked the grounds of that house remained young. By this time, another family had moved in—a young couple with four little sons. And for a while, everything seemed fine.

But a scream reached Helen one night, so loud that it was carried all the way down the hill to her house. She put on her robe and slippers and went downstairs, where she was told by an older brother to wait until he went to the house to investigate.

When he returned an hour later, his face was ashen. In a shaking voice, he reported that the father had somehow fallen from his bedroom window, headfirst. He had broken his neck.

Half a year later, his sons were dead too.

Helen tried to push that memory from her mind —four tiny bodies wrapped in sheets. It had been over thirty years ago, she told herself. But if time heals all wounds, it hadn't yet, after all those years, healed the pain she felt inside when she thought of those four little boys.

She walked over to the window and gazed out at the big white house. Two lights were lit, and through a ruffle-curtained window she could see the silhouette of a child. There was a new family in the house now.

She would not let him have this one.

5

Melanie felt Gary's lips against hers. She responded dreamily, sighing with the feeling of warmth he gave her. In her somnolent state, his hair seemed thicker, his lips fuller. When he whispered, it was with a passion that seemed out of another time.

"I do love you so," he whispered.

His grip on her body tightened as he lifted her a bit off the bed to kiss her. She felt her body heat rise as he rocked her, her breathing deepening into sleep.

Then she opened her eyes for a moment to see a man who wasn't Gary. The figure disappeared in the few seconds it took for Gary to roll over in his sleep. Melanie's heart began to pound with fear. It would be hours before she fell asleep again.

* * *

Gary woke at two o'clock in the morning to the sound of his own coughing. His eyes began to tear with the sting of cold as soon as he opened them. He sat up and looked at Melanie, sleeping soundly under a huge mound of blankets. It was no wonder he was freezing, he thought, reclaiming his own covers.

Outside in the hallway, the ancient metal radiator banged loudly. But when Gary put a trembling palm against the one standing near his bed, he felt no heat rising from it. He threw aside his covers and climbed out of bed to take a closer look. Somehow, the valve had been turned off in the night. He twisted it, heard a spitting sound, and started back to bed again. Damn these old houses and their faulty heating systems. Maybe they should have bought a brand-new house—less atmosphere but everything would have worked.

Now there was a draft coming from somewhere. Gary scanned the room for its source, squinting to stretch his vision through the darkness. He spotted the opened closet door and guessed that the small window above the top shelf had blown open. In the darkness, he pushed away suits and coats and picked up his foot to place it on the first shelf.

But instead of landing quietly on the wooden plank, his foot fell heavily to the floor. It was as if he had miscalculated the number of steps on a dark stairway. But Gary had miscalculated nothing. There was simply no shelf for him to step on. Confused, he swung his hand over his head until he touched the light cord, then pulled it.

The bulb swung a bit, casting dramatic shadows over the shelves Gary had, only a few weeks ago, called solid and sturdy. Now they were broken neatly down the center, as if someone had karate-chopped them from top to bottom in one clean stroke. The few items that had been placed on them had fallen to the floor. The closet reeked of aftershave.

Not believing what he saw, Gary reached out and grabbed one of the shelves. He had misjudged them, of course. They were merely plaster, or cheap imitation wood. If he tried, he could break off a piece as easily as if it were peanut brittle.

But the shelf, in spite of his efforts, remained intact. He gritted his teeth, put all his weight against the wood, and still couldn't crack it. By now, his shock had turned to anger, though logic told him there was no one to whom he could direct it. No one else in this house could have broken these shelves like this. It would have taken an axe—and someone a lot stronger than any of them.

Gary thought about searching the house but finally decided that whoever had done this was long gone. If it had been done tonight, he would have heard something. No human could destroy something so thoroughly without making noise.

He looked at Melanie, debating whether or not to wake her. He decided against it, reasoning that nothing could be accomplished now. If law school had taught him one thing, it was never to take as truth what one saw in the dark. In the morning, Gary thought as he shut the closet door tightly to keep out the draft, he would ask questions.

* * *

Melanie walked into the kitchen to find Gina and Kyle huddled on the same chair. Gina had an arm around Kyle, and the little boy was rubbing a finger under his red nose. Melanie frowned.

"Are you two feeling all right?" she asked. "You look like you're coming down with something."

"We're just cold, Mom," Gina said. "It was freezing in my room last night! Kyle's, too. I think our radiators got turned off in the night. Did yours?"

"I don't think so," Melanie said. "I was warm when I woke up. We'll have Daddy fix them when he gets up, okay?"

She lifted the teakettle from the stove and started to fill it. It was still hard to imagine how water had come from this empty pot a day ago to burn her little daughter. An aluminum teakettle, innocent on its own, had somehow turned into a thing of evil. . . .

She suddenly threw down the kettle with a yowl. The scorching hot water from the tap had leaked through a hole in the dented metal. She gave her hand a hard shake to take the pain away and watched a bright red mark appear where the water had splashed her hand.

She felt a hand press her shoulder. Gina's so quick to comfort, she thought. But when she reached up to place her hand on her daughter's, she felt nothing but the plush of her bathrobe. The pressure was constant, but there was no hand.

Melanie turned and looked at Gina, who still sat with Kyle. The girl returned her mother's gaze with a befuddled one of her own and started to get out of the chair.

"You okay, Mom?"

"Huh?" Melanie faltered. "Yea—yes, I'm fine. I just spilled water on my hand and hurt myself a little. The kettle's broken—we'll do without oatmeal today."

"Yay!" Kyle yelled. "I hate oatmeal!"

Gina clapped a hand over his mouth and sternly reminded him that Nancy and their father were sleeping. Kyle shrugged, but lowered his voice when he said, "I'm still cold, Mom."

"Me, too," Gina put in.

"I'll make some cocoa," Melanie offered, sucking at the red mark on her hand.

She was thinking of the touch she had felt on her shoulder. It was such a strange thing—like that vision she had while in bed with Gary. If someone asked her, she would have sworn on a Bible that the man bending over her was real. But she had heard somewhere that dreams sometimes go on for a few seconds even after the eyes are opened. Some dream, she thought with a quiet laugh. Gary would appreciate the competition! Well, she never went for tall, dark men—like the one she had seen.

"Hi, Daddy!" she heard Gina say. The reply was a grumble, and Melanie turned to see a frown where Gary usually wore a good-morning smile. He sat down heavily in a chair and stared at the coffee cup Melanie put in front of him.

"The kids say their rooms are cold," she told him.

"My radiator's off," Gina said.

"Mine, too," Kyle put in.

Gary looked up. "Really? I had to turn mine on last night."

"I was warm all night," Melanie said.

"I'm not surprised," Gary answered. "You stole all the blankets."

"I did?" Melanie asked. "I've never done anything like that before. I wonder what made me do it last night?"

"I couldn't tell you," Gary replied, "but you were certainly bundled up."

"Well," Kyle drawled, "*I* froze my toes!"

When he discovered the poem in his last sentence, he began to tap his spoon against the edge of his cup, chanting it.

"Froze my toes! Froze my toes!"

"Quiet, Kyle!"

It wasn't Gina, but Gary who silenced the boy this time, reminding him that Nancy was still asleep.

"Gary," Melanie said quickly, "could you just check on her? I don't want her room cold."

"Will do," Gary said, taking a quick sip from the still-full coffee cup.

He walked up the stairs, thinking to himself that he'd tell his wife about the shelves when the kids were gone. No use frightening them. But it had been a trial to hold in his anger.

Kyle's room was nearest, so he entered it first. It was simple enough to turn on the radiator. But he had a strange feeling about the closed door to his son's closet. He reasoned that he was doing it "just out of interest" when he opened the closet door. His casual air faded when he saw the shelves, broken exactly as his had been. On the floor, every toy model he had worked on with the boy for so many hours was smashed.

He slammed the door. He didn't want to think about this now. He knew that no matter what explanation he came up with, nothing would make sense.

He walked into Gina's room and picked up a stuffed animal that had fallen on the floor. Still holding it in his arms, he went to the radiator to turn it back on. Then he turned to the closet, expecting to find the same thing he had found in Kyle's. His suspicions were justified. Up above the broken shelves, the tiny window flapped in the breeze, banging against the tree that stood just outside it. An icy wind seeped into the room.

Gary threw the stuffed toy across the room to vent his anger. In Nancy's room, he again fixed the radiator, moving softly around the sleeping child's bed. When he opened her closet, it was only the worry of waking her up that kept him from crying out.

Those shelves, too, were broken.

6

Melanie drove her car down the long road that led into Belle Bay, tightly clutching the steering wheel. Halfway between her house and the center of town, the road took a swing to the right and ran along the beach for a half mile. The morning wind of late October stirred little chops of waves from the nearby water and sent the soothing aroma of salt water into the half-open car window. She sucked in the air, letting it refresh her, but still kept a tight grip on the steering wheel. She clutched it in terror, because she was certain something strange was going on at the house, and that morning she had had to run away.

The road turned back again and met the main highway. Melanie followed this until she saw a sign announcing that Belle Mall was to the right. She turned, then drove past the line of stores until she came to the end of the road.

At the duck pond, she turned off the engine and got out of the car, heading for a green bench that sat at the water's edge. As she settled herself, a half-dozen mallard ducks came swimming over, expecting her to feed them. When she didn't move, they quacked in anger and swam away.

Melanie watched them, staring at the iridescent green head of a drake. She had come here to think, hoping the peaceful emptiness of the park would help her. She closed her eyes and pieced together the events of the morning.

She couldn't recall a time when she had seen Gary so upset. Within minutes after he had gone upstairs to check on Nancy, he had returned to the kitchen with an unusual spark of anger in his eyes. Someone had axed the closet shelves in all the bedrooms, he seethed.

"What?" Melanie whispered in disbelief.

Gary stood in the doorway with his chin tucked into his neck. His jaw was clenched and his face was red. The arms that had held Melanie so gently the night before hung stiffly, ending in clenched fists.

"Daddy?" Gina said carefully.

Gary let out a long sigh at the sound of her worried voice and shook his head. He assured her that he wasn't angry at any of *them,* but at the stupid senselessness of the whole thing.

"What would anyone gain by doing a thing like that?" he demanded.

"Shouldn't we call the police?" Melanie asked.

"I don't know," Gary said. "Let's get the kids out of here first. Nothing seems to be missing, and I'm sure no one's hiding here."

He slammed his fist on the table in a resurgence of his anger when Melanie gently reminded him that the house was big and had a lot of empty rooms.

"Damn it, Melanie!" he roared. "Will you let me do the thinking!"

"Gary," Melanie retorted, "I have as much right as—"

Kyle was suddenly on his feet.

"My models are in my closet!" he cried, racing to the stairs.

"Kyle, wait a second!" his father called after him.

Gary didn't want his son to learn about the broken models in such an abrupt way. But Kyle was already shuffling back down the stairs, clutching the remains of a plastic army tank and sinking his teeth into his lower lip to bite back tears. He handed it to his mother.

"Dad and I made that on my birthday," he blubbered. "All my models are buh-buh-broken!"

"Kyle," Melanie said soothingly, kneeling down to hug him. She looked up at Gary over the curled head and demanded: "Who would do such a sick thing?"

"I'm scared," Gina said then, very softly.

"Don't be, honey," Gary said. "Daddy'll straighten this out. Kyle, I'm sorry about all this. It was a crappy thing to do and I'm going to make somebody pay for it."

"Yeah," Kyle sniffled, pulling away from Melanie.

"I'll tell you what," Gary suggested, "we'll go over everything when you get home today. I'm sure most of them can be fixed."

Kyle studied the army tank carefully, wanting to believe his father's words. He looked at Gary and said, "Really?"

"Really," Gary said. "Now get your coats before you miss the bus."

He bent down to hug his son and planted a kiss on Gina's dark hair. He and Melanie watched them walk down to the bus, each waiting for the other to speak. But neither was ready with a theory.

Perhaps Nancy's "mean man" had something to do with it. . . .

"Excuse me!"

Melanie's eyes snapped open, and she saw a young woman staring at her. She straightened herself and rubbed her eyes, then looked up. The young woman held out a set of keys. "I found these on the path and wondered if they were yours," she said.

"I—I think so," Melanie said, taking them. "Yes, they are. Thanks."

"Sure," the young woman said. She started to walk away, but when she saw Melanie put her head down in her lap, she stopped. "Are you all right?"

Melanie nodded, then shook her head. She wasn't all right. She felt dazed, as if she had just waked up from a deep sleep. She rubbed her eyes again.

"I just feel a little dizzy," she admitted. "I had a rough morning."

"I believe it," the woman said, taking a seat beside her. She was a good head shorter than Melanie, with fine blonde hair that reached down to her thin waist. She took Melanie's hand.

"I'm Janice Lors," she said. "Local librarian. I work just down the block from here, so I decided to come outside for my coffee break. It's always so quiet in there on weekday mornings!"

Melanie laughed. "I'm Melanie VanBuren," she said.

"You know, I recognize most of the faces in this town," Janice said. "There are so few of us here in Belle Bay. Why don't I recognize you?"

Melanie started to explain, "We just moved here a few weeks ago," when Janice interrupted her.

"The *Times!*" she cried, snapping her fingers. "You did an illustration for the cover of the *Times* magazine section last year. I remember it because it was a story on the singles scene."

"Am I really worth remembering?" Melanie asked with a laugh.

"Oh, yes," Janice assured her. "If you're ever in town, drop by the library. I want you to sign our copy of that issue. Maybe we could do a display on a Belle Bay 'Artiste Extraordinaire.' "

"That's a first," Melanie said. "I've never been asked for an autograph before. As a matter of fact, you're the first person I've met in this town."

"What?" Janice asked with surprise. "What have you got for neighbors—snobs?"

"We have only one," Melanie told her. "An old lady who the mailman says is senile."

She felt stronger after this chance meeting. Janice Lors' cheerfulness was catching. The young woman sat for a half hour with Melanie, oblivious to the time, and told her all about the parts of Belle Bay that she had not yet seen. "There's an art club that meets on Tuesday night in the basement of the church," Janice said. "You might be interested in that."

"I would," Melanie said. "Sometimes I just like to get out of that big old house."

"Where exactly do you live?"

"We live on Starbine Court Road," Melanie answered. "At the top of the hill. Our property line is halfway into a forest on one side, and that's just a half mile from the beach."

"You must mean the old Langston place," Janice said. "I'd love to live in a place like that. I'm surprised it took this long to sell it. How'd you get so lucky?"

"I guess we—"

"Don't answer that," Janice said. "I didn't mean to be nosy. If you ever want to find out more about the house, just ask. We've got newspapers and magazines on microfilm to way back when at the library. There's even a collection of diaries and letters about the town."

"It sounds fascinating," Melanie said. "I'll take you up on the offer some day."

"There have been stories about the place," Janice told her. "But any house built way back in the 1700s is bound to have some tales behind it."

"What kind of stories?" Melanie asked, trying to sound casual. But Janice immediately picked up her uneasiness. She gave Melanie a questioning look.

"I'd like to hear about them," Melanie pressed.

"Well, why don't we make a date for lunch tomorrow?" Janice suggested. "I don't know much about the old place, but what I do know, I'll tell you then."

"Are you in a hurry to get back to work?"

"Look," Janice said, "maybe I shouldn't have said anything. There isn't much to the stories, just gossip that's been passed down for generations. The more a story is told, the more farfetched it gets." She smiled. "Isn't that a bit of neat philosophy from an old-maid librarian?"

"Old maid?" Melanie laughed. "How old are you?"

"Twenty-nine," Janice answered, "which is too damned old to be playing the singles scene in a town like this, if you ask me." She sighed. "Oh, hell, it's fun. Come on, I'll walk you back to your car."

As they walked, Janice pulled out a pack of cigarettes and offered one to Melanie. When Melanie shook her head, Janice said, "No one else likes 'em either."

She shoved them back into her pocket. "I got these in the city. They were handing them out free a few days ago. These girls with boxes tied around their necks and dumb straw hats. I went around the block four times just so I could get more of them. They must have recognized me after a while." She stopped to laugh. "And I can't stand these! Sure I can't unload a pack on you?"

"I don't smoke," Melanie said. "I quit."

"The worst kind," Janice mumbled.

They had almost reached their cars when a voice called out from behind them. Melanie and Janice swirled around to see a stooped old woman, aided by a young nurse, emerging from a nearby car. The nurse held fast to her arm until she had steadied herself against her walker, and walked slowly beside her, keeping pace with the woman's slow gait. Although she was weak, bent over and wrinkled with age, there was a fierce determination in her eyes that mesmerized both Melanie and Janice and held them fast until she reached them. When she did, she looked Melanie straight in the eye and said:

"There is danger in your home, young woman. He's a murderer. He'll destroy your family!"

Melanie was taken aback by the fanatical insistence in the woman's voice. The man's face that she had seen over her in bed the night before flashed in her mind, with the echo of Nancy's words "mean man." She couldn't speak. It was Janice who came to her rescue.

"Say," she snapped. "What do you mean, scaring her like that? Just who are you, anyway?"

"Please," the young nurse said, "she's just an old woman. I take her out once a week for fresh air, and, well, sometimes she forgets herself."

"I most certainly do not!" the old woman hissed.

The old woman eyed Janice and ran a pointed tongue over her lips. She knew this woman. Had seen her grow up. Why, she was one of that high-school gang that used to pelt her house with eggs on Halloween. Why should Helen Jennings tell this brazen young thing her name?

"Well?" Janice pressed. "Who are you? And what do you want with my friend?"

The words "my friend" had a strange effect on Helen. Her eyes softened, and she smiled slightly.

"Helen Jennings," she said at last. "I live next door to Mrs. VanBuren."

"Fine," Janice said. "Now why don't you go home and leave her alone?"

At that, Helen's calm front fell away. She leaned over the front of her walker and grabbed Melanie's sleeve.

"Please, you must listen," she pleaded. "For years I have cried out in warning, but not a soul will listen to me! I've seen innocents like your own children die by his hands! I've seen them suffer hideously because he hates them so!"

"Stop that!" Janice cried. "Just get lost, will you?"

She took Melanie by the arm and pulled her away, cursing softly. She headed toward her own car, ignoring Helen's cries. She could feel Melanie stiffen and pulled her a little closer. Melanie stared ahead, still absorbing the words hurled at her by the old woman. *Who* would kill her children? Why would Gina, Kyle, and Nancy have to "suffer hideously"?

. . . Screaming on a miniature rack designed just for them, painted with teddy bears and tin soldiers. Turn the handle and out comes . . .

"Hey!"

She thought she heard Janice's voice in the distance. Her eyes stared blankly at a face that was close to hers. Melanie felt someone shake her.

"Wake up!"

With a start, she blinked and looked at Janice.

"Have you landed yet?"

"Huh?"

"Are you all right?" Janice said. "You looked like you were off in space."

Melanie let out a long sigh. She shuddered quickly in one jerking movement, and she wrapped her arms tightly around her body.

"She upset me," Melanie answered.

"Who, that old bat?" Janice said. "Ignore her. She's as senile as they come."

"But there have been some strange happenings in my house," Melanie said.

"Which are probably very easy to explain," Janice said.

Melanie nodded in agreement, but she secretly wanted to talk to the old woman. She seemed to know something about the house that no one else did.

"What say you and I meet for lunch today?" Janice suggested.

"I couldn't," Melanie said. "Not today, anyway. I've got a million things to do—go to the supermarket, stop at the laundry, pick up a package at the post office. . . . How about tomorrow?"

"Sounds fine," Janice said. "I'll see you then. Meet me at the library, okay? Now go home and get yourself busy with a painting and forget your nutty neighbor."

Melanie watched Janice walk to her car. With each step her long blonde hair swished back and forth, just barely touching the bottom of her rabbit-fur jacket. From the back, Melanie thought, she looked just like a teenager. Why would a pretty unmarried girl like Janice stay in a small, dull town like this?

As she drove home, Melanie was certain this chance meeting with Janice had given her some sort of strength. But that strength didn't prepare her for what she found inside the house. Her courage drained away at the sight of Gary twisted at the bottom of the stairs. His head was bent at an odd angle, revealing a bruised neck.

7

When Melanie left, Gary had gone upstairs to reexamine the shelves. He was no longer angry, but more worried about his family's safety. God help them if it was that easy to vandalize this place without being seen . . . if there was some maniac running around who enjoyed destroying things for no reason. They were using only half the rooms in the vast house. There were plenty of empty rooms and closets for anyone to hide in.

He picked up the two halves of one shelf in his bedroom and tried to fit them together. From above him, the window moved in the wind to tap against the outside of the house, as if to remind him it was still open. The branches of the tree outside touched the window ledge, as if they were grabbing at something inside the closet.

He went to the linen closet in the hallway and pulled down a small stepladder. From over his head there came a low whine, and he looked up at the square indentation in the ceiling that led to the attic. The noise began as a thin wail, then sounded incredibly like a child crying.

"Squirrels," Gary said, spitting it as if it were a curse word.

The first window to be locked would have to be Nancy's. She didn't need those late-autumn gusts drafting in her room to add to her problems. Gary rested the ladder against the small yellow dresser next to her door and walked softly to the bed. Although she was usually awake and playing at this hour, she was still sound asleep, sucking at both thumbs. Gary thought to himself that sleep must help her forget the frightening experience she had had.

Gary opened the closet door slowly, so that the creaking wouldn't wake her up, and placed the ladder inside. He climbed to the top and reached for the window to pull it shut. Satisfied that it wouldn't blow open again, he climbed down and headed for Kyle's room.

He stopped for a moment to pick up one of the models and remembered his son's tearful face that morning. Well, he thought with a sigh, they would build new ones, and Kyle would forget all this.

When he finally returned the ladder to the hall closet, he listened for the sounds of squirrels. But this time no sound came from the attic above.

He walked out and headed for the stairs, where he gave the sphinx a pat on its brass head.

"I suppose that after all these years you've seen a lot of weird things happen in this place," he said. "This must all seem pretty ho-hum to you."

The shining Egyptian statue did nothing. It stared forward into forever, unable, or unwilling, to respond. It was another voice that Gary heard, low and gruff, filling the empty hall behind him.

"Leave her!" it demanded.

Gary turned around and looked down the hall. Though he could see no one, the voice seemed to be only a few feet away. It roared again.

"This time she is mine!"

Gary shook his head and took a step forward, certain it was some kind of a trick. He thought with excited anticipation that he was about to confront the person who had broken the shelves.

Suddenly, icy fingers wrapped around his throat. He gasped for air, ripping at his collar. But he could not stop the pressure of the unseen fingers against his neck. His arms flailed against the air, trying to push away something they could not feel. He choked, whooping in high-pitched breaths.

"You shall give her to me!" the voice cried. *"You will not hurt her again!"*

Gary tried to speak, but his words were clipped short when his tongue involuntarily pushed forward, as if to lick up any small bit of air it could. His eyes rolled back and he let out one long sigh. Then, as suddenly as they had grabbed him, the fingers fell away, and Gary felt his knees bend beneath him. With dulled reflexes, his arm swung out too late to grab the twisted rung of the banister before he fell down the stairs. The last thing he saw before he hit the bottom was a milky-white cloud at the top of the stairs.

His assailant watched him, his long-dead heart almost beating with his fury. The strength that had hurt the daughter and broken the shelves hadn't been enough to frighten him away, the being thought. Perhaps this would serve as a better warning. . . .

* * *

March, 1818

The stains just wouldn't come out. The young maid leaned forward heavily on her scrub brush, scouring and scouring. Yet when she rinsed the suds away, the mark was still there. She rubbed her hand under her nose, tucked a stray hair back into her cap, then challenged the task once again.

Mrs. Baxter had been adamant that the stains be removed from the rug. So Adele worked until her fingers were raw, ready to burst into tears when she rinsed the rug to find the spot again. How could Mrs. Baxter make such an impossible demand? Adele Collins was only thirteen, and it just wasn't fair to expect this of her.

"Hush," she told herself firmly. "Papa sent you here to work, and work you shall. You aren't paid 50 cents a week to complain!"

Two black slippers and the hem of a long black gown suddenly appeared before her. Adele looked up to see her mistress. The woman returned Adele's smile with a cold stare. Adele tried not to frown at the sight of Mrs. Baxter's pale tired visage; but it was difficult, especially when it was so easy to recall how rosy and alive those cheeks had once been.

"Is it coming out?" Mrs. Baxter asked, her voice far away.

"No, my lady," said Adele. "I'm sorry, but I'm trying."

It was the fifth time she had asked that question in the last half hour. Adele had shown a good deal of patience with her mistress, but even her kind spirit was beginning to fray. She thought for certain that if Gwendolyn asked it once more, she'd hand her the brush and make her try to clean up the mess herself.

Mrs. Baxter sat awkwardly down on the steps and leaned her head against the carved post. Her hair glistened in the light of the chandelier the girl had lit. Adele knew there was no use starting a conversation, for Gwendolyn's mind had lost itself somewhere in the short time since her husband's "accident."

Adele shuddered. *Why is it,* she thought, *that horrible things happen only to good people?*

She had only been with the Baxters since they had moved into this house three months ago. This big white house on the hill had been in a terrible state then, thick with dust and dirt from two decades of neglect. Adele couldn't understand why no one had bought the place after the first owner passed away; it was big and roomy and very nice to look at. Oh, her father told her stories about evil there, but since it didn't stop him from sending her to work, she had paid no attention to them.

It was just two weeks after she first moved into the house that she began to wonder if the stories might be true. She had waked up one night to the sound of footsteps shuffling across the rug to her bed. But when she opened her eyes, no one was there. And the door was tightly closed. She felt incredibly cold and decided to go to her bureau for another blanket. The cold became worse as she moved across the room, groping forward in the pitch darkness. She knew that all she had to do was walk a straight line and she would touch the smooth oak of the dresser. But instead, her hands touched the bare chest of an unseen intruder, who stood in her path. Adele let out a small, startled cry and backed away.

"Who's there?" she demanded. "Say, or I'll scream. I swear I shall!"

The only answer was a low, evil laugh. Then, before Adele's scream could emerge, it was blocked by a strong hand. She felt herself being pushed back to her bed. Her feet stumbled up the step backward, and she fell, her body at an angle over the side of the bed. She heard the sound of lace ripping from her nightdress. Adele had no knowledge of sex, but she knew he intended to hurt her, badly. She trembled, not struggling. She couldn't—the man was too heavy on top of her. He pressed close to her ear and whispered.

"You shall not have your mother's life again, witch-child," he said, in a faint British accent. "She is mine now! She has returned."

And then he wasn't there. Adele, sprawled against the side of the bed, couldn't move for her fear. Was he there in the darkness, waiting? She kept perfectly still, listening. Then all was black.

The next morning she found herself under her covers, as if she had been there all night. Still shaken, she rolled from the bed and went to splash water on her face. Looking in the mirror, she studied the lace of her nightdress. It hadn't been ripped.

"You dreamt it," she told herself. "What a silly! And besides, who would accuse you of hurting your mother?"

Yet there were other bizarre events. Adele, not a superstitious girl, could live with books that disappeared and candles that blew out when there was no wind. But when Mr. and Mrs. Baxter fought because of it, she felt she couldn't go on working here. Who would believe they had been so loving once, when they first moved into the big house?

And they had been. Adele had seen the signs of their love. "I love you so much," Adele had often heard the handsome Dane Baxter whisper to his wife.

"And I love you," Gwendolyn would sigh.

They had said it. Adele had heard them. So she knew they meant very much to each other. That's what made it so terribly frightening when they began to fight. It was over little things, like disappearing vases, figurines that neither could find. Then the little spats became violent arguments, initiated when Dane found a piece of sharply glistening glass under his pillow. Gwen denied ever having seen it and expressed shock that her husband might have been seriously hurt. Three months ago, Dane would never have thought such things of his wife, but now he accused her of attempted murder.

But Gwendolyn hadn't left the glass there, and Dane's would-be murderer was angered to find that his trap had failed. One thing did work in his favor, however. Dane moved out of the bedroom, leaving his wife to sleep alone. Gwen tossed and turned in her sleep, praying fervently that her husband would believe her and return to her bed. That night, her prayers were answered, but not in the way she had hoped.

She pretended to be asleep when she felt the bed sink under Dane's weight. But when he kissed her softly, she reached up to hold his face in her hands. How cold he felt! Even his lips. But Gwendolyn didn't care. He was here again, and that was all that mattered.

"Please stay with me forever," he said.

"Forever," Gwen whispered.

"I love you so!"

"And I love you," Gwen answered. *"Je t'adore."*

Someone was pounding at the door. Thinking it was Adele, Gwen whispered that they should ignore her. But the voice behind the door belonged to a man. As soon as she heard it, she felt the burden of weight on her body disappear. Confused, she lit the lamp and looked around the room. It was empty.

She went to the door and opened it wide, her heart beating loudly. Dane was standing there, a look of anger on his face. He was completely dressed. He didn't look at all like someone who had just made love.

"Why did you lock that door?" he demanded.

"It was not locked!"

"Then why could I not open it?" Dane asked. "You are hiding someone in here—I heard you!"

"Dane," Gwen said, "I must have been talking in my sleep. There is no one here!"

"I heard a man's voice."

Dane pushed her aside and entered the room, throwing open the closet, checking under the bed, and moving dressers aside. Gwen wasn't lying—there was no one in here. But he had heard a voice, and the door had been locked!

"There is a secret passage here," he shouted. "You have hidden him!"

"How ridiculous!" Gwen cried. "To think you could accuse me of such a thing!"

But Dane was already pounding at the walls and tugging the chandelier. Nothing moved in the walls, yet still he was convinced his wife was hiding a lover. Of course, that would explain her lies about the missing articles. She had stolen them to give to her lover! Dane turned to look at her, his eyes wild. How could she dare to stand there like that, haughtily mocking him while another man listened from a deep shadow?

"Stop laughing," Dane said.

"I am not laughing."

"Silence!"

Gwen fell backward when her husband's fist reached her eye. She touched it gingerly, shocked, and drew back a finger spotted with blood. How could Dane do such a thing to her? She opened her mouth to call to him, but he had already left the room.

He spotted the man standing at the top of the stairs, one hand resting on the golden sphinx. He was dressed in a naval uniform that was at least two decades out of date. Was this the man his wife had taken to her bed? Dane couldn't understand why. This fellow looked downright ridiculous in that costume. But Dane didn't laugh at him.

"What were you doing with my wife?"

The man didn't answer. Dane reached out to grab his throat, but when he reached him, his hands sliced through the neck and touched each other. There was nothing there—nothing but a blast of cold that ruffled his hair.

And then something grabbed at his own throat. He backed up, terrified, trying to get away. What was this? Was he mad? But if so, then why did he feel the pain? He choked and gasped, struggling, helpless.

But he wasn't helpless! He had put a dagger in the pocket of his robe. His hand reached for it. But what would he do with it? How could he stab something that wasn't there? He was desperate. The blade sliced through the coldness. The fingers around his neck loosened, but the pain was only lessened for a brief instant. Suddenly, Dane felt something cuff him under the chin, hard. He fell backward, tumbling, falling head-over-heels. The dagger was still useless in his hand. When he hit the bottom landing, he fell on its sharp point. Blood gushed from the wound in his heart, staining the rug. Both Adele and Gwendolyn had watched the scene in shock. By the time they reached the bottom of the stairs, Dane was dead.

And so Adele found herself scrubbing to remove the stains. Who could believe such a thing would happen to Master Dane? Who could believe the beautiful, spirited Mrs. Baxter had turned into something akin to a walking corpse? Adele shivered.

Once again, she poured clean water over the area. This time, her efforts were rewarded. Sighing, she stood up and wiped her forehead. Then, lifting her bucket, she went to dump the water, leaving Mrs. Baxter to sit on the stairs.

"She won't be lonely much longer," Adele said out loud, as she threw the water out the back door. She turned into the kitchen and replaced the scrub brush and bucket just inside the cellar door. "When her mother and father arrive, they will certainly cheer her."

The day after Dane's death (she still couldn't bring herself to call it murder), Adele, in desperation, had written to Gwendolyn's parents in her childish hand, telling them their daughter needed them. They lived all the way in Philadelphia, but she expected they would come as soon as they received the letter. That had been five days ago.

She heard the sound of horses' hooves and ran to the parlor window. Someone had pulled a horse and carriage to the side of the house. Adele ran back into the kitchen, out the back door—the only door servants were allowed to use—and around to the front drive. She led Gwendolyn's parents into the house, where her mistress still crouched on the stairs.

Gwen's mother gasped at the sight of her daughter. Gwen didn't move an inch when her mother approached, but still kept her eyes fixed on the chandelier. When her father passed a hand in front of her eyes, she didn't blink.

"Dear Lord," he whispered, crossing himself with a wrinkled hand.

"She talks sometimes, sir," Adele told him, "but very little. Usually she sits and stares, just like that."

"Has she had a physician?" George Kingsley asked.

"Yes, sir," Adele replied. "I called one here when we found Mr. Baxter. Oh, sir! It was awful! Just awful! Do you see that wet spot on the rug? I spent hours cleaning the blood!"

"Oh, George, what are we to do?" Hedda Kingsley wailed.

She sat down beside Gwen and pulled her close, smothering her in her ample breasts. She rocked her daughter, who at last had turned to acknowledge her presence. Gwen stared at her for a few moments, then said, "Mama? Where is Dane?"

"Hush," Hedda cooed.

"We must get her away from this house," George insisted, "and under proper care. What physician could leave her like this?"

"Doctor said it was nerves," Adele said, "and that it would pass in time!"

"Paugh!" George cried. "We are taking her away tonight."

"I already packed some of her things," Adele said. "Someone can return for her other belongings."

"And what of you, child?" Hedda asked.

"Oh, my father visits me every Saturday," Adele

replied. "When he comes tomorrow, I will ask him to take me home."

"But you will be here alone!"

"I'm not afraid, ma'am," Adele said, smiling. "And it's only for one night."

"It's only for one night." How often did she repeat that in the hours that followed. Soon after the Kingsleys had left with their daughter, Adele began to feel unnerved. She was the only soul in this house. The only living soul, she thought. She listened attentively for any sounds. Finally, late that night, she slid down under her quilt and fell asleep.

Some time later she was wakened by a voice—the very same voice she had heard months earlier, accusing her of wanting to harm her mother. She answered sleepily, insisting that she loved her mother dearly.

"You have sent her away!" the voice hissed. "You have sent her to her death!"

"You're just a dream," Adele mumbled, turning over and falling asleep again.

She never felt the pain. She slept through the blaze that shot up from her pillow, then licked over her hair and down her body, destroying only what it had to destroy and nothing more.

When her father arrived the next day, he found her lying in a fetal position—or what was left of her. With a cry, he picked up the grotesque shape, so like a dead tree in winter. Her legs were stumps, and bones jutted from the tips of her fingers. There was nothing left of her face, no mouth, no nose, no eyes. He shivered to think he was holding his daughter, wrapped inside a heavy blanket. In spite of what he saw, he prayed this wasn't his little Adele. But he knew the truth.

Someone would pay. He searched every room. No one was there. He felt tears welling in his eyes, and he fled the house. Behind him, he heard the distinct sound of wild laughter.

* * *

Melanie hated waiting rooms. A sort of tense heat always filled the air, making them unpleasantly stagnant. The uneasiness was almost choking. That uneasiness enveloped her for the second time this week, and she could feel it sucking away at her nerves. She paced the floor for a few more minutes, then dumped herself into a chair to stare at the wall.

Across the room, Nancy leaned toward a fish tank, unable to kneel because of the bandages around her legs. She traced the slow path of a little goldfish with a chubby finger. Then, she turned and hobbled over to a pile of magazines, walking like a tiny mummy. She inspected the one on top, yawning widely. It was so quiet in the little room that she was beginning to get drowsy again. She had been sound asleep when Melanie woke her to take her daddy to the doctor, and still didn't feel very playful. Nancy wanted her mother to read to her but she had such a sad look on her face that the little girl went over and sat with her instead. Melanie had to help her up onto the bench, and she wriggled until she settled herself between her mother and the armrest. Melanie put an arm around her and Nancy studied her mother's pale visage with large, blue eyes.

Melanie sprang to her feet when the door opened, nearly knocking her daughter to the floor. But the man who entered was only a janitor who had come to feed the fish. He chirped at them, calling them by name. Greedily, the fish swam to the surface, sucking at the food in small, jerking movements.

The janitor looked over at Melanie, who had disappointedly sat down again, and eyed her with understanding. He seemed to be telling her that he had seen many others here too. He knew, he knew. He nodded slightly and left.

Melanie looked at her watch. Somehow that little shake of the janitor's head had calmed her. She finally spoke to her daughter.

"It's two-thirty already," she said.

"Can we go eat now?" Nancy asked.

Melanie hadn't thought of food since she had brought Gary to the hospital, and she realized that she was as hungry as her daughter. Poor kid, Melanie thought. The banana she had been handed to eat in the car on the way here wasn't enough to satisfy a five-year-old's appetite. Melanie knew she would have to get them both something to eat before they wore themselves out.

"Let me see what the doctor says," she said. "You wait here, and Mommy will be back in a minute."

She went to the nurses' station and asked the RN to contact the doctor who was in charge of Gary. She pointed out that it had been nearly two hours—surely they were finished by now! With the smile of a professional, a meaningless smile, the nurse complied, and in minutes a plump, red-faced man appeared.

Dr. Padraic O'Shean smiled at Melanie. "Your husband is sleeping well, Mrs. VanBuren. We've given him a mild sedative."

"How is he?" Melanie wanted to know.

"No bones were broken," O'Shean said. "His wrist is sprained, badly enough to need a cast, but I think it will heal quickly. But there are bruises on his neck that I . . ." He stopped to think, pulling at the lapels of his brilliant white jacket.

"Mrs. VanBuren, I have some questions I'd like to ask you. Won't you come with me to my office?"

"Well—" Melanie mumbled, faltering under the powerful authority of this man. "I was kind of thinking of having lunch. You see, my little girl—"

"Of course!" O'Shean said with a laugh that reminded Melanie of an old engraving of Santa Claus. "We'll have something sent up."

Melanie went into the waiting room again and brought Nancy out into the hall. Hand in hand, the two followed the doctor to his office. Inside, Nancy ran up to his desk and stood on tiptoe to examine the biological statue there. She poked a finger at a plastic heart and gasped when it popped out and bounced across the floor. She scrambled after it, just barely reaching it before Melanie snatched it up from the floor.

"Sit down, you," Melanie ordered, smacking her

daughter's little arm. Embarrassed, she handed the plastic organ to the doctor.

"I'm sorry," she said. "I think it's broken."

"Nonsense," O'Shean replied, reclaiming the heart and pushing it back into the figure's chest. "It's supposed to come out. Do you know what it is, little girl?"

"Her name is Nancy," Melanie told him.

"Nancy," the doctor repeated with a grin. "Do you know what this is?"

The little girl tightened her lips and shook her head. Her round blue eyes stared at the little thing that had made her mother angry. She didn't care what it was! It was such a hateful thing!

"It's a heart," O'Shean explained. "You've got one, too. Right here."

He poked a fat finger gently at her chest. Nancy frowned and squirmed away from his touch. Amused, the doctor straightened himself.

"Don't you believe me?"

Again, Nancy shook her head in silence. That wasn't a heart! Hearts had two round bumps at the top and a point at the bottom and they said "I Love You." This couldn't be a heart. There was no love in it!

"I'm sorry about her," Melanie said. "She had a bad experience a few days ago and she's been a little nervous since then."

Dr. O'Shean sighed, looking down at the pouting child. He unhooked his stethoscope and handed it to her.

"Would you like to hear your own heart?"

Reluctantly, Nancy reached out and took the instrument. She stood perfectly still as the doctor placed it in her ears. She heard the *boom-bum-boom* of her heart and thought of a drum. She loved drums, with their loud, rhythmical beats. Was her heart shaped like a drum? Or was it like that hated thing in the plastic man?

"Now," the doctor said, "you play with that while your mother and I have a talk."

Dr. O'Shean directed Nancy to a big couch far across the room. He turned from her and walked to his desk. Hoisting himself up onto it, he rested a well-padded hand on his knee and leaned forward. Melanie sat in the chair he indicated.

His tone all at once became serious. "Were you alone with your husband this morning?"

Melanie started, not expecting such a blunt question. She explained that she had been out shopping for about an hour and a half, and Gary had been just fine when she left. A bit angered over something, but . . .

"A bit angered?" O'Shean echoed. "Why?"

"What does that have to do with this?" Melanie asked, not impolitely.

"Perhaps in his anger he stumbled," O'Shean hypothesized, "and fell. But that doesn't explain the bruises on his neck. Somebody must have tried to injure him."

Suddenly infuriated, Melanie stood up abruptly and glared at him. It was bad enough that he asked questions that really didn't concern him. But to insinuate that she had had something to do with Gary's accident was more than Melanie would take.

"I think I know what you're saying," she told him. "But I swear *I* never hurt him! For God's sake! I've got two witnesses to prove I was out of the house this morning!"

Dr. O'Shean widened his eyes and slid back on his desk, away from Melanie's gaze.

"Mrs. VanBuren," he said, with reassurance raising the tone of his voice, "I never said you injured your husband. I only wanted to know if you had been there when it happened. Your husband refuses to discuss this with anyone. But you might be able to help us find out what happened, exactly. The police will want to know."

"Oh, God," Melanie groaned. "I forgot to call them."

"As soon as you get home," O'Shean suggested.

Melanie nodded. At that moment a nurse came into the room with their lunches. Dr. O'Shean suggested that she take Nancy into the pediatrics playroom.

"Anyone could see those bruises didn't come from you, Mrs. VanBuren," O'Shean went on, taking such a huge bite of his sandwich that Melanie was certain he'd take his finger with it.

"The fact that you wouldn't want to hurt him is beside the point," O'Shean said. "The distance between the thumb mark and the finger marks indicates a hand much bigger than yours. And your husband certainly could have fought back if you were the assailant. The sprained wrist, however, probably happened in his fall."

"I'm glad you haven't marked me as a suspect," Melanie said with unconcealed relief. "Well, since you've started this, I'll tell you the entire story."

She began to recount the morning's events, from the broken shelves to Gary's twisted form at the bottom of the stairs. O'Shean didn't comment, but took it all in with interest and finally offered his own explanation.

"Perhaps," he suggested, "someone had broken into the house, knowing of the fine antiques to be found there. A house that size might have secret passages and hiding places with priceless items in them. So, in order to find them, the thief broke the shelves."

"Without Gary or myself hearing?"

"I can't explain that," O'Shean admitted. "But perhaps the thief didn't find what he was looking for. Suddenly, he realized he couldn't leave the house without being caught. So he hid in one of the spare rooms. When he tried to escape the next morning, Gary found him, and a struggle followed."

"When you were a child," Melanie asked with a smile, "and people would ask what you wanted to be, did you say a doctor or a detective?"

"You guessed," Padraic O'Shean laughed. "I haven't lost the touch of sleuthing. Forgive me if I've gone too far, but I cannot help being concerned about my patients."

"Don't apologize," Melanie said. "Yours is the most logical answer to what happened this morning. I appreciate it."

She put a slender hand to the side of her head and leaned back against the chair.

"Oh, God," she sighed. "You know, I stayed out

all morning on purpose. And to think Nancy was alone in that house with Gary knocked out cold!"

She closed her eyes in thought. It was *hideous*. Though she tried to fight it, her mind was connecting the events of the past days. That voice she had heard in the hall the morning she found the beautiful gown. Had some maniac been hiding in one of the house's many rooms? It would be easy enough. Perhaps the man who had tried to kill Gary was the same one who had attacked Nancy!

She thought for a brief moment of Terry Hayward. He was the only person she knew who could do anything so sick, and yet she felt strongly that it *wasn't* Terry. The fact that he didn't know where they lived was enough to make her dismiss him as a suspect, but still she was certain *someone* had been in the house.

"I don't know what we're up against," she said. "I think, though, that I heard a man the other day."

"I'd guess that much," O'Shean said. "The finger marks . . ."

"No, no," Melanie interrupted, shaking her head. "There was a man in the house a few days ago. I heard him."

"If that happened," O'Shean asked, "why didn't you tell your husband?"

Melanie opened her eyes and looked at the doctor. She couldn't answer his question.

8

Both Gina and Kyle had been itching to get home that day to find out more about the broken shelves. They sat on the bus together, the center of attention among a group of children, who had heard the tale that morning. One little girl made Gina repeat the story four times, listening wide-eyed.

"I'd sure be scared if I were you, Gina," she said.

"I *was* scared," Gina told her. "My daddy was really mad, and he never gets mad like that."

"My father yells all the time," Lorrie said.

"Well," Gina said, "Daddy was mad because he cares about us. I mean, whose father wouldn't be upset to find all the closet shelves broken?"

"And my models," Kyle put in. He took Gina's hand. "You know what? I couldn't think of a thing all day but my models. Dad and I worked on those for hours and hours!"

"It was a mean person that did that," a little boy said. "I hope your dad gives him a bop on the nose when he catches him."

Kyle nodded at him, then leaned very close to whisper in Gina's ear.

"Do you think it was the same guy who hurt Nancy?"

Gina shrugged, trying to hide her fear.

"Hey, it isn't fair to tell secrets!" a boy across the aisle cried.

"Quiet down back there!" the bus driver snapped.

"Hey, Gina—there's a cop car at your house!"

From this point on the road, the entire mansion was visible, and parked at its front was a black-and-white police car. Gina and Kyle glanced at each other, both wondering why the police should show up so late. Their father had called them first thing in the morning.

"Gina, something else happened," Kyle said.

"They've just come back to talk again," Gina insisted.

But she too was anxious to get up to the house for an explanation. When the bus driver pulled to the bottom of the hill, both children jumped off without saying goodbye to their friends.

"Hope everything's okay!" the bus driver called.

They ran up to the house, covering the ground with leaps and bounds. As they reached the porch, a handsome young policeman came out of the door to greet them. His name was Tony DiMagi, "Officer Tony" to the kids who knew him. Gina blushed under his smiling gaze, feeling a brief twinge of puppy love. But her face soon became solemn again and she frowned. She wanted to know what Officer Tony was doing here.

"Your mom can explain that better than I can," Tony said. "She and your dad had a crazy morning, but everything seems to be all right now."

Gina rushed into the house to find her mother, but Kyle remained behind to talk to the young cop. He liked Officer Tony, who let him wear his cap and touch—just a little—the gun strapped to his waist.

"Did you ever shoot anyone?" Kyle asked.

"No!" Tony said. "And I hope I never have to, either. I like people too much to kill anyone."

"Say, are you here because of those shelves?"

"Sort of," Tony said. "And also because your dad had a bad accident and we want to know why."

"Is my dad okay now?"

"Well," Tony said, "you'll have to ask your mom to explain everything. She's inside."

At that moment, another cop came from inside

the house. Jack Hughes, Tony's partner, was a good fifteen years Tony's senior, with graying temples and a rugged face that spoke of a long, tough career. He was as bulky as Tony was slender.

"I didn't find a thing," he said.

"Me neither," said Tony. "The downstairs is clean."

"What're you looking for?" Kyle asked.

"Some things," Tony said, "have to be a secret, Kyle. Police work, you know." He turned to his partner. "He's the VanBurens' son."

"Hi," Hughes said.

"Listen, Kyle," Tony said. "Go inside and talk to your mom. She needs you, I think."

Kyle ran into the house with a quick "goodbye" to both cops.

"You've always been great with kids," Jack said.

"I wish Mandy and I had had a few," Tony said.

"Don't think about that now," Jack answered. "Brooding over your divorce isn't going to make it better. Forget it. Out of sight, out of mind."

"Except for alimony," Tony joked.

"Alimony," Jack Hughes repeated. "C'mon, kid, let's forget about Mandy. You're young. You've got a zillion sons in your future."

"God," Tony laughed. "You make me sound like Henry VIII!"

Inside the house, Kyle had found his mother in the living room, a tearful Gina in her arms. He didn't cry when he heard what had happened to his father—he was by nature an optimist—but his mouth turned into a deep frown. He asked if they were in trouble now.

"No, we're safe," Melanie told him, though she wasn't quite sure herself. "There's no one in the house now, or the cops would have found him."

"Maybe he's a murderer and he's hiding in one of the rooms," Gina said dully.

Melanie looked down at her daughter, shocked that this beautiful twelve-year-old could voice the same theory that she herself had thought of. She tried in vain to deny the possibility. But there were such feelings of doubt in her own mind that she couldn't keep them from getting in the way as she tried to reassure her children. It was Officer Tony who came to her aid.

He had let himself into the house after talking for about fifteen minutes with Jack Hughes, and now he knocked at the door to the living room. They had found nothing at all, he told Melanie. No footprints, nothing disturbed.

"I think your doctor was right," he said. "This fellow was a prowler who happened to get caught. Your husband was in the wrong place at the wrong time."

"So he tried to kill him," Melanie said.

"I'm not sure," Tony said.

"But," Melanie wanted to know, "if that's the case, why won't Gary discuss it with me?"

"He doesn't want to frighten you, I guess," Tony said.

"It frightens me more when he broods like that," Melanie said. "Gary and I have had some trouble communicating. But he usually doesn't clam up this much when we aren't having a fight!"

"This whole thing is pretty bizarre," Tony said. He looked at Kyle. "Who knows, this may be my first real case. And you can bet Officer Tony'll get his man!"

Even Gina began to smile. They talked to Tony for a while longer, as they waited for the detective squad to come and dust for fingerprints.

Kyle walked with Tony and Jack through the house, listening eagerly as they explained what the detectives were doing. He watched them dust the banister and photograph the stairs, and he made a decision there and then that he wanted to be a cop when he grew up. Just like Officer Tony.

* * *

"I warned them, Belle," Helen Jennings said to the cat that rested in the bend of her arm. "I warned them, but they never listen to me."

She had seen the ambulance two days ago, and this morning the husband had been brought home. His head hung, as if pulled forward by the sling around his neck, and his wife, the girl named Melanie, supported him as he walked up the porch stairs into the house.

Helen opened her arms and let Belle jump to the floor. "He got the father this time," she said.

The cat turned its head and yowled in reply, then twitched its tail and ran from the room. Helen reached for her walker. She moved slowly to the telephone and eased herself into the chair next to it. Settling her head back against its worn upholstery, she reached for the receiver. This was her chance. Maybe now Melanie would be willing to listen.

"Operator," she said when a faceless voice answered, "give me the number of a VanBuren family in Belle Bay. The address is Starbine Court Drive."

"Hold, please," the woman said. The line buzzed for a few moments, then clicked. "VanBuren?"

"Yes, that's it."

"I'm sorry, the number is unlisted," the woman said.

"Nonsense," Helen retorted. "Look again."

"I am sorry, madam," the woman snapped back. "The number is unlisted."

"It can't be!" Helen cried. "You're lying! I must have it!"

"I-don't-have-the-number," the operator said in clipped tones.

The line went dead.

Close to tears, Helen replaced the receiver. She would have to go in person to the house, to warn them of the danger. She had an obligation to save them from the man who walked the grounds of their house.

She got up again and went over to the window. She could see the hill that went up to the VanBuren home. It was so steep! Helen was uncertain if her heart could take the stress of pumping energy to her legs so that she could reach the top.

"I must do it," she said with determination.

She pulled on a fur coat that had long ago been in fashion and fastened its remaining rhinestone buttons. Clutching the neck closed, she went out the back door, holding an ancient diary under her arm. The air was cold, laced with the scent of wet leaves. The soles of her shoes collected fallen leaves as she headed for the VanBurens' house. The very slight rain chilled her.

With a deep breath that pulled the cool air of autumn inside her and revitalized her lungs, she began her slow climb up the hill. Every few feet, she stopped to rest, a gloved hand pressed against her chest to massage away the dull pain. When at last she reached the top of the hill, Helen, her weakened legs a badge of honor, wanted to cry out in triumph.

She stopped in front of the door, teetering on the bulging floorboards of the porch. When she rocked, she heard them creak beneath her, and the thought occurred to her that when *he* had walked here, when he had had weight to bear down on these boards, they had not creaked.

But the thought of him did not depress her as much as the thought of facing Melanie again. The woman (woman? girl!) hadn't listened to her the other day. Why now?

Helen reached up and tapped the U-shaped knocker against the wood. She held her breath, expecting the door to be slammed in her face before it had been swung completely open. But to her surprise, the greeting she received was a pleasant one. Melanie's smile was warm, but her eyes were as distant as they had been that day in the park. Helen looked into those dull eyes and was certain *he* had already taken his toll on this family. With a friendly greeting, she followed Melanie inside.

Helen accepted the younger woman's offer to take a seat in the living room and settled herself to wait patiently while Melanie went to the kitchen for tea. Helen chose a plush velvet chair; her small frame was nearly lost in it. The antique furniture brought back memories of her childhood, but Helen couldn't feel nostalgic about this place. There were too many bad thoughts connected with it. She looked at the huge stone fireplace and wondered if *he* had leaned against it once, an arm resting on its mantel, a glass of port in his other hand. Looking oh so handsome . . .

And those bay windows. How many times had she seen faces looking out of them, faces that would be no more within a few months' time? She had seen the VanBurens' faces at those windows, and she intended to see them there for many years to come. She looked up when Melanie entered the room and smiled.

"You have some lovely antiques in here," she said.

"My husband collects them," Melanie told her, handing her a teacup. "Most of the furniture you see was in the house when we came, and Gary bargained with the realtors to buy it. Why the last owner left all this valuable furniture I have no idea, but it was fortunate for us; I just can't imagine modern furniture in a house with seven fireplaces, can you?"

"Never," said Helen.

Melanie sat across from her and waited for the old woman to speak. But Helen merely sipped at her tea, silent. At last, Melanie thought she understood what was expected of her.

"I was a bit rude the other day," she said. "But there was so much on my mind. You see, my husband had found . . ."

"I know, dear," Helen soothed. "Things happen here that we don't understand. Every other family went through it, too, but they wouldn't see. Funny how we're all so willing to admit danger only when we're right in the middle of it. But you'll see, I'm sure."

"You spoke like that the other day," Melanie said. "And it frightened me. Please, don't start about those things again."

"Those things?"

"Murdered children," Melanie said quickly. She watched Helen raise her cup. When it was set down again, it looked as if she had only touched her lips to the liquid. The cup was still full.

"Oh, of course," Helen clucked. "Here, I brought this for you."

She handed the book she had brought with her to Melanie.

"My own great-great aunt wrote that," she explained, "in 1797. If you read it, you may understand some of what has been happening around here."

Melanie looked up, startled, but Helen quickly reached out a hand and placed it gently on her knee. She had been watching the house, she said, and she had seen the ambulance take Gary to town. And, she added, she had heard the screams the morning the little girl was hurt.

"I do hope the child is all right?"

"She's fine," Melanie said, unnerved that this woman had been spying on her family. She looked down at the book in her lap and opened it. The name *Nora Jennings* was written across the top of the first page, over the date January 1, 1797. Melanie thumbed through the record of the first few months and saw that every yellow page had been filled with elaborate script.

"They didn't have much to do in those days, did they?" she commented. "I couldn't keep a diary like this myself!"

"Indeed," Helen said, "there is a lot of information. My family has lived next door to this place for over two hundred years. She talks of this house a great deal. For instance, she wrote that the first man to live here was a British naval captain."

"We guessed that," Melanie said. "It's obvious. The house was filled with maps and nautical paintings when we moved in. I'm an artist—I've decided to paint a seascape for my next work."

The two women smiled at each other, Helen genuinely interested, Melanie trying to be polite. She wasn't quite sure if she welcomed this woman's visit. But if it meant finding out what had caused Gary's and Nancy's accidents, then she did welcome her. She rose to her feet and went over to the mantel, lifting a piece of scrimshaw in her hands and pretending to study it.

"It's beautiful," Helen said. "But it seems wrong that such a delicate piece is in such wicked possession."

Melanie eyed her in such a startled way that Helen lost no time explaining herself. She reached over to the coffee table and set down her cup.

"My dear," she said, "I meant the original owner of this house, of course. He was a truly evil man."

"Oh?" Melanie asked with forced interest. She sat down and looked at Helen, her eyes sober.

"Mrs. Jennings," she said.

"Miss, dear," Helen corrected.

"Miss Jennings," Melanie repeated. "You seem to know a good deal about this house. About its history, I mean. You said the other day that there was danger in my home. I was inclined not to believe you then, but so many things have happened since that I'm willing to at least hear you out."

"Thank God," Helen said with a sigh. "I'll put it simply. This house is haunted by a man who has taken the lives of many. His most recent cruelty is still so vivid in my mind that I simply can't discuss it. But believe me—you are in danger in this house!"

"Haunted?" Melanie echoed. "Really! I might believe the place has a jinx on it, but—"

"Can you explain these things in a better way?" Helen asked.

"Well," Melanie said after a pause, "anything is possible, isn't it? When my husband is better, I'll discuss it with him."

"Has he told you anything?"

"No," Melanie said. "He needs to rest first—he'll tell me when he's ready."

"Whatever he tells you," Helen entreated, "believe him. You must believe him."

"I believe everything Gary tells me," Melanie replied. "Mrs.—Miss Jennings, it's nearly time for din—"

Before she could finish, Helen took the hint and pulled herself up on her walker. In one last effort to convince Melanie, she looked at her and said, "Read the diary. It will tell you everything."

She looked around, almost trying to spot an apparition. Outside, a loose wire that ran from the television up the side of the house tapped against the window. Helen turned her head to the sound, expecting to see a face in the window. But no one looked through the panes into the living room.

Melanie walked with her to the door.

"Can you get home all right?" she asked. "I, uh, hate to leave the children, with Gary sick."

"I'm fine," Helen said. "You will read the diary, won't you?"

"By all means," Melanie promised. "Antiques fascinate me. I'll return it as soon as I'm finished."

After a quick goodbye, Melanie opened the door for Helen and watched her move down the porch stairs with the skill of someone much younger. Then she closed the door and leaned against it. The whole meeting had been a waste of her time, she thought. For some silly reason she had hoped Helen might know of some hermit who hid out in the woods—and that the *he* Helen spoke of was some kind of maniac. And all that Helen had meant was a ghost!

Melanie went into the living room and picked up the diary. She opened it to the first page and sat down with it on the couch. She became so wrapped up in it that she didn't lift her head—didn't see the horrid little scene being played down the hill.

When she had nearly reached her front gate, Helen felt someone tug roughly at the long gray braid that ran down her back. With a gasp, she tried to turn around, but a strong arm clamped her neck and held her fast.

"Please," she begged. "I have no money!"

There was no answer. Reaching an arm that had suddenly pulled free, Helen swung it over her head in self-defense. But her hand sliced through the air and felt nothing but a strange, icy cold. This was it, she knew. He had found her out. The grip around her neck tightened. She screamed.

"Nnnnnooooo! Please let me g—"

A sparrow turned its head toward the ugly cracking sound.

A split second of eternity had passed when a single leaf fell from the tree above her to land on her sightless eye.

9

Melanie hadn't planned to read the diary at all. She had wanted to start in on the pile of art magazines stacked up by her chair. But here she was now, at midnight, still absorbed in Nora Jennings' writings.

Gary was lying with his head half-buried under a pillow when she walked into the bedroom. He slept like that now, since the accident. To Melanie he looked as if he were hiding. She slipped her dress over her head and climbed into the bed next to him. She pressed herself against his back and threw an arm around him.

Was he hiding from something? Had his accident really been so terrible that he couldn't talk about it, even after three days? Even to his wife? She thought of Helen's warning that she should believe everything Gary told her.

"Anything," she whispered. "I'll believe anything you tell me."

Gary's eyes sprang open. He turned his head and stared through the dark at her, pushing his pillow toward the headboard. For a moment, he didn't speak.

"I'm sorry," Melanie said. "I woke you."

Gary shook his head, his hair making a faint sound against the sheets.

"I was awake when you came in. How come you're up so late?"

"I'd been reading a diary our next-door neighbor

brought over," Melanie said, hoping to draw him into a conversation. "She's a really nice old lady named Helen Jennings, but she's nutty as a fruitcake. Anyway, the diary has some things about this house in it that she thought we'd be interested in."

"I'd like to hear about it," Gary said, sitting up.

He pulled Melanie into his arms. She sighed, settling herself, and began to recount what she had read in the diary. Gary listened attentively, alert for the first time in days.

"The first owner of this house was a man named Jacob Armand," Melanie began. "He was a captain in the British Navy in the late 1700s. The girl who wrote the diary is Nora Jennings. She's Helen's great-great aunt, and she's fascinating! She wrote the diary in 1797!"

"That's something," Gary said, impressed. "Does she say much about this house?"

"A lot," Melanie replied. "She's definitely Helen's relative—they're both busybodies. Do you know that old lady has been spying on us? She says this place is haunted—by some fellow who's out to kill us all. I think she was talking about this Jacob Armand. She must be loony."

"You're right," Gary said, trying to hide the look of fear in his eyes by turning his head. "She must be crazy."

Great act, Gary, he thought. Call the old lady crazy to keep that title away from you. Maybe you can forget those hands the other day. The ones you couldn't see. . . .

"So," he said suddenly, cutting off his thoughts, "tell me what she said in the diary."

"She spent a lot of time writing about some girl Jacob had," Melanie said. "She wrote that she had seen her in town with two little girls. But Jacob was definitely not her husband. So either she was a widow, or maybe she was having an affair."

"Nora Jennings wrote that?" Gary asked. "I always thought those Colonial girls were such prudes. You know, 'pure of mind and body.' "

"She was," Melanie said. "She started to write

something like that, but she stopped. She said it would be un-Christian. But it's obvious what she meant."

"Anyway," she went on, "Jacob Armand seems to have been an interesting person himself. Nora listened in on her father's meetings with his friends a lot, and she wrote about what she heard. Jacob paid a sort of protection fee that was collected by a servant of the Jenningses. I guess it was to keep the neighbors from burning his house down, since he stayed loyal to the King of England."

"Sounds like the Colonial mafia," Gary said. He lowered his voice in an imitation of Marlon Brando. "You has come to see da Godfadder?"

"That's terrible," Melanie said with a giggle.

"Well . . ."

Melanie gave his arm a squeeze and smiled up at him. She much preferred this happy Gary, with his bad imitation of Brando, to the introverted man she had brought home from the hospital. With him cheerful again, she wasn't sure if she cared to ever know the truth behind his accident. The only thing that mattered now was that he was happy again.

"You're terrific," shc said, kissing him.

He let go of her to slide down under the blankets next to her. He could feel her warmth, hear the breathing that passed through her nostrils deeply and slowly. His tongue found hers, his hands the richness, the smooth silk that was her skin. He held her close, caressed her. When he made love to her, it was with an animal force that wore them both out. He told her again and again how he loved her. For only a brief moment, Melanie noticed that the strange accent she thought she had heard when they had made love before, was gone. Then the moment exploded and the thought was split in two.

"I love you so much," she sighed, clutching him tightly as her heartbeat began a descent to its normal pace.

"Don't ever stop," Gary said, rubbing his face over her neck. She was so warm. . . .

* * *

Melanie leaned over the breakfast table and looked at Gary with smiling eyes.

"I've got a great idea," she said. "Let's go down to the beach for a picnic today."

"In the middle of autumn?" Gary asked. "I don't think that's such a hot idea."

"Why not?" Melanie wanted to know. "It's not that cold yet. Do you know we've been in this house for almost two months, and we haven't done a thing together as a family?" In the city, before Terry, they'd always done things as a family—trips to the zoo, boating in Central Park, going to see the dinosaurs in the Museum of Natural History. Perhaps, Melanie thought, they should plan an excursion back into the city some weekend. She felt so cut off from her previous life. She missed shopping in Bloomingdale's, walking along Fifth Avenue, visiting the art galleries. A weekly call from her agent kept her up to date on what was happening in the New York art world, and occasionally friends would call to gossip and tell her about the new plays and restaurants. But back in the city she'd be afraid of seeing Terry's face in every crowd, on every park bench.

"Okay," Gary consented. "It sounds good to me."

"It sounds *great,*" Melanie said. "We'll take the hibachi down to the beach."

"What're we going to use for charcoal?" Gary asked. "I doubt if I could get any now."

"So," Melanie said, "we'll use firewood. That would be okay, wouldn't it?"

Gary shrugged. "I guess so. The kids can help carry it."

"Then we're set," Melanie said with a smile. "We'll leave after lunch—so we can have dinner on the beach."

The children were bundled up more than usual for the picnic, since Melanie was sure the beach would be extra cold. Kyle, with his blond curls and very rosy cheeks, looked like a picture of his Dutch grandfather. Melanie decided that she would have to do a portrait of him, looking exactly as he did now.

The three children were walking ahead of their

parents, and Kyle and Gina's arms were laden with wood. Kyle was whispering to his sisters from the corner of his mouth. Melanie smiled when he looked back at them from time to time.

"Mommy and Daddy sure are nice to each other now," he whispered.

"That's because they made up, silly," Gina told him. "And I'm glad they did, too. They're nicer to us, even! You know what? I'm going to ask if I can have a slumber party for my birthday this year!"

"Oh, really?" Nancy asked with enthusiasm.

"Uh huh," Gina replied, nodding her head so that the pompom on top of her hat bounced. "I never asked to have a big party before. I hope they say yes."

"They will," Kyle reassured.

"Well, don't say anything yet," Gina said.

Kyle twisted his fingers over his lips as if he were turning a key. Nancy made a quick cross, with the wrong hand, over her heart. Then the three of them began to giggle.

"What's so funny?" Melanie asked.

"Can't tell you," Gina said, looking back at her mother and trying to hide a smile.

"Oh, I get it," Melanie said. "Trade secret."

"Huh?"

"Never mind, Kyle," she said. "Gina, that wood isn't too heavy, is it?"

Gina shook her head and ran back to join her parents. Her father was carrying the hibachi so awkwardly, she thought. His bandaged wrist jutted out beyond it, and she leaned closer to read where she had signed the cast.

"Do you remember that time we were cooking burgers out on the balcony of our old apartment?" she asked.

"And the neighbor's dog went crazy barking because of the smell?" Melanie said.

"What you don't remember," Gary added, "is that I threw him one. That's the one I said fell over the side."

"Gary!"

"He's kidding, Mom," Gina said. "Aren't you, Daddy?"

"Sure," Gary replied. "But I was going to before it dropped. He was a cute little fellow."

"Can we get a dog?" Gina asked hopefully.

"I was waiting for that," Melanie said.

"Maybe," Gary said, "once we get a little more settled."

"Wow!" Gina cried, running ahead to tell her brother and sister the news.

"That's not such a bad idea," Melanie said. "Maybe a nice German shepherd."

"You mean an attack dog," Gary said, reading her mind.

Nancy suddenly sat herself down on a flat rock and began to pout. They'd been walking for a while, and the beach was nowhere in sight. When, she wanted to know, were they going to get there?

"Yeah," Kyle said. "It must be a hundred miles from here!"

"In just a few minutes, honey," Melanie said. "It *is* a long walk from our house."

"Can't you hear the gulls?" Gary asked.

Nancy sat silently for a moment, listening. Then she nodded her head. Yes, she said, she could hear the gulls.

"Well," Gary told her, "the gulls are right on the bay."

Encouraged, Nancy got to her feet again and rushed ahead. Her little legs, the burns now healed, moved quickly, and she was soon far ahead of the others.

Something moved behind the trees next to her. She turned toward the sound, to see something blue and flowing disappear into the thick of the pines. Nancy blinked, waiting with her heart pounding for the mean man to appear. But the woods were empty.

When Gary caught up with her and bent down to hug her, he didn't know her slight scream was one of terror.

"Daddy!"

"A penny for your thoughts, Nancy," Gary said.

"Can I have a dime instead?" Nancy asked with a grin, all thoughts of the mean man gone.

"I'd give you all the dimes in the world," Gary said, "if I had them. But all I can offer now is chicken. Sounds yummy?"

"Real yummy," Nancy said. She clutched at her father's coat and walked with him the rest of the way.

On the beach, Gary set the hibachi down on a flat rock. Melanie suggested the children gather shells to decorate later while they waited for Gary to cook the chicken. She would even let them use some of her paints.

With that promise, the three children ran down toward the water and walked along its edge. Shells were lifted and examined, only to be thrown down again when a chip or break was discovered.

Gina wandered ahead of Kyle and Nancy, humming a tune to herself and putting shells into her sweater pockets until they bulged. Each was designated for a different friend, and Gina had the idea to make Christmas presents of them. She was certain her mother had so many paints that she could color each one differently.

Something hooked her ankles just then and sent her flying forward into the sand. Her teeth slammed into her lower lip.

"Witch-child!" she heard a low voice growl.

She started to turn around to yell at Kyle or Nancy for tripping her. But the two children were yards behind her, running. She sat on the sand, rubbing her lip. The bay was calm. Gina stared out over it, to the thick beige grasses on its other side. She had heard a voice, had felt strong hands shove her from behind. And yet she was all alone.

"Just like Daddy's accident," she whispered, still staring at the marsh.

Oh, she had thought a good deal about that. How Daddy had been nearly strangled, then pushed. How he couldn't remember who the man was. Gina shivered, remembering the terrible phone calls from that man Nancy called Uncle Terry.

Hello, kiddo! I'm going to . . .

Gina shook her head, trying to clear her mind. She didn't understand a word the man had said, but she didn't have to. She had been afraid then, and she was a little afraid right now. But then, Mommy and Daddy were right down the beach. And here came Kyle and Nancy. She erased the solemn expression from her face.

"Gina!" Kyle cried, helping her to her feet. "What happened?"

"I tripped over something," Gina said breathlessly. "Is my lip bleeding?"

Kyle stood on tiptoe to get a closer look. "Just a little. Wanna go back?"

"Okay," Gina said. "But don't tell Mom and Dad, okay? They'll think I'm a klutzo."

"I don't think you are," Kyle said.

"Did you hear someone say something just before?" Gina asked.

"No, I didn't hear anything," Kyle admitted. "There isn't anyone else here, Gina. Maybe you heard a gull."

Gina nodded, although she knew it was no gull she heard. Perhaps, she thought, it had been her father's voice. It had seemed so close, yet she might have been imagining things. It had sounded like "witch-child," but could her father have been asking her mother "which side?"

"Race ya!" Kyle cried suddenly, running up the beach.

"I don't want to race!" Nancy cried.

"I'll walk with you," Gina said. She called up the beach to her brother: "We're not included!"

"What are you going to do with all those shells?" Nancy wanted to know.

"I'm going to make Christmas presents out of them," Gina told her. "I'll help you make some, if you want."

"Okay!"

"You know what?" Gina said thoughtfully. "I'm going to hide them in a special place. There's a really deep drawer in my old desk, and if I push the shells back really far, no one could ever see them!"

Gina made Nancy promise she wouldn't say a word about her secret drawer. The two girls skipped up to the rest of the family, giggling. The fire Gary had made was roaring, filling the air with a delicious scent. In a few minutes, they were eating, talking, and laughing. It was easy to forget anything bad had ever happened to them.

10

Gina arranged her shells on her dresser in size order and chose the best ones for her parents' gifts. She would use some of them to outline a little hand mirror to give to her mother. For her father, she'd paint the biggest shells so that he'd have a nice place to put his paper clips and rubber bands. And, as she had told Nancy, she'd keep them hidden in her desk.

One of the cubbyholes was deep enough to push the shells back into without their being seen. But the little door refused to open when she tugged at it.

"Oh, come on!" Gina cried, pulling hard. She didn't expect it to snap open so quickly, and she gasped, knocking the side of her hand against the trimming on one side of it. It flipped aside, and a panel in the desk slid open. Gina poked her hand inside the dark hole, delighted to have found a secret compartment. The tips of her fingers touched something cold, and she pulled at it.

"Oh, neat!" she cried, seeing a pearl-handled pistol. She ran from the room. "Mom! Mom!"

Melanie's first reaction upon hearing her daughter's cries was to pray nothing had gone wrong again. When Gina stepped into the studio, she gasped. The little girl was aiming a gun at her.

"My God, Gina!" she cried. "Put that down! Where did you get it?"

"I found it in my desk," Gina told her, handing

over the pistol. "There's a secret compartment in it, Mom!"

"Really?" Melanie said. "How'd you find it?"

"The little door got stuck and I hit against the side when I pulled it. There's a panel that looks just like it's part of the desk, but it slides open."

"Another mystery to add to our list of funny happenings," Melanie said. It sounded more casual than she meant it.

"Yeah, but this isn't as creepy as other things that go on here," Gina said.

"Do those things bother you?"

"Sometimes I worry in school," Gina told her. "The other kids want to know what's happening, but I don't want to tell them any more. And sometimes I have nightmares."

"Oh, honey!" Melanie cried, putting an arm around her. "I never realized you kids paid any attention to all this. If you have nightmares, come into bed with Daddy and me."

"I can do that?" Gina asked.

"Sure," Melanie said, kissing the child's dark hair. "It's a big bed."

Gina snuggled against her mother and touched the gun.

"Why do you suppose it was hidden away like that?"

"Oh, just to keep it safe," Melanie said. "Just the way we keep guns in drawers and not out in the open."

"But if it was a secret compartment, how could anyone know the gun was there?"

"It wasn't always a secret, Gina," Melanie said. "Whoever had this gun knew how to get to it."

* * *

Perhaps the owner had known how to open the panel, but this knowledge had been of little use to her when she wanted to use the gun. The last person to see it was a woman named Jesse Prentice, who had lived in the house just after the end of the Civil War. She had hidden the gun in the panel, not daring to leave it in plain sight. She was afraid the raiders would come back to her house again. On a day she had been to town, they had come to her house to kill her husband and kidnap her baby son. And Jesse was certain they'd be back to steal the treasures of the house.

But she would wait forever for them, because they didn't exist. There were no raiders planning another attack on the house. In fact, the same man who murdered her husband and took her child away meant to protect her from any harm. He loved her. He would take care of her. But in order to take care of her, he had been forced to murder not only her husband, but her infant son.

Jesse stood perfectly still as the news that her baby had been found in the bay was gently broken to her. Then, dry-eyed, she closed the front door and walked up to her bedroom. The pistol she had hidden was loaded. One bullet would be enough.

Jesse pushed against the molding around the secret panel and waited for it to ease open. Nothing happened, although she had pushed the trimming as far as it would go. The strip of wood remained tightly shut, sealing the gun away from her.

A cold wind blew up behind her, and she turned to see if she had left the window open. But it was closed, and the curtains were still. She turned back to the panel and pounded at it, the tears she had held back gushing now in torrents. Jesse Prentice wanted to die. Why wouldn't they let her?

She buried her face in her arm and slammed her fist against the desk top, again, and again, and again . . .

. . . until it hit something hard and cold. The letter opener! She stopped crying only for a few moments to look at it before slashing it over her wrists, again and again.

Her lover watched her, unseen, confused. Why was she doing this? Didn't she know she was safe now, that he would protect her?

He threw himself over her body and began to scream.

* * *

Melanie placed the gun on the table and asked Gina to find her father. Gary and Kyle were outside in the barn. Both looked up when Gina opened the big doors and walked inside. She headed for the light of her father's flashlight.

"Guess what?" she asked. "I found a secret compartment in my desk!"

"Oh, wow!" Kyle cried. "I want to see!"

"First guess what I found inside," Gina said.

"A book?" Gary suggested.

"Uh-uh."

"A doll?"

"No, a gun!" Gina told him.

"C'mon, Kyle," Gary said. "Let's go inside and see."

When he was nearly to the door, Kyle's foot caught on something protruding from the dirt floor. He stooped down to pick it up. But what he thought was a rock turned out to be the corner of a small box that had been buried there. He dug at the earth around it, pulling the treasure from its hiding place.

It was a tin box, very small, and when he opened it he found a tiny package with a note tied to it.

He realized that the barn was suddenly very dark, and he looked up to find his sister and father gone. He stood up and walked outside, opening the package.

"Why would anyone bury a stick?" he wondered, confused.

He took it up to his mother's studio and handed it to his father. Gary was holding the pistol, and he frowned when his son gave him what seemed to be a bent twig. But on closer inspection he found it was, in fact, the slender bone of a human finger. It had been charred black.

"This note was with it," Kyle said, handing him a slip of paper.

"I'll bet it has an interesting story behind it," Gary said, showing it to Melanie. "It's a bone."

"Oh, yecch," Gina groaned.

"Read the note, Gary," Melanie said.

Gary unfolded the yellow paper. He lifted his

glasses from his pocket and slipped them on as the children fidgeted anxiously.

"The writing's kind of faded," he said. He began to read. "This is all that remains of my beloved Lydia. By this and by God I swear my eternal love for her, and by this I shall avenge her death. JNA, September 10, 1797."

"JNA," Melanie said. "Jacob Armand?"

"It could be," Gary said.

"The year is right," Melanie said. "Remember the diary? I guess Jacob really did have a girl, just like Nora Jennings wrote. And he loved her a great deal."

"Enough to keep part of her with him for all time," Gary said.

"Who's Jacob Armand?" Gina asked.

Her question was ignored. Melanie had caught sight of something Kyle was holding in his hand, and she let out a cry of astonishment. She pointed at it, too shocked to explain why it terrified her. Confused, Kyle tightened a chubby fist around the blue and gold brocade that had wrapped the charred bone.

11

Jacob Armand had built his home far from the town, for privacy and as a safety precaution against those who would destroy his property. As a result, very few people traveled up the hill to his home. The VanBurens had been the first to use the road regularly in some thirty years. With them came the milkman, the mailman, and the newsboy.

But not a soul had been on the road since Helen Jennings left the house that Saturday afternoon. On Monday Gina and Kyle set off for school as usual, gloves and hats added to their coats to protect them from the bitter winds that had blown up overnight. Though it was only two days before Halloween, winter promised to arrive, at least with respect to temperature, within a few days. Gina held tightly to a box containing her witch costume for the school play, for whatever extra warmth she could get from it.

They found Helen in a crumpled pile. At first there was no reaction from either child. They had seen death before, in the face of a wino who had fallen in the gutter in front of their city apartment. They hardly knew Helen Jennings any better than they had known that bedraggled old man.

Though the icy air had preserved the body to a degree, it was still an abhorrent picture. Her puffy cheeks were split in the center by thin, blued lips that stretched into a ghastly smile. Eyes like prunes had fallen back into her head, staring. One thin arm had been thrown over her head, and now its skin was stretched and pulling.

Reality stopped against something in both Kyle's and Gina's minds that was there to protect them from this horrid sight. And then Gina let out a gasp and grabbed Kyle's hand. The two ran back home, bursting into the kitchen, both shouting at once.

"Okay! Okay!" Melanie cried, taking each child by one shoulder. "Gina, tell me what happened."

"We found an old lady on the hill," Gina said breathlessly. "She's—uh—dead, Mom."

"Oh, God," Melanie whispered. "Did you know who she was? Did she look bad?"

Gina shook her head. "She wasn't as bad as the wino, Mom."

"I don't know who she was," Kyle said. "I think maybe that Mrs. Jennings you were talking about."

Melanie, not taking her hands away from the children's shoulders, called to Gary.

"The kids say they found an old lady on the hill," she explained when he appeared in the doorway. "I think it's Helen Jennings. Gina says she's dead."

"Christ," Gary mumbled. "Where is she, exactly?"

"Right near the bus stop, Daddy," Kyle said.

"For God's sake, Gary," Melanie said, "get her out of there before that bus comes with all those kids on it." She turned to the children. "Do you want to go to school?"

"*I* do," Gina said quickly. "For once I've got something neat to talk about."

"Me, too!" Kyle put in.

Nodding, Melanie sank down into her chair. Gary had already gone out, carrying a large piece of canvas that had been used to wrap furniture when they moved into the house. Gina, without a word, ushered Kyle out the door.

By the time the bus pulled away, with the two children on board gasping for breath, Helen Jennings was wrapped and in Gary's arms. He held her awkwardly, his injured wrist pushed out beyond her body so that she rested more on his upper arms. He was happy that he had reached her in time; he had seen the children on the bus craning to look out the window after Kyle and Gina got on board.

He carried her up to the house and laid her in a trough in the barn. It seemed a callous thing to do, but he wasn't about to sit her at the kitchen table.

Melanie, after a few moments of respectful silence dedicated to her eccentric neighbor, had phoned the police. By nine A.M., Helen Jennings was packed into a tiny cubicle to wait in darkness while her next of kin was sought.

From the discovery of her body to her delivery into the hands of the coroner, every act was performed dutifully and with little emotion. The VanBurens had little reason to mourn her death. As far as they knew, she had never done anything for them.

* * *

Janice brought her rubber stamp down hard on the last book of the night and pushed it toward the man who stood in front of her desk. Ten minutes later, she was bundled up in rabbit fur and suede, heading out the door. She laughed at her reflection in the glass display case, thinking she looked a bit too much like a refugee from Antarctica.

She had been thinking of Melanie VanBuren that day. For some reason, she wanted to befriend her, even though Melanie hadn't kept their lunch date. Perhaps, Janice reasoned, it would be fun to get to know a near-celebrity. It wasn't everyone who got an illustration in *The New York Times*.

The rain that had been falling lightly had changed and was now coming down in heavy drops. Janice turned up the speed of her wipers and watched them swish back and forth noisily, throwing off the rhythm of the song she was trying to sing. She said out loud, "The Starship disco'll probably be empty tonight." She lit a cigarette. "Oh, hell," she sighed, "maybe the creeps'll stay in out of the rain and I'll meet somebody decent."

She turned her car onto Starbine Court Road and headed toward the hill. She switched it into low gear so that it could comfortably take the steep climb to the top. When she brought it around the driveway, she stopped it with a gentle pressure to the brake. But in spite of her care, the old thing coughed and shook before settling down to wait for her.

Melanie registered surprise when she opened the door to find Janice Lors standing on her porch.

"Janice, hello!" she cried. "Come on in—I didn't expect to see you after I didn't call about having lunch. I've been so busy . . ."

"Hey, don't worry," Janice said, slipping out of her jacket. She handed it to Melanie. "I'm sure you've been caught up with moving-in chores."

"That and other things," Melanie answered.

"You don't know how glad I am to see someone who isn't wearing a uniform," she said.

"Oh," Janice answered. "I left mine at the library. You know, the bun and glasses."

"I can't see you in that," Melanie said with a shake of her head.

"Neither can I," Janice answered, looking around. "My God, look at this place! What's behind all the doors?"

"Oh, most of those are closets," Melanie said. "And empty. I suppose we'll fill them as years go on, but since wc moved out of an apartment, there really wasn't much to bring."

"Oh, jeez," Janice said, "I'd have them filled in five minutes. Can I see the rest of the house? I've never been in a mansion."

"Sure," Melanie answered, leading her down the hall. "I'll give you the grand tour. Anything to get my mind off this day."

"What's wrong?"

"Oh, let's not discuss it right now," Melanie said quickly. "This is the first chance I've had all day to relax."

She led Janice through all the downstairs rooms, delighted to hear her friend gasp at the beauty of it all. Janice had to take a closer look at the fireplace in the dining room and couldn't help touching the pieces of antique furniture.

"And look at those neat nautical paintings!" she cried. "In every room! Did you do them?"

"Oh, no," Melanie said. "Those came with the house. The first man who lived here was a sailor, Jacob Armand."

"Romantic name," Janice said. "So, let's see *your* work."

Melanie took her to the upstairs studio, where stacks of her paintings remained covered with sheets. Unlike the rest of the house, which was walled in dark wood, this room had been painted white, and when Melanie turned on the light, Janice squinted in the brightness that bounced off the enameled walls. She went to the canvas on the easel, a painting of a lighthouse.

"Pretty," she said. "Do you ever display?"

"I've had several shows," Melanie told her. "My last one was way back in May. But we've just been too busy with the house." She walked to another easel. "When I get a chance to finish it, this is my current project."

Janice smiled at the portrait of Nancy and Gina, nearly finished, but left without its last touches for weeks. She shook her head, smiling at the pretty faces.

"My daughters," Melanie said proudly.

"You're kidding!" Janice cried. "Aren't they adorable!"

Melanie pointed to each. "My youngest, Nancy, and this is Gina."

"God," Janice sighed. "What dolls."

"I have a son, too," Melanie said. "His name is Kyle. I'd introduce you, but they're sleeping now."

"I'll have to come here some Saturday afternoon to meet them," Janice said, "when they're not in bed." Suddenly, she looked up at the huge floor-to-ceiling windows and chuckled: "Do you sunbathe in here?"

"I suppose I could," Melanie laughed.

"In the nude, no less," Janice suggested.

"Oh, God!" Melanie cried. "I don't think so! Come on, let's go downstairs."

Janice ran her finger over the brass sphinx at the top of the stairs, declaring it was kind of cute. Then she went down with Melanie, admiring the carved banister. She felt relaxed in the warm amber glow that bathed the bottom landing.

"This place has *romantic* stamped all over it," she said when they walked into the living room. "My God! Another fireplace! And look at the bay windows! Oh, geez, Melanie, this place is beautiful!"

"Beautiful, maybe," Melanie agreed, "but I think it has a jinx on it. Since I saw you last week I've lived through a murder, an attempted murder, and God only knows what else. The police were here all day."

"You weren't kidding about the uniform then," Janice said. "Poor thing. Tell me about it."

"The day I was with you," Melanie began, "I came home and found my husband lying on the floor at the bottom of the stairs. I think he was pushed."

"Pushed?" Janice asked. "You aren't sure?"

"He hasn't said so," Melanie told her, "but there were bruises on his neck that the doctor said might have come from fingers. We think he ran into a burglar and there was a fight. But we don't really talk about it. Gary doesn't seem to be too inclined to tell me the whole story, and I don't believe in pushing."

"But is he all right?" Janice wanted to know.

"He sprained his wrist," Melanie said. "But the doctor said it'll heal quickly. But here's the other strange thing that happened—remember that old lady we saw at the parking lot?"

"Yeah?"

"She was at my house Saturday," Melanie said. "She told me stories about this place—that it was haunted."

"She told you that in the park," Janice pointed out, "and I think you were ready to believe her."

"*Now* I might be," Melanie admitted, "after what's been going on here. Helen—that's her name—gave me a diary to read that her great-great aunt had written in 1797. It gave me a good deal of information on this house."

"So," Janice said, "does it have any weird stories behind it?"

"I don't know," Melanie said. There was a hint of disappointment in her reply. "The darned thing disappeared the day after I started reading it. And I'm afraid I can't ask Helen to fill in the blanks. She was killed Saturday, on her way home from here."

"Oh, no!"

"Oh, yes," Melanie said. "My children found her on their way to school this morning. She'd been lying there since Saturday afternoon."

"How did they take it?" Janice asked, leaning forward in her seat.

"Better than I could," Melanie admitted. "They couldn't wait to run off to school to tell everyone. Anyway," Melanie went on after a pause, "the police were here for a few hours today. I couldn't give them much information, though. But they're convinced that there might be a connection between my husband's accident and Helen's death."

"How did she die?" Janice asked.

"They weren't too willing to talk about it," Melanie said, "but one of them—Tony DiMagi—confided that her neck might have been broken, judging from the finger marks. Of course, since Gary has his wrist bandaged up, he's not a suspect."

"Thank God," Janice said for her. "It sounds like someone wanted to strangle both people—bruises on both their necks, I mean. Gross! Who could it be? Some very respectable local figure who's a psychopathic killer? Spooky." Melanie stood up. "Can I offer you a drink?"

"No, thanks," Janice said. "I'm saving my stomach for the Starship."

"Starship?"

"A disco," Janice said. "Not that I care for the music, but once in a while somebody worth bringing home shows up."

"I remember the singles scene only vaguely," Melanie said. "It must be fun."

"Well," Janice said with a sigh, "when you get to be twenty-nine and you don't have a man, it's kind of a drag. But in this day and age, I guess I could go it alone. I did it for four years at Ohio State University." She clapped her hands together and leaned back. "So! Tell me what else has been going on here. It might do you good to get it off your chest."

"Oh, it would take me all night," Melanie said. "But the most recent thing—a little thing—was a gun my daughter found in her drawer. Gary says it might date back to the Civil War! And there's something else, too. My son, Kyle, found a human finger bone buried out in the barn. Somebody wrapped it up in a blue and gold cloth."

"Sounds pretty sickie," Janice said.

"I think so," Melanie agreed. "The thing that got to me was that cloth. About a week or two ago, I found a pearl ring, and a silk gown, wrapped in the same cloth. That was two separate occasions. I thought the gifts were from Gary, but now that I think of it, they couldn't have been."

"Why didn't you ask him in the first place?" Janice inquired.

"We used to have a game we played when we were first married," Melaine explained. "We'd leave little gifts around the house for each other and not talk about them."

"That's sweet," Janice commented.

"After I saw that cloth Kyle was holding when he brought in that terrible thing," Melanie said, "I asked Gary about it. He didn't have the slightest idea what I was talking about."

Janice shuddered. "That's creepy!"

"Creepy isn't the word for it," Melanie sighed. "My family is in some kind of danger, and that damned cloth has something to do with it."

"Does Gary think so?"

Before Melanie could reply, Gary appeared at the door with Tony DiMagi. The young cop had returned to the house to give back a law book he had borrowed earlier that day.

"Can you believe he finished it already?" Gary asked. "Two hundred pages!"

"I'm impressed," Janice said, smiling at the handsome young cop.

Introductions were followed by another offer of drinks by Melanie. Tony declined, saying he had to get the car back to the station. He started for the door, buttoning his coat. But as he moved to open it, a scream came from upstairs.

Gary looked at Melanie for only a split second before running, with the others, up the stairs. At the door to Kyle's bedroom, they were stopped by great, dark curls of smoke. Tony pressed his hand to the door, then pushed it open.

Kyle was sitting on his big bed, screaming, in the midst of roaring flames.

12

Kyle was crouched on his knees in the center of his bed. All around him, the light of the fire danced, making brilliant flecks of color in the tears streaking down his face. It was a fierce blaze, flowing angrily around the bed and digesting everything in sight.

Tony's trained mind took only a split second to assess the situation: the fire was concentrated and could be put out easily with an extinguisher. He turned to shout at Melanie to find one.

"Aren't you going to radio headquarters?" Gary demanded.

"No time for that! Move it!"

Under the authority Tony had suddenly assumed, Gary jumped and ran from the room, announcing he would call the fire department. He coughed in the smoke and held his bandaged wrist up to his mouth until he reached clear air. At the bottom of the stairs, he leaned over the banister and lifted the receiver—for nothing. There was no sound through the wire.

"Shit," Gary mumbled, slamming it down. Now what would he do?

Pounding the banister on his way back up, Gary gritted his teeth in anger. What the hell was this? How could the phones be out? There hadn't been any storms.

The thought was cut off when something shoved hard against his back and sent him flying forward. He hit his lip on the top stair, and the faint taste of blood rose on his tongue. He tried to stand to continue his ascent, rubbing at his cut lip and cursing in his impatience. And then he heard the voice.

"You cannot stop me!"

Gary's mind raced back to the day he was attacked, when he had heard this same voice. His heart thumped in anticipation of the cold grip. *(Oh, God! Oh, God! He's trying to keep me from Kyle!)*

He rested his head on the step for only a second, breathing in heavily for strength. Then he attempted to continue, only to be hindered when something hooked around his ankles and painfully dragged him to the bottom of the stairs, *thump, thump, thump.*

"You cannot stop me!" the voice hissed again.

"Eat shit, you sadistic bastard!" Gary screamed, not knowing at who or what his anger was aimed. He shot to his feet and ran up the stairs, something deep within telling him speed was his only means of escaping the fearsome presence. When he reached Kyle's room again, the combination of running and breathing the heavy smoke made him gag. He stumbled to the bed and took the wool blanket Tony held out to him.

"The phone's dead," he shouted, choking.

"It's all right," Tony screamed. "I think we can put it out when your wife brings the extinguisher! Just keep smothering the flames with the blanket!"

Gary did as he was told, moving around the bed in a constant motion, trying to find one spot where the flames were low enough that he could reach his son.

"Why can't we pull him out?" he shouted.

"The bed's too high to reach him!" Tony yelled back. "And our weight would collapse it! Even one man is too heavy for that thing."

"Damn it, it's solid oak!" Gary told him.

"You think so?" Tony asked, aiming below the bed. Two of the crossbeams had split and were angled toward the floor.

"But what do we do?"

"What we're doing," Tony said, trying to reassure him.

"Bull!" Gary cried. "I want you to get my kid out of there!"

"I told you . . ."

"Then I'll do it!" Gary yelled, moving closer to the inferno. He reached a hand through it, hoping to quickly grab his son—the way one might pass a finger through a birthday-candle flame in order not to get burned. But the moment his arm began to reach, the flames shot up, as if something were working a bellows at them.

"What was that?"

"I don't know!" Tony admitted. "Come on, we can still put it out! Keep at it!"

As he heard his son coughing and crying, Gary felt terribly helpless, wondering why Tony didn't do more, wondering what more he *could* do. The flames were higher, nearly blocking his vision of his son. Kyle was screaming his head off, sitting in the middle of all this, for the moment untouched. The flames seemed to be avoiding their prey, and yet Gary knew he was being teased, that something planned to hurt his child when it felt the time was right.

"You sadistic bastard!" Gary seethed again to that unknown malevolence.

While the men were working at the fire, trying to get through the flames and arguing about how to rescue Kyle, Janice was frantically trying to find Melanie in the dark hallways. The main hall was glowing from the fire, but the two branch halls were pitch black. Finally she managed to discern an open door. She went through it and found herself in a closet. She also found Melanie, standing very still, staring up at the ceiling. In the dim light of the closet's single bulb, Melanie looked like a corpse. Her eyes were bloodshot, and her face had lost its color.

"Oh, my God!" Janice cried. "What's wrong with you?"

She tried to pull Melanie from the closet, but her friend's feet were rooted.

"What happened?"

Melanie found her voice.

"Someone kissed me!"

"Oh, don't be silly!" Janice cried. "There's no

one here but me, and I didn't see anyone leave the closet. Did you find the fire extinguisher?"

At that question Melanie seemed to wake up. "It's on the wall behind you," she said, pointing. Janice turned, yanked the extinguisher off the wall, and led Melanie back out into the hallway.

"Come on," Janice said, "they need it. The fire is getting worse." The two women hurried back to Kyle's room. Janice shoved the extinguisher at Tony and took his blanket.

Just then a bedpost fell. It collapsed in such a swift movement that it left a dark blur through the air. Inches away, Kyle shook with screams. Melanie began to cry.

"Stop it, Melanie!" Gary snapped. "Get to work on the fire! Here!"

He tossed her his blanket and went to find another. He tore apart drawers, finding nothing, then at last finding an old wool jacket. It was small, but good enough. He turned around in time to see a flame attach to Kyle's sleeve. The child frantically pounded it away, and it left a black mark on his blue flannel pajama top.

(He's starting, Gary thought. He's had enough fun and games, and he's going for my kid!)

"But *who's* going for my kid?" he asked out loud.

"Gary?" Melanie asked.

"Nothing!" her husband insisted. "Hey, why isn't that extinguisher working?"

"I'm *trying,"* Tony yelled, almost impatiently.

He knew enough not to show it, but Tony was as frightened about this whole thing as everyone else. He just couldn't understand why the fire wasn't going out. It had been a good five minutes. He felt his throat growing sore from the smoke, and his body was chilled by sweat. Suddenly foam spurted from the extinguisher. Tony worked at the flames until they began to subside. He sighed heavily and moved the foam over the remaining spots of fire.

And then it was gone. Tony stared at the blackened bed. Something was very wrong here. Not the child whimpering in his mother's arms, not the smoke that still hung in the air, nor the stifling heat. It was there. And then he saw it.

"Funny," he said.

"I don't think so," Gary snapped. "My son was nearly kill—"

Tony cut him off, pointing. "No, look. Don't you see that the fire didn't spread? It seems to have been concentrated around the bed, and that carpet is too old to be fireproof. I've never seen anything like it!"

"Very few things surprise me in this house any more," Gary said. Then, feeling the emotional after-effects of the ordeal, he turned to confront his son. "Kyle, were you playing with matches?"

"Gary!" Melanie gasped. "Kyle would never do a thing like that!"

"Don't butt in," Gary told her. He wrestled the child from his mother's grip and held him firmly by his small shoulders, leaning down to meet him eye-to-eye. "Tell me the truth, Kyle—were you playing with matches?"

"I-I was sleeping, Daddy!" Kyle wailed, his eyes brimming.

"Then how did that fire start?" Gary horrified by the strangeness of the event, wanted terribly to place the blame on something simple—like a little boy with matches.

"I-I don't know!" Kyle insisted, looking up at his father with pleading eyes.

"Gary, stop it!" Melanie cried, taking the boy into her arms again. "Kyle's never told a lie in his life, and you know—"

Whatever she was about to say was cut off by the sounds of new screams from down the hall. Melanie let go of Kyle and ran toward Gina's room, only inches in front of Gary and Tony. When they burst through the door, Melanie gasped. Like an instant replay on a Saturday football game, the scene of a few minutes ago was being repeated. Only now the victim was Gina, and the fire was twice as bad as the one in Kyle's room. Tony didn't have to consider long to realize it would take more than an extinguisher and blankets to put it out.

"I'll call in," he shouted over the din of the flames. "Get some blankets and work at it until I come back up!"

He ran from the room, the light of the fire guiding him through the dark hall. Halfway down the stairs, he felt a touch on his shoulder and turned to face Janice. When she asked if she could help him down here, he told her to look for more wool blankets. Janice turned into the first door she came to and entered the dining room. It was dark now, and across the room, the fireplace loomed like a gaping black hole. Janice kept her eyes turned from it, even after she turned the light on. Something about the void bothered her.

"Crap," she said when she had pulled open three drawers to find only silverware and linen tablecloths. And there was no rug she could pull up—it was all wall-to-wall.

Over her head, she could hear the sounds of running footsteps. A moment later, they were drowned out by nearer ones, and she walked out to the hall to meet Tony. He shoved an extinguisher in her hand and said, "Take this right upstairs, then come down again. I'll need you!"

Janice hurried up to Gina's room, where Melanie and Gary were pounding the flames with blankets. The fire shot all the way to the ceiling, helped by the heavy canopy. Gina was sitting upright, alternately coughing and choking. Janice pushed the extinguisher at Gary, then ran downstairs again.

Outside, she found Tony fumbling with his police radio, trying to pull some reaction from it. But it was as silent as the phone inside.

"Something's gone wrong with this thing," Tony said. "Can you drive to town to get help?"

"Sure," Janice said, turning to run to her car.

She got inside, turned the key—and nothing happened. Giving the dashboard a punch, she tried again, pumping the gas. In her rearview mirror, she could see the orange flames in Gina's bedroom window and the shadow of someone running.

"Move it, you old bomb!" she yelled, pumping the gas harder.

With a sputter, the engine finally revved, then hummed. Janice rolled it forward, watching Tony's reflection in the mirror. Then something up ahead caused her to lower her eyes. A swift movement of shadow. She squinted and pushed her head forward, trying to discern what it was. As she moved closer to it, she saw the shape of a tall man moving along the edge of the hill.

She honked her horn to flag him down and ask his help. He moved right past her without turning. When he neared her window, she tried to get a good look at him, but in the darkness and light rain his face was obscured.

She looked up at the mirror again. Tony had lifted the hood of his car and was leaning over the engine. The strange man came up behind him, slowly. Janice did a double-take at the scene. How in the hell, she thought, did he get there that fast?

"Stop worrying about dumb things and move your body out of here," Janice said to herself. "If he's a weirdo, Tony can handle him. He's got a gun."

Under the hood of his police car, Tony was using a rare string of curse words, holding a bundle of cut wires in his fist. They had been sliced, carefully, then tied together to make their reassembly all the more impossible.

"Arson," he said plainly, suddenly wishing Jack Hughes were here. If only his senior partner hadn't had the flu!

He was thinking just that when a strong, cold wind blew up behind him, and the hook of the car hood came crashing down on his spine.

* * *

Up in Gina's bedroom, Gary and Melanie were still trying to put out the fire. Melanie was crying, and by now Gary felt like joining her. He was confused, and yet he knew exactly what was going on. The unseen thing was out to kill his kids, and there was nothing he could do about it.

"Melanie, give this a try," he said breathlessly, handing her the extinguisher. He wiped the sweat from his forehead. "I'm exhausted."

Even so, he took a blanket from her and pounded at the flames. They shot as high as those on Kyle's bed and even higher where the canopy was draped. And, like Kyle, there was no way to get to Gina. Gary shuddered. This damned thing was just too weird.

Melanie struggled with the extinguisher, finding it awkward at first. Gina screamed and screamed, her skin bright red from the heat, and yet still untouched by the flames. Melanie didn't wonder about that, but Gary knew.

On the other side of the house, Nancy slept soundly, exhausted after a very busy day. Something dark loomed over the little girl's bed, holding her stuffed yellow rabbit dangerously close to her face. Nancy did not feel the softness of the plush that touched her cheek. She mumbled in her sleep and turned away, dreaming. The figure pressed the rabbit closer and then suddenly threw it across the room. It sensed something.

At that very moment, Melanie became so frustrated with her helplessness that she forgot the danger and crossed the flames to Gina's bed. She wrapped her arms around her daughter and looked for a chance to escape. The flames began to hypnotize her, and she became oblivious to what was happening.

"Are you out of your mind?" Gary demanded.

She said nothing.

"Melanie, you'll be hurt!"

But that wasn't what was intended for the fire. When the dark presence in Nancy's room realized what Melanie had done, it knew its plan to kill the children had failed. Melanie must never be harmed.

"Daddy, I'm cold!" Gina screeched.

Suddenly, it *was* cold. In fact, the whole damned room was *freezing*. Gary felt a shiver rack his body, and goose bumps formed over his skin. As he worked at the fire, still calling to Melanie, his teeth began to chatter. It was as if the temperature in the room had dropped fifty degrees.

An incredible wind blew up just then, ruffling the curtains and blowing Gary's hair into his eyes. In the half second it took for Gary to brush it away, the fire disappeared completely. Gary looked at it in amazement, for only the blackened bed gave evidence of what had happened here just a second ago. He let the extinguisher fall to the floor and passed his bandaged wrist over his forehead. His body, alternately heated by the flames and chilled by the mysterious cold, shook violently. He walked over to the window to open it and let the rain blow cooling spatters over him. The sound of a siren reached him from down the road, growing louder as the truck approached the house.

"I wonder what happened to Tony," he said then.

He turned back to the bed, where Melanie was hugging Kyle and Gina. Gary went to her and stroked her cheek, his eyes asking what had happened. But she had nothing to say.

Gina leaned her head back and looked up at her canopy, or what was left of it. A tear rolled down her cheek and caught on the edge of her lip. She unconsciously reached her tongue around to lick it, staring up in confusion at what had once been her beautiful bed.

But no more. The rich white velvet had taken on the sickly gray of the smoke, and the canopy now hung like the leaves of a weeping willow. The rug around the bed was pitch black for about two feet, then was completely unmarred. Gary thought about what Tony had said when they had put the fire out in Kyle's bedroom. Here again, the fire seemed to have concentrated in one small area, as if someone wanted to destroy only the bed. *(Or the children.)*

He dropped to his knees and crawled to where the pink floral design of the carpet stopped against the black. He rubbed his fingers over the area, then leaned down and sniffed at it. But he couldn't tell if anything had been put on part of the rug to make it fireproof. It was as if someone had wanted to harm the children, but not the rooms around them.

A man dressed in a fire chief's uniform burst into the room, followed by two other men.

Gary stood up. "We took care of it. I-I can't explain what happened."

"The children are all right?"

"I think so," Gina mumbled. Kyle nodded slowly.

"Thank God for that," Melanie said. She turned to the chief. "What took you so long?"

The chief looked at the two men with him and frowned.

"It seems something went wrong with officer DiMagi's radio," he said. "A woman named Lors came to us in person."

"Why didn't anyone call us on the phone?" a fireman asked.

"It was dead," Gary answered.

The fire chief went over to the window to signal that everything was under control. Down in the driveway, where Police Chief Bryan Davis had found the body of Tony DiMagi, a rookie cop stood staring at Tony's car with enormous, sickened eyes.

The chief started out the door, saying to his two men, "Check this place out—every inch of it."

"Gary," Melanie said, "we'll let the children sleep in our room tonight, okay? Then we can move them into the rooms across from Nanc—"

The remembrance of her youngest child jolted through Melanie and set her running. Gary understood. He followed his wife around the hallway, leading the two firemen. They burst into the little girl's room, where the child lay sleeping under a mound of blankets. Melanie went over and touched her lightly. She was fine, she was just fine.

The two firemen returned to Gina's room to talk to the children. Gary gave his wife a hug to encourage her and ran downstairs to answer a furious pounding at the door. He opened it to let in a husky cop.

The man snapped out a badge that identified him as Police Chief Bryan Davis. He moved further into the house, a sober look making him appear quite stern. His voice, though deep, was quiet.

"Do you need an ambulance?" he asked.

"No one was hurt, thank God," Gary said. After a moment, he added, "I'm Gary VanBuren."

"I know who you are," Davis said.

"Where's Tony, by the way?" Gary asked.

Davis ignored him. "Tell me everything that happened here tonight."

Gary related the events of the past hour, up to the start of Gina's fire. He explained why Tony had been up at the house in the first place and how the two of them had believed the fires were no accident. He saw Davis' expression change at that statement, but went on with the story.

"When the fire in Gina's room started," Gary said, "Tony ran down to his car to radio for help. I haven't seen him since."

"The Lors woman came down with him, didn't she?"

"I don't really remember," Gary admitted. "Everything was happening too fast. You understand."

"Yeah," Davis said softly.

A policeman opened the door and asked, "Ambulance requesting leave, sir. Anyone else?"

"No, go ahead," Davis said with a wave of his hand. "Tell them to get the hell out of here."

"What does he mean 'anyone else'?" Gary demanded.

He heard the motor being revved, the sirens. He put a hand on Davis' shoulder and turned him around. In the man's eyes he could see tiny speckles of tears.

"What the hell is going on out there?"

"Officer DiMagi is dead," Davis whispered, pushing his hand away.

"What?"

"He was caught under the hood of his car," Davis said quickly, as if the words were poison to be gotten rid of. He eyed Gary's cast. "How long have you had that on?"

"About two weeks," Gary said. "Jesus, I can't believe this night!"

Davis squeezed his eyes shut and pounded his fist on the table. Those cut wires under the hood—still in Tony's hand. *Tony!* The best damned cop that ever came to Belle Bay.

He could see it. He could see it. Two blue-trousered legs dangling over the grill of the car, like a scene from a Japanese horror film. The car like one of those plastic monsters. And the hook . . .

He snapped open his eyes and gave his head a sharp shake. Duty. Calm and collected—that's right. Always keep your head. Even when you lose one of the best men you ever knew. They never explained this at the police academy. They never explained the hurt.

"I'll have to take fingerprints," he said. "You'll come down to the station."

"Why?" Gary demanded. He thought for a few seconds, then said, "That was no accident, was it?"

Davis shook his head slowly. "I don't know."

"I can't leave my wife and children alone," Gary said.

"We'll talk tomorrow," Davis said. "I'm posting an all-night guard on this place."

"Thanks," Gary mumbled. He wasn't really certain if the guards were to keep others out or them in.

13

When at last sleep came to her, Melanie's dreams were shrouded in a cloth of blue and gold. Her children screamed for her, but no matter how many halls she turned down, no matter how many doors she opened, she couldn't find them.

Open the door—inside there is a package wrapped in blue-and-gold brocade. Huge, hundreds of times bigger than real life. They seem to float in an invisible pool, packages in every room. Huge white clouds loom behind them, like a Dali painting.

She opened another door. This time, the cloth began to move away from the treasure it wrapped. *(There is nothing there to see.)* It was coiling itself, tight, and moving like a sidewinder toward a man who stood with his back to her.

He couldn't see the rope standing on end, reaching for his neck. Melanie opened her mouth. No screams. The man turned to her, as if he had heard her silent plea. It was Gary, pop-eyed, a blue tongue dangling from his mouth. . . .

Melanie bolted upright, awake. Her heart pounded in the silence of the room. Next to her, Kyle and Gina were sleeping soundly. Her movements hadn't disturbed them.

Melanie rolled off the bed. She felt somewhat smug, because she had at last discovered the culprit behind all the things that were wrong in this house. A cloth of blue and . . .

"You're really going crazy," she whispered, stepping out into the hall.

It was dark. One day soon, she thought, she would have to ask Gary to put some fixtures in here. She opened the door to the room he had taken across the hall, just to have a look at him. It was good to know he was here.

She wanted to read the diary again, to learn more about the house. It had to be *somewhere* downstairs, because Melanie was certain she had put it on the coffee table that night and hadn't read it since. Since she couldn't sleep, she would try to find it. To read it might ease her tension, she thought. It would answer questions.

She started toward the stairs, moving quickly, wanting to be down them and into the light. But as she neared them, a strange sound came from above her. It was like the crying of a child. She stepped closer to the linen closet, and the cries became clearer. What was up there?

She opened the door and looked inside at the dark shelves. The cry stopped for a few moments, then started again. It seemed to be saying "Mama, mama. . . ." Then it choked and died away.

Melanie looked up at the ceiling. It was a trick, she told herself. Someone's hiding up in the attic and trying to lure me up there by sounding like a child. He is waiting for me.

"The police tore that place apart," she reminded herself out loud, "and they found nothing."

Then she remembered the guards who were posted downstairs. She went quickly down the steps, but saw no one. She headed for the darkened living room.

"Ma'am?"

Melanie nearly hit the ceiling. With a gasp, she turned around to see one of the guards standing behind her. She smiled at him sheepishly and said, "I thought I heard something upstairs. Can we check?"

"That's what I'm here for," said the policeman.

Melanie let him lead the way up the stairs, and up the narrow steps to the attic, following close at his heels. The attic was dark and musty, not a place she liked to be in so soon after her horrible dream. But she felt secure with the young cop, who kept his hand ever in reach of his gun. The two poked through the clutter of boxes and old furniture, finding nothing. At last, the guard said, "Maybe it was squirrels."

"My husband mentioned them a while back," Melanie recalled. "Oh, you must be right. Besides, there isn't a place here where anyone could hide."

"I should be going back down now," said the guard.

"Go right ahead," Melanie told him. "I'd like to stay up here for a few minutes. I can't sleep anyway, and it might be fun to rummage through a few old trunks.

"I'll be right downstairs, then," said the cop. He disappeared through the square hole in the floor. Melanie looked around, then picked up an old leather case lying on top of the nearest pile of boxes. The initials JNA sent chills through her.

She put the case down again and walked around the room. The cries had stopped completely now, but still she kept her ears and eyes open. It didn't matter that the guard hadn't found anything. Just the thought of it made her shiver.

Something sparkled in the beam of her flashlight, and she moved forward to investigate. Her fingers touched cloth.

It was the blue-and-gold brocade, yards and yards of it wound around a bolt. It leaned against an antique wooden mannequin. There was a picture pinned to it of a young girl dressed in a lovely gown, done in the simple style of a Colonial artist—all out of proportion in uneven ink strokes. Melanie guessed that the fabric had originally been intended for making the gown that the figure was wearing. She picked up the end of it and saw that two pieces had been cut away. Pieces just the right size to wrap the gifts she had found.

She started to look further around the room, driven by an excitement that protected her from fear. Then the crying began again. Melanie turned toward it, aiming her flashlight. The beam hit the metal of a doorknob that was barely visible above a big old trunk.

Even as she walked toward the door, Melanie was telling herself she could be walking into the hideout of a madman.

She couldn't stop. She shoved the trunk away from the door, thinking it was strange the police hadn't seen this in their long, detailed search. A strange, comforting thought hit her. How could there be anyone in there, with this trunk here? It couldn't have been pushed from the inside, naturally. *(Perhaps unnaturally . . .)*

The noise was mice, of course. But Melanie had to be sure. She lifted a small telescope from the floor to use as a club. Holding it up, ready to strike, she entered the room.

She saw no one. She walked further inside, keeping her back to the wall and looking right and left in a constant motion, to be certain no one was hiding there. She took in her surroundings. The room was papered with a toy soldier motif. A teddy bear, its ancient plush rotting away, lay forlornly at the foot of the small bed. Melanie smiled for a moment, realizing she was in a nursery.

But the gentle sweetness that had once been in here was gone now. There was something terrifying and ugly about its emptiness. It made Melanie wonder to God what she was doing here.

Go down and get Gary. . . .

Still holding her telescope up, ready to strike, she went over to the dresser and pulled at drawers, finding an array of little boys' clothes. A piece of wood broke off in her hand and fell to the floor. A streak of ice shot through her. The dresser had been burned. And the bed?

She walked over to it, and found that the mattress had been set on fire. All that was left of it now was blackened springs. It stood there before her, something to tell her that the evil in the house wasn't natural. It told her that someone had succeeded long ago in doing what they hadn't done tonight. Murder.

Suddenly frightened, she turned to run from the

room. But the cries came again, pulling her back. She stopped short, just a foot in front of the door, feeling her heartbeat. She didn't want to turn. . . .

In the bed, four little boys screamed silently, reaching out to her. Light danced in the tears on their faces, the light of fire. But there was no fire.

"I'm not seeing this," Melanie said with determination.

Her eyes focused on the youngest of the boys, a tiny child who couldn't have been more than two. His big blue eyes were wide with terror. She read his lips, moving slowly as if he were eating sticky candy.

Ahhhhh . . .

Mahhhh . . .

MMAAMMMAAAA!!

He wanted his mother! Melanie took a step toward him, the innocence of a child crying for his mother making her forget that there was something very wrong, very evil here.

One of the older boys collapsed, knocking the little one down. His hair began to shrivel away, his skin suddenly blistered. As if the scene were being run on a too-fast old-time movie camera, the pajamas blackened and disappeared in invisible flames.

"NO!" Melanie screamed, running to the bed.

She reached out to pull them away—and found Helen Jennings in her arms. The woman pulled away and slapped her, her long nails grazing Melanie's cheek.

Fool! You did not listen to me and now he'll kill them all!

"You're dead!" Melanie screamed.

He'll kill them all! Aaaahhhh!

"NNNNOOOOOO!!"

Melanie screamed as she ran.

This is only a dream, she told herself. *Please, dear Lord, make it a dream!*

Her badly shaking legs carried her, too slowly, down the stairs and into the hallway. From above her, she heard an angry, masculine voice, then a woman's screech. But she didn't stop to hear more of it.

Her arms groped forward to guide her when her tears blocked her vision in the darkness. Then she couldn't run any more. She sank to her knees and began to cry in her terror. She wanted Gary.

She suddenly felt strong arms around her. She bent her head to bury it in Gary's shoulder, trembling in the darkness.

Her body shook violently, and she cried until there were no more tears left inside. Whimpering like a little animal in a trap, she pushed herself closer to him and said in a choked voice, "I'm so frightened!"

"I know, my love," the voice said. "I'm so sorry you were hurt."

She felt herself being pulled up to him, his grip around her tight. It was a strange feeling in this pitch-black hallway, where not even the light of the moon cast any illumination on them. The lips she touched were cold, yet they responded to her with an unusual warmth. His hands massaged her back. Something, Melanie thought, was wrong with that. The hands were too smooth, not like a plastered wrist should feel.

"Gary?" she asked, backing away. She didn't trust what she couldn't see.

"My love," the voice whispered, "there is no need for fear now. I shall protect you from those who mean you harm."

A bright light caught her eyes just then, and she squinted to see one of the guards standing behind it.

"Mrs. VanBuren?" he asked. "I heard you call out."

"I-I'm all right," Melanie mumbled, edging closer to Gary. "My husband can take care of me."

"I'll take you to him, then," the guard offered.

Melanie eyed him strangely. What did he mean? Then she turned to look at Gary, to ask if he understood what the guard was saying. But Gary wasn't behind her. There was no one there at all. Melanie screamed.

"Here, here," the guard said, helping her to her feet. He led her to Gary's room, where her husband was tightening the belt of his robe. Gary took her in his arms.

"My God," he said, "what happened?"

"I found her on the floor of the hall," the guard

told him. "Mrs. VanBuren, please tell me what happened. Did you see anyone?"

Melanie nodded, then shook her head.

"I don't know," she whimpered.

"I'll check it out," the guard said.

"Helen Jennings was right," Melanie said softly.

"Come inside and lie down," Gary said. "What happened to you?"

"H-Helen Jen-nings was right," Melanie said again. "There's someone in this h-house!"

"Yes, I know," Gary soothed, brushing the hair from her eyes. "The guards will find him."

Melanie shook her head, hard.

"N-no," she said. "He's-he's . . ."

She buried her head in Gary's shoulder and mumbled, "I-I couldn't see anything. He was in the hall and I thought it was you and it was-wasn't. . . ."

Gary pushed her gently down on the bed and stood up. He removed a gun from the drawer next to his bed and walked into the hall. Melanie, seeing him go, started to rise, but Gary told her firmly that she would be safest right here. He wanted to find that bastard, and he wasn't about to let two guards get the best of it.

He could hear the sound of doors being opened and closed as the guards inspected the upstairs. He had a strong feeling, a hunch that nothing would turn up. It was more than a hunch—he knew for a fact that the search was fruitless. How can you find what you can't see?

Gina and Kyle were sleeping quietly, just as they had been when Melanie left the room a while earlier. Gary recovered them, thinking it was no wonder they slept that way—locked together. The poor kids were probably nervous wrecks by now.

In Nancy's room, he found the little girl sitting up in her bed, tears rolling down her cheeks. She took one look at the pistol in his hand and began to cry loudly.

"Oh, honey!" Gary cried, putting the gun behind his back and walking to her. "Did all the noise wake you up?"

Nancy nodded. "I heard crying upstairs, Daddy."

Gary kissed her and promised that everything was quite all right. Nancy didn't know about the guards, or even about the fires. Gary put her covers on and kissed her lightly.

"Daddy will take care of everything," he said. "Now, you go to sleep, sweetie. I'll check on you again later. Okay?"

"Okay, Daddy," Nancy said, closing her eyes.

He left the room to check on what she meant by "crying upstairs." That meant the attic, of course. Was it the squirrels he had heard a few weeks earlier? *(Or the sound of a bodiless voice.)* He went to the closet and opened the door, looking up at the ceiling. The square panel had been moved.

He climbed awkwardly to the top. But the investigation of the attic wasn't to be his own. One of the guards had already seen the moved panel. He flashed his light in Gary's face, ready to pull out his gun. Gary said, "My little girl said she heard someone crying up here. Did you find anything?"

"Your wife and I were up here earlier," the guard told him. "We didn't see a thing. But there's something over here that looks like a nursery."

"The landlord told me about a sealed-up room," Gary recalled. "I meant to have the door opened to use it for storage."

"It's still furnished, for some reason," the guard said, stepping inside.

Gary followed, eyeing every inch of the floor and walls. The dressers were pressed flat against the now-peeling wallpaper, and the closet was child-sized, too small to hide an adult. The bed? Gary walked over to it.

"I've checked under it already," the guard said. "But, uh, I think you should take a look at the bed itself."

"Oh, Christ," Gary said when he saw the burned mattress. "Do you know if that was done recently?"

"I don't think so," the guard said. "A fire big enough to destroy half a bed wouldn't get by unnoticed. If it had, this whole house would have burned down."

"Then it's—uh—possible that this has nothing

to do with the fires tonight?" Gary suggested, wanting it to be so.

"I really don't know," the guard said. "I'm not a detective. But I suggest we tell Captain Davis about this."

"I'll do that," Gary promised. "Look, don't tell my wife what we found, okay?"

"I won't," the guard promised.

Gary took one last look at the nursery before leaving it to go downstairs.

"What an idiotic place for a nursery," he mumbled.

In the hallway, he and the guard were met by the other cop. The report from all sides was similar—nothing had been found. It was suggested that Melanie had been sleepwalking and had had a bad scare. That was the only explanation that made sense right now. There was no way anyone could have left the house without being seen.

Gary, because he wanted to believe the guards' words, agreed with them and returned to Melanie. He told her what they had said, that she must have been seeing things.

"I didn't see anything," Melanie whispered.

"Or hearing things, I mean," Gary said. "We've looked everywhere. Even the attic."

"You didn't see the little boys?"

"What little boys?"

"They were burning," Melanie said plainly.

Gary rose from the bed, not taking his eyes from her. She was in some kind of shock, he thought. He took a sleeping pill from the medicine chest in the bathroom adjoining the bedroom and handed it to her with a glass of water. She took it without asking what it was.

In a few minutes, her breathing evened out. But there was no sleep for Gary that night. He stared through the darkness of the bedroom, listening until he could no longer hear the guards' voices downstairs. If they were discussing the possibility that there had been someone in here, they were right. But Gary knew they would never find him. He also knew that his wife had had a frightening run-in with the very force that had tried to kill him.

14

Janice swung her arm at the alarm clock to silence it and pulled her covers tightly around her shivering body. She drew her knees up into her chest and tensed her muscles, trying to drive away the cold.

She didn't want to get up this morning. Shaken by the fires at Melanie's house, she had gotten a little too drunk at the Starship disco. Well, she was in charge of the library, and it could damn well wait until she was good and ready to open it. Right now she just wanted to sleep.

But the alarm was ringing again. No, the telephone. With a groan, Janice turned over and lifted the receiver.

"H'llo?"

"Miss Janice Lors?"

"That's my name," Janice replied, yawning widely.

"This is Captain Bryan Davis of the Belle Bay Police," the voice said.

Janice was suddenly wide awake. She straightened herself against her pillow and took on a more serious air. She didn't wait for Davis to finish his introduction.

"It's about last night, isn't it?" she asked, smoothing her mussed hair as if Davis could see her.

"Yes," Davis replied. "We tried to reach you later in the night, but couldn't. Where were you?"

"Out," Janice snapped, letting him know she

thought it was none of his business. Then, after a moment's thought, she added, "I went to a disco."

"Tell me about it down here," Davis said. "When can you get here?"

"I have to open the library," Janice said. "Say eleven, okay?"

"Eleven," Davis repeated. He hung up.

Janice slipped off her warm nightgown with regret, as the cold air of her apartment was painful. She stepped into a warm shower and let the hot flow massage her thoughts away. Janice enjoyed the fun side of life and hated anything that stood in the way of it. So now, she thought, breathing in the warmth of the steam, she was being called in by the police. All the times she and her crowd had gone out together, from their days of underage drinking to more recent escapades of singing through the streets at late hours, Janice had never been pulled in. Today, she would finally know what it was like to be questioned. And somehow that scared her more than if she were going there to answer a summons for one of her earlier misdemeanors.

* * *

The drive to the police station took Janice through the heart of town, then around the duck pond and up another road. Belle Bay was a small community, easily covered in ten minutes. But Janice was so lost in thought that the drive took her nearly twenty. She didn't notice the Thanksgiving decorations on the house doors or the great piles of leaves that had been raked off dozens of front lawns. All she thought about was the upcoming confrontation with the police.

She went over the events of the previous night, wondering if it would sound too much like a rehearsed speech when she rattled it off to them. She hoped Tony would be there. He seemed like such a nice guy, and she wouldn't mind getting to know him.

"Officer DiMagi died last night," Captain Davis informed her ten minutes later when she asked where he was. He turned his eyes for a moment, so that he would not have to take in another look of shock. Janice looked at him, and then at the officer who sat on a bench on the other side of the room. This other man was Jack Hughes, who had ignored his aching throat and head to come down here today. Both men wore black armbands, and Jack Hughes was holding something in his hands. A cap—Tony's?

"I can't believe it," Janice managed to whisper. "I just met him last night!"

"Miss Lors," Davis said, in a voice that cut through the quiet hum of the room, "did you see anyone leaving or approaching the house when you came to report To—Officer DiMagi's failed electrical system?"

"I'm not sure I want to answer anything," Janice said carefully. "Do I need a lawyer?"

"You're in no trouble," Davis reassured her.

"Well," Janice said, pulling herself up tall. "Go ahead. I just won't answer if I don't want to."

"Please," Davis said with professional politeness, "the more cooperative you are, the sooner we'll find out who killed Tony."

"Killed?" Janice echoed. "Jesus."

"Answer my question," Davis pressed.

"Let me think," Janice said. "I did see someone at the house, but it was after the fires. He was walking on the road up that hill."

Davis sat up straighter. Across the room, Hughes leaned forward and looked at his captain with widened eyes. Before Davis could speak, he asked, "What did he look like?"

"Big," Janice said, holding her hand up to indicate the man's height. "I'd guess about six foot six."

"Did you see his face?" Davis asked.

"It was too dark," Janice said. "But I know he was wearing a cape of some kind. I saw him from the back when I looked in my rearview mirror. He had very dark hair and the cape was blue. He was talking to Tony, I think. I don't know what happened after that."

Now Hughes was on his feet. Davis gave him a quick look, then ran his eyes over Janice. The blonde woman sat cross-legged in high boots and a well-fitted jumpsuit. Common sense told him she couldn't have made up her story. The only reason to do so, he reasoned, would be to cover for herself. And, as slim as she was, she couldn't have pushed the car hood down so strongly. Was she covering for someone else?

"Did you report this?" Davis asked, a bit more sternly than he had intended.

"I suppose," Janice said with a shrug, "that I forgot about it in the confusion. Getting help to Melanie and those little kids was more important."

"Yeah," Davis said. "Look, I want to talk with Officer Hughes. Could you wait outside?"

"Sure," Janice said pleasantly, though she was unnerved that they had something to discuss that she wouldn't be allowed to hear. What did they think of her?

Hughes walked over to the captain's desk and leaned against it, watching Janice close the door behind her. He noted that her hands had begun to tremble.

"What do you think, sir?" he asked.

"We have a choice," Davis said, looking at the end of his pencil, ragged where his teeth had chewed it. "Either she's guilty, or she isn't."

"Why would she kill Tony?" Hughes said, trying to fight the feeling of enmity his mind was forming toward her.

"Somehow," Davis said, "I don't think she did. Logic fights against it. Look at her, Jack! She couldn't be taller than four eleven and a half—maybe five feet. She'd have trouble reaching up for the hood without Tony knowing it."

Hughes nodded. It made sense. Everything Captain Davis said made sense, he thought with a mixture of admiration and jealousy. Davis always had a perfect explanation for everything. That was how he became captain.

"Then what do you think about her caped man?" he asked, wondering if Davis, for once, didn't have an answer to a certain question. That was, who had killed Tony?

"Maybe someone else at the VanBuren house saw him," Davis suggested. "We'll go down there right after lunch. I've had a guard on the place all night."

"What about Gary VanBuren?" Hughes suggested.

"It doesn't seem right to think he did it," Davis said. "He's a wisp of a guy, and besides, he's got one of his wrists in a cast."

"I know that," Hughes said. "But that doesn't mean he isn't a prime suspect."

"I'd go easy with him, though," Davis said. He explained himself. "Jackie, you weren't there. You didn't see it. I know it must have taken a tremendous force to push that hood dow—"

Hughes cut him off. "Please, sir. I don't want to hear again about how Tony died. It makes me vicious."

Davis sighed and thought for a long moment, turning his pencil in his fingers. He began to bounce it on the desk.

"Something bothers me," Davis said. "In all that rain last night, there should have been footprints. There were Tony's, and Janice Lors'. But no third set. It doesn't fit right."

He went on bouncing the pencil, one of his ways of steadying his thoughts. Then he leaned forward and said with an all-knowing voice, "Then again, we weren't looking for footprints last night. I'm sure they were there and we didn't take notice."

"I'm surprised you admit a thing like that," Hughes said evenly. "I mean, failure in the line of duty. Footprints would be the first thing to look for."

"Don't forget who you're talking to before you go making accusations," Davis said, though not as austerely as he should have. He couldn't bring himself to bully Jack Hughes. The man, though rebellious at times, was one of the best in the department. A rare, good cop.

He softened the look on his face. "I'm going to take Vic Towers down there with me this afternoon. We'll let you in on everything that happens."

"What do you mean, 'let me in'?" Hughes demanded. How could they dare to leave him off this case? "My God, Captain, Tony was my *partner!*"

"I don't think," Davis said carefully, breathing in a sigh that spoke of his many years as a cop, "that you're up to it. Jack, you couldn't even come to the *phone* yesterday, let alone go out on a case. You look terrible—you look like you ought to be in the hospital. I need all the men I have, and I'd rather keep you off for a few days than have you laid up for weeks. Don't you understand?"

"No, I don't," Jack said evenly. "But you're right, sir. You're right."

"I know I'm right," Davis said. He took on a firm tone. "You're to keep off this case and in bed. That's an order, Officer Hughes."

"Yes, sir."

The reply was respectful, but there was no mistaking the look on Jack Hughes' face. It was a look of untapped anger. Davis knew the man was defiant enough to disobey the rule.

* * *

Daylight often works like the best medicine to ease a mind troubled in the night. When sunshine lights a room, an ugly face on the floor becomes a sweater carelessly thrown there, and an apparition turns into a robe hung a bit crookedly on a door hook.

Daylight had been shining for hours when Melanie reacted to it. The room seemed innocent in this bath of sunshine. Melanie's first thoughts were of the previous night. Did the nursery look this innocent now?

Gary came into the room with a cup of coffee for her. He handed it to her, and with a slight smile asked how she was. Melanie's smile was just as slight. She didn't answer him, but asked instead, "How're the kids?"

"Fine," Gary told her. "I kept them home today. Last night was a bit much. Just so things look smooth, Nancy's here, too. I said I'd take them out somewhere. Maybe we'll drive into the city to see the Rockettes."

"We can't do that," Melanie reminded him. "The police are going to be here, aren't they?"

"To hell with them," Gary said.

"Never mind," Melanie answered. "You can't avoid this issue, Gary. My God—a young man was killed here last night, and you want to go off to New York City!"

"Just to help us forget," Gary told her. "To help calm the children."

Melanie reached out for his arm and pulled him toward the bed until he sat down.

"We've got to talk about this," she said. "Ignoring the things that have happened here isn't going to do the children—or us—any good. *Please,* Gary, let's get this all in the open so we can figure out a way to handle it! I'm much too worn out from last night to take another minute of this!"

Gary noticed the desperation in her voice. She was still upset about running into that "someone in the house." Someone she couldn't see, as he had been unable to see the hands that had nearly strangled him just a couple of weeks earlier. He sighed, as if released of a great burden. He was finally able to tell Melanie the exact truth of his "accident."

"But," he said when he finished, "it happened very quickly. I can't even say for certain that I *was* attacked. It just felt that way. I want to believe that the voice was my imagination, and that I had just tripped over a rip in the stair carpeting. I've been trying to convince myself, Melanie!"

"Gary," she said with a sigh, "why did you think I'd make fun of you for that? Why wouldn't I believe you?"

Gary shrugged, unable to explain himself. But far from being embarrassed, he was quite happy. At long last the secret that tortured him was out. And Melanie believed him. He leaned over and kissed her hard, giving her a silent thank you.

"I have things to tell you that I've kept to myself," Melanie admitted, "little things that meant nothing until last night. I think they're connected in some way with your mishap."

She told him again about the little gifts she had found and how she had been shocked to see that bone tied in the very same fabric that had been used to wrap them. She explained how she had heard a voice in the hall, and that when she opened the door to find the package, she believed Gary had sneaked back up there to leave it for her.

"But you didn't, did you?" she asked.

"I don't think so," Gary said.

"Don't be so careful with me!" Melanie snapped. "I'm not a child, you know."

"I'm sorry," Gary said, pulling away from her. "No, I didn't." He thought for a moment. "Melanie," he said, "what about Terry Hayward? It makes sense—he threatened us, so that would explain the accidents, even the fires, if he knew a way to get in and out of here that we don't."

"I can't believe that," Melanie said. "First, there's no way Terry could know where we live. And second, how could he know more about this house than we do?"

"Somebody does," Gary answered. "And there's something else that makes me think of Hayward—the gifts. Obviously a token of love."

"No, Gary. I *know* it isn't Terry. So much has happened here lately that can't be attributed to anything human. First, little Nancy, then you, and the fires. Why haven't we seen a culprit yet?" Melanie sighed. "But something else happened last night that horrified me more than anything that's happened to us. I saw and heard things—evil things. Gary, I'm convinced that Helen Jennings came here with a warning for us that day. She said there was evil in this house!"

"She was a crazy old woman," Gary insisted.

"No," Melanie said evenly. "She was sincere. And I believe her now. Helen tried to caution us before these things happened last night. If we had listened to her, there would never have been a fire last night at all. And poor Tony . . ."

She cut herself off, thinking deeply.

"Melanie," Gary said, "all this talk of 'evil' is insane. I refuse to believe that the things that went wrong here were caused by anything other than nature and some mortal. A damned insane one—and I can tell you I'm more afraid of him than something I can't see."

(Can't see—those words again. Gotta stop saying that.)

"Hear me out, Gary," Melanie requested with a

wave of her hand. "Last night, I ran into *someone* in that hall, even if the cop didn't see him. I was running from the attic, and I was so terrified I couldn't think straight. Gary, I saw something in that attic that turned my stomach. I saw four little boys in a bed, screaming in a fire! And I couldn't save them! When I went over to the bed, they were gone. Helen Jennings was there!"

"For God's sake, Melanie!" Gary cried, as if he were losing patience. "You were sleepwalking. Helen Jennings is dead."

"I know that," Melanie said with a click of her tongue. "But who were those little boys? If you don't believe they existed, go up and look in the attic. There's a nursery there, and the bed's half burned away."

"I've been up there," Gary said. "I can understand why you were so frightened, considering that spooky old place. Don't you see, Melanie—when you saw the burned nursery, you thought of Kyle and Gina, and you imagined those little boys as a representation of our kids."

"Why do you always sound so much like you know it all?" Melanie snapped, getting out of bed.

She stormed into the small bathroom, her blonde hair flying over her face. Gary sat on the bed, hearing her turn on the faucet. She was whistling something, an angry tune that made no musical sense. She cut herself off suddenly, and came back into the room, her hair tied back.

"Helen Jennings scratched me last night," she said triumphantly, indicating her jawbone. Gary saw three evenly spaced scratch marks there. "If I imagined everything, where did these come from?"

Gary didn't bother to attempt an answer. He had none.

15

Gary didn't go to work that day. The explanation to his secretary, who said his week-long absence was causing quite a stir among his clients, was as brief as he could make it. He said only that something had gone wrong at the house the night before and he was staying home to take care of it. He made a perfunctory promise that he would be in the office the next day, if only to go over his papers with her.

A twinge of guilt led him to his study, where he pulled out his briefcase to put in a little at-home work. But the telescope stand and map and all the naval pieces kept pulling his eyes from the papers in front of him. What he had once admired now made him nervous.

There wasn't much time for thoughts like this, though. By one o'clock the locksmith he had called arrived. Gary planned to have every window and door lock changed, at any cost, to keep his family safe. It didn't matter that he couldn't even see what endangered them. The locks were Gary's way of solidifying what Melanie called an "evil." They made that bodiless voice something tangible, something he could touch and fight.

He toyed with the theory that someone had a way of getting in and out of the house in spite of the locks. If anyone had a key, he was out of luck now. But his second idea would take a little more effort than just calling a locksmith—a secret passage. Why not? Gary reasoned that in a house this old there might very well be a secret tunnel that led from the cellar out to some cave on the beach.

He was on his way to Melanie's studio when he heard Gina call upstairs that the police were here. At first Gary was annoyed with the intrusion. But logic told him it was better to get the questioning over with now. As Gary headed back downstairs, he saw the guard who had stayed during the daylight hours leading Captain Davis and another cop (not Hughes, Gary was surprised to see) into the living room.

He followed them into the room and sent Gina to bring her mother down. Gary noticed that Davis had a more relaxed, professional look on his face now. It was a far cry from the saddened face he had seen the night before, a face ready to twist with tears and anger. But Bryan Davis had finished with his grief. He now displayed the cool manner that he used in every situation that involved a serious crime, speaking as if the victim were someone he didn't know.

"Did you see anyone in or near this house last night, with the exception of your family, Janice Lors, and Officer DiMagi?" Davis asked, wondering if they had come in contact with Janice's caped man.

Gary shook his head and answered in the negative. Melanie, who had just stepped into the room as Davis was asking the question, told him they had been upstairs the entire time Tony was out in the driveway. Davis replied that Janice Lors had seen someone.

"A tall man dressed in a cape," he said.

Melanie gasped. Gary took her hand in his and tried to avert the policemen's attention from his wife's face. Her wide-eyed stare told them she knew something of this. Gary hoped she wouldn't start talking about ghosts and things.

He had no cause to worry. Melanie knew as well as he that talk of evil and haunted houses would only turn the police against them. It would sound too much like playacting, as if they were both pretending to be insane, so that if Gary were accused of killing Tony, he could use that as an excuse.

Instead, she said calmly, "My little girl, Nancy, had boiling water thrown on her by some strange man.

We thought she was imagining it when she said he was tall and wearing a long cape. But she wasn't seeing things, was she?"

"Where is she now?" Davis asked.

"I'll get her," Gary said, leaving the room.

"Something else happened here last night," the guard reported. Melanie held her breath, praying he wouldn't tell of her running through the hall.

"We went up into the attic again," he went on. "We must have missed it before, but there was a child's nursery up there. I think the door must have been hidden by a trunk or something. But Mrs. VanBuren had been up there, and she came down to—to tell us what she had found."

"What were you doing up in the attic?" Davis asked.

"I don't have to have a reason for walking through my own house," Melanie said stiffly.

Before Davis could answer her, the guard went on with his report. "The thing that's strange is that the bed was half burned away, just like the kids' beds last night. But I doubt if there's a connection. That room hasn't been used in thirty or forty years."

"It could be," Davis said, "that someone set fire to the bed recently to make it look like the bed had been burned that long ago."

"Why would anyone do that?" Melanie wanted to know, trying to push aside her thoughts of the little boys.

"Well," Davis explained, "then it would make it look like the fellow who's been doing all this is very old. A younger man couldn't have been alive at the time the fire in the attic might have been set, if it was set in the nineteen-forties."

Gary walked into the room, holding Nancy. He was accompanied by Kyle and Gina, who had been prepared for this interview. They knew that they had to tell Davis everything that had happened. Davis smiled at Nancy and asked, "Do you remember that man who hurt you?"

Nancy's smile faded. "Uh-huh!"

"Well," Davis went on, being as gentle as possible with this tiny child in spite of his need to get quickly to the truth, "want to tell me what he looked like?"

"He was real tall," Nancy said in a fascinated tone.

"Tell Captain Davis what he was wearing," Melanie prompted.

"A cape," Nancy said immediately.

"A cape?" Davis echoed. "What color, honey?"

"Blue," Nancy replied.

Davis looked at Melanie and Gary. Had this child been rehearsed? Had Janice Lors been rehearsed? He still didn't know if the man really existed.

He tried to trap them. "He had blond hair, didn't he?"

"No," was Nancy's firm reply, followed by a shake of her blonde-curled head.

Davis was convinced. He knew the little girl was telling the truth. Honesty was easier to see in the eyes of children than in the eyes of adults. He went on with the questioning, speaking with Kyle and Gina.

"I don't really know what happened," Kyle said, thinking hard about Davis' question. "I was asleep. The smoke woke me up."

"You didn't see or hear anyone?" Davis asked.

"No, sir," Kyle said. "I was sleeping."

Gina could give no more information than her brother. Finally, Davis asked them to run off and play while he spoke with their parents.

"I don't have much to go on," he said. "Except a vague description given to me by a little girl and a young woman. I'm not even sure it will be believed in a court."

"I guess I'd be the first suspect," Gary said.

"I'd just be sure I could prove how badly that wrist is hurt," Davis said.

"There is one other person you might consider questioning," Gary said. "A fellow named Terry Hayward. He lives in Greenwich Village."

"Gary, Nancy's description doesn't fit him," Melanie said softly.

"Are you sticking up for him?"

"No, but why lead the police on a false trail?"

"I'll take any lead at this point," Davis said. "What makes you talk about this Terry Hayward?"

"He was harassing my family with crank phone calls when we lived in the city," Gary said. "And he even threatened to kill my wife."

Bryan Davis listened carefully as Gary related the story, then took down the man's address from Melanie. He pulled on his coat and stuffed his note pad into his pocket.

"If you see anyone, give me a call. I'll check this guy out and let you know."

"I have to have the phone fixed," Gary said. "The phone company is a bit slow about that."

Davis stopped. "The phones were dead last night?"

"I didn't tell you?" Gary asked.

"Maybe," Davis said. "I don't remember."

"That's why we didn't just call you," Gary said.

"I'll send a team down here to check it out," Davis said. "I'll talk with you again."

When he left, Melanie sighed heavily and put her arms around Gary.

"I'm sick of 'teams,'" she sighed. "Locksmiths, cops, everybody!"

"But they might help us out," Gary insisted. "Then we can find this maniac and be rid of him."

"I wish it were that simple," Melanie said wearily. She broke away from Gary's embrace and walked upstairs. When she was out of sight, Gary opened the door to the playroom. He brought Kyle out into the hall.

"We're going to play a game," Gary said. "I want to see if there are any secret passages under this house. Want to help?"

"Wow!" Kyle cried eagerly. He took the flashlight Gary had pulled from a utensil drawer in the kitchen and followed his father down the cellar stairs.

"Now, here's what you do," Gary explained. "Run your hands over this wall and pat it. That's to see if there are any loose bricks."

With an excitement that can only be experienced by a little child, Kyle slapped his palms over the cool cement, covering every possible inch. When four walls were inspected with no results, he suggested pulling at the posts on the stairway to see if they were fixed with a trick wire. Gary looked at him with surprise and said, "Smart boy, Kyle! Why didn't I think of that?"

"I saw it on TV once," Kyle said.

But nothing in the basement hinted there might be an entrance down there. The ornaments on the old wooden stairs were fastened securely, as were the various gas lamps and torch holders.

As disappointed as his son, Gary went back upstairs and returned the flashlight to its drawer in the kitchen. Kyle was sent back to play with his sisters, after being promised that Gary would tell him if he found anything.

Gary pulled on his jacket and went outdoors. Something about the crisp autumn air helped set his thoughts in order. It was dark outside today—the gray clouds blocked the sun and threatened snow. Snow! Gary thought. That would really fix things. No one could possibly get into the house then without his footprints being seen.

Gary leaned against a tree inside the woods and stared back at the house. It was still beautiful, in spite of the fires and chokings and boiling water. How was he supposed to feel about all that? He felt anger that someone had dared to hurt his children. And disgust. And fear . . .

. . . but he felt fear a lot lately.

He shook his head and started to walk back to the house. A dry leaf crunched behind him and a voice ordered him to stay right where he was. At its command, Gary raised his hands into the air and turned around—slowly, to find a .22 in perfect line with his heart.

But not for long. Its owner dropped it to his side quickly and mumbled an apology. Gary took a step toward Jack Hughes and demanded to know what he was doing here.

"I—I couldn't get Tony off my mind," Hughes said hoarsely. "I just had to come here to have a look for myself. I thought I'd find something the others didn't."

"Your captain and another cop were here earlier," Gary said. "I'm sure they would have looked in the woods if they thought they'd find anything. I don't like the idea of you sneaking around my property with a loaded gun. I've got little children."

"So do I," Hughes said, sheathing the pistol. "I'm really sorry."

"Sure," Gary obliged. "I guess you're just doing your job."

"No, I'm not," Hughes admitted. "I'm not on this case. Davis left me off because of my health." As if to verify this, he coughed.

"I won't tell anyone I saw you," Gary promised. "This time. But please don't be wandering about my property any more."

"I won't," Hughes said, knowing it was a lie.

Gary turned to walk away. When he entered the house he found Melanie in the kitchen, preparing dinner. He offered to do it himself, to let her rest, but she insisted she could do fine. Besides, she said, he had that sprained wrist to worry about. She pulled a bunch of carrots from the refrigerator and began to peel them.

"Say, Gary," she asked, "have you seen that diary around? I've looked for it over and over and it just doesn't seem to be anywhere."

"No, I haven't," Gary replied. "Did you look in the library?"

"Yes," Melanie said. "Gary, I've been thinking about what I read. Helen Jennings brought it over for a purpose—so that we'd know more about the first owner of the house. I think she was using it to give us the answer to what's been going on here. The evil she spoke about—the clue to it is in that diary. I think I understand what she was trying to tell us."

"Melanie," Gary said carefully.

"No, Gary," Melanie said. "It makes sense. I think this place is haunted. Maybe by Jacob Armand, the man mentioned in the diary. Do you think it could be?"

Gary widened his eyes at Melanie's statement. A ghost! It would make things very clear, wouldn't it? It was the perfect explanation for the unseen hands and bodiless voices. But Gary shook that thought from his head. He was becoming too drawn in by a simple explanation. He couldn't just say he agreed.

"I don't think so," he said finally. "I'm sure as ever that we'll find this crazy idiot and he'll be as real as you and I."

"I wish you'd give me the benefit of the doubt just once," Melanie griped.

They heard the sounds of the children giggling in the playroom and looked at each other in wonder. No one would guess what had happened here last night if they saw Kyle and Gina now. Gary and Melanie were amazed at the spring-back power they had.

Kyle, Gina, and Nancy were playing explorer. Kyle had told them what he had done in the cellar with Gary, and now his two sisters wanted to share his fun. The fireplace was toyed with; every wall was patted. Nancy climbed onto the window seat and was checking the windows. She stopped for a moment to look at the shining new lock there. Then she shrieked in laughter at Kyle's funny imitation of Sherlock Holmes.

But it took only one sight to stop her laughter—one quick glimpse, through the glass of the window, of the man who had hurt her so many days ago. She stood there, so still she might have been a statue, her chubby body pressed against the glass, her round eyes staring in awe at the stern face that considered her. Then she jumped from the seat with a scream and ran to Gina.

"It's him!" she cried. "It's him, he's outside!"

Gina and Kyle looked up at the window and saw nothing.

Nancy pulled away and ran toward the kitchen, screaming for her mother. She ran into Melanie's arms, sobbing, screaming that the "mean man" was outside. Melanie looked at Gary.

"Maybe you should get the gun. . . ."

But Gary had already had that thought. He was running down the stairs and toward the front door now, breathing heavily. He all but pulled it from its hinges in his haste to get to the front porch before the intruder got away.

The night had a kind of deadly silence that makes one fear something is going to drop unexpectedly from one of the trees above. A slight wind, heralding a storm, blew the leaves around the porch floor. Gary stepped carefully into the darkness, able to see only as much as the porch light allowed. There was no moon tonight.

He kept trying to tell himself that he was a grown man and that he was the one who was armed. He tried not to think that the man he was stalking was some kind of maniac who thought nothing of terrorizing little children.

(Who could make himself invisible and hurt those who crossed him.)

He went back inside after a few minutes, reasoning that the new locks would keep them safe. The children were sent from the kitchen, but Nancy still clung to her mother.

"How could he have disappeared so quickly if he was human?" Melanie demanded. "Neither Kyle nor Gina saw him. Gary, that was Jacob Armand out there —I'm sure of it!"

"I can't believe that yet," Gary said softly.

Melanie watched him close the door, then turned to the refrigerator for a treat to divert Nancy.

* * *

In spite of Melanie's bizarre "dream," and in spite of the fact that he couldn't remember seeing the man who attacked him, Gary was still willing to put the blame on a mortal. Nancy had very definitely seen someone at the window, and it was a good guess that that someone was Terry Hayward. Without telling Melanie, Gary went to work the next morning with plans to visit the man's apartment and confront him, to put a stop to this for once and for all.

"I'm glad to see you back," Warren Lee said when Gary walked into the office. "How're the kids?"

"They're doing okay," Gary said. "I would be making the understatement of the year if I said they were shaken up a bit. But they're calming down."

"Kids are great about those things," Warren said with a smile. "How's your wrist?"

"Scratchy," Gary told him.

Warren grinned and handed him a pile of papers. "This ought to take your mind off it," he said. "And you'll be glad to hear we've gotten a millionaire divorce. That'll mean big bucks, if we do right by the old lady."

"Oh, damn," Gary moaned. "Look, Warren—I've got so much on my mind that I couldn't think about these right now."

"But this is a big case," Warren pointed out. "And I can't handle it by myself. Gary, you'll have to leave your home problems at home, no matter how awful they are!"

"It's a little difficult to push your children's safety out of your mind," Gary said, shuffling through the papers. "Warren, would you take a ride downtown with me at lunch today?"

"What's downtown?"

"Remember that guy Terry Hayward?" Gary asked. "The weirdo who made all those crank phone calls? I think he might be the one who's been pestering my family."

"How'd he find out where you live?"

"I don't know," Gary admitted. "Nobody's been asking questions here, have they?"

Warren shook his head.

"Then Terry's the most likely suspect," said Gary.

"You told the police, I take it."

"Yeah," Gary answered. "They're going to question him. But I want to get to him first."

At noon Gary and Warren hailed a cab for the twenty-minute drive downtown. Along the way, Gary told Warren all the details of the bizarre events. Warren listened carefully, then said, "It sounds like you've been invaded by a poltergeist, instead of a real person."

"A what?"

"A poltergeist," he repeated, "sometimes called a 'noisy ghost.' They usually show up in houses with adolescents and cause lots of trouble. Gina's about that age, isn't she?"

"She'll be thirteen on Thanksgiving Saturday,"

Gary said. "God, Warren, Melanie would love you. You both think along the same lines."

"She's talking about ghosts?"

"Something to that effect," Gary said, pulling out his wallet to pay the cabbie. When they were on the sidewalk, he went on, "But I want to see a human culprit."

They walked into the Christopher Street apartment building, and up to the fourth floor, looking around until they found the apartment number Melanie had given Davis. Gary pounded at the door.

"No answer," Warren said.

Gary tried again. This time, an old man opened the door and peered over the chain. He scowled at them.

"You cops?" he asked. "I seen enough cops for one day."

"We're lawyers," Gary told him. "We want to see Terry Hayward."

"How come everyone's looking for that guy?" the old man said. "He don't live here."

"Looks like the cops got here first anyway," Warren said when the old man shut his door.

"I want to talk to the landlord," Gary said, heading for the stairs.

The landlord was a landlady, a fat woman who puffed at a string of cigarettes. There was a smell of cats in her apartment, and the place looked as if it hadn't been cleaned in months. Warren was hesitant to sit on the dusty couch, but Gary was too interested in learning about Terry to care. Both men declined when offered a drink.

"So you're a friend o' Hayward's?" the landlady asked. "He's popular these days. Two cops was here askin' about him."

"Do you know where I can find him?" Gary asked.

"Just like I told them cops," the woman answered, "you might try Potter's Field. He's been dead for three weeks."

"Dead?"

"You heard me right," the old woman said. "I figured it was coming. You never know these days, do you? I took him in 'cause he was nice and clean-cut. I don't take weirdos in. Anyway, all of a sudden he turns into Mr. Nasty. Musta been mixed up with pills and booze—so many people do that now."

"How did he die?"

The fat woman took a slow drag from her cigarette, then leaned forward, squinting her eyes.

"Electrocuted himself," she said. "I wouldn'ta found him at all if I didn't go up to collect rent. When he didn't answer I used my key to get in—and Jeee-sus! The smell! Like if you burnt meat and left it sitting for a week. It almost killed me."

Gary shook his head. "That's a hell of a way to die. How'd he do it?"

"The cops said he was blow-drying his hair," the woman explained. "They said the cord was really worn down, and the wire was exposed. But the weird thing is that there was an inch of water on the floor when I found him. I was sick, I tell you. The way his hair floated it was like he wasn't real."

"I'm sorry that happened," Gary said, standing. A cloud of dust rose with him.

"Well," the woman said, "you can't keep the weirdos away, no matter how hard you try."

Gary thanked her for her time, and they left quickly.

"Well, you've done what you can," Warren said. "Let the police finish it."

Gary nodded, but the fear stayed with him. Melanie's conviction that they were dealing with the supernatural unnerved him. He desperately needed someone to pin the blame on—someone human. And his only suspect was dead.

16

In a time that was very far into his past, yet still clinging to his inner soul, Jack Hughes had been a gang member. The Deadly Knights. At the time, he was only thirteen, but he was already adept at beating the system. He knew that he just had to roll his large brown eyes and feign innocence to melt almost any judge.

Until one day, the system beat him. He and the rest of the gang had been caught in the middle of a rumble with their rivals, the Knives. (Hughes still clenched his fists when he thought of the name.) But he was one of the luckier ones. He was placed in a foster home, and for the first time in his life he was made to feel he could stand on his own. By the time he was eighteen and ready to start his life over again, the gang had dispersed—death, jail, execution. One or two went straight. And Jack Hughes went to college. The police academy followed, with Hughes in the top third of his class at graduation.

But his distaste for authority never left him. His stubborn, defiant character made him the "bad boy" of the department. But it was also one hell of an asset on the streets. His first assignment was the Upper West Side, and his name soon became a household word there. His superior work in tracking down and arresting a gang of hoods that had been terrorizing old people got him a medal and a promotion. And a transfer—to quiet, gentle Belle Bay.

It had once been gentle, anyway. Quiet? Yes, it was still quiet. Quiet like this damned squad car was now that Tony wasn't sitting beside him.

Hughes had made a mistake the night before by pulling his gun too quickly. Like a damned fool, he had almost put a bullet through Gary VanBuren. He wondered if he had come face to face with Tony's murderer. Could it have been Gary?

But the man had kept his promise to keep quiet. Tonight, Hughes would be more careful, because in spite of everything he'd said to Gary, he didn't intend to stop coming here until he was satisfied no more could be done. He owed it to Tony, he told himself.

It was that thirteen-year-old hood that still lived inside him that made him do it, made him disobey a direct order to stay off the Tony DiMagi case and ignore the fact that he should be back home in bed with his flu.

This time he left the car at the bottom of the hill. He couldn't help glancing back at the old woman's house, all boarded up now with a "For Sale" sign posted on its front lawn. Davis had been down here with a search warrant, only to report he had found nothing. But, Hughes thought, maybe tonight . . .

Hughes pushed his door shut and walked toward Helen's house. Every window was covered with a wooden slab. At the side of the house, the untrimmed ivy grew over one window—a window that for some reason hadn't been boarded. Hughes pulled at the vines, ignoring their stinging needles, and ripped them away from the house. Without looking to see if anyone was watching, he lifted his gun from its holster (worn under a blue civilian jacket) and smashed the window.

He was in the kitchen. For some reason, the food Helen had last placed on the table was still there, waiting for her. Hughes saw a piece of rotting chicken, and next to that a loaf of bread that had gone green and fuzzy. There were small insects crawling over it, having an enormous repast.

The thought tugged at his stomach, hard. He hurried from the room, trying to convince himself that it was only the flu that still held fast to him that was making him feel so sick. He passed through what seemed to be a short hall and entered the first door he came to. Hughes felt along the wall until he touched a light switch, then clicked it. The pitch black stayed in the room.

"Damn," he said, "they've got the electricity cut off."

He turned back to the kitchen and climbed through its window. The run to his car was a short one, and he was back inside the house in minutes with a flashlight.

The living room looked like something out of the eighteen-nineties, except for a television set and a recliner. But the rest of the furniture was quite old, and the stuffed chairs, leaking now, even had little lace doilies placed over their backs.

You could almost hear them talking in here. Hughes didn't quite know who "them" was, but he guessed that at one time Helen had sat here with her family, chatting and laughing while the women sewed and the men smoked fat cigars.

His flashlight caught the mantel, and he walked over to it, lifting each of several tiny portraits in his hand. The gold plate on one said "Helen, Aged 3, 1899." Hughes set the picture down again, carefully.

He walked into a hallway, stepping inside every room. His hand was always ready to grab his gun, but Hughes had a feeling there was nothing to be found in the house. It was almost impossible to keep from being charmed by the place. How could a killer hide here?

"He could," Hughes told himself.

He found himself in a sewing room, and he nearly fell when his foot caught on a pile of fabric that had been thrown on the floor. He kicked it aside and looked around. The sewing machine, still with a piece of fabric inside it, was an ancient foot-pedal model. It was strange—it seemed as if the house would wait like this forever for Helen to come home again.

Upstairs, he found five huge bedrooms, though only one looked as if it had been used in recent months. He went inside and pulled open Helen's closet door. She had had only a few dresses, each hung carefully on a padded hanger. The closet was so big he could stand comfortably inside.

An indentation in the wall, near the floor, caught his eye when he aimed the flashlight down. Hughes kicked at it, and it gave way to reveal a storage space. He guessed it might lead to the closet in the adjoining bedroom.

But it could also be a hiding place. He bent down to look through it. He was pushed roughly away by an odor that was so strong it reached him even through his stuffed nose. It was the smell of death.

Hughes flattened himself on his stomach and pushed a hanger into the tunnel to pull out whatever it was that had been caught in there. When he turned his head to the sight, it was one so horrible that even the street-wise cop flinched. It didn't belong in this lovely little house. It was a cat, dead from starvation. Her mouth was still open, with tiny bits of wood stuck in her teeth. She had tried to gnaw her way out of the trap.

Hughes jumped to his feet and ran from the room. It seemed impossible, but he somehow managed to reach the kitchen window and climb through it before losing the lunch in his stomach.

"You damn idiot," he said to himself when he stood straight. "You've seen worse than that. What if the bastard *is* in there?"

If he was, he could be caught another time. Right now, Hughes decided to check the woods again. Perhaps, he thought, he would go down to the beach to look for a cave, where someone could hide.

He still had cat hairs on his coat. He noticed them when he got back to the car. His already sore throat had become unbearably painful from the vomiting. Jack Hughes, usually a very strong man, was embarrassed that the sight of a dead cat had made him so ill. But sick or not, he wasn't about to go home.

He opened the glove compartment of the car and took a box of cough drops from it. Popping one into his mouth, he leaned against the door and debated whether or not to keep the flashlight. There was a moon tonight, but the trees would no doubt cast shadows that would confuse him and hide the enemy. The enemy! Hughes thought wryly. It sounded like the damned army.

Hughes moved into the woods without the light—reasoning it could be seen too easily from the house. His hand was ever ready to grab his gun. It was not only ready, it was hopeful. Hughes wanted more than anything to be able to use it.

He suddenly bent over and had a coughing fit. Maybe there was something in the wind that didn't want him to find Tony's murderer. It seemed everything was against him tonight. The cold was his worst enemy, chipping away at his lungs like an ice pick. He felt dizzy.

He had a frantic urge then to scream. The cat hairs were still there; he brushed them away again with vigor.

His eyes started to droop, and there was nothing he could do to keep them completely open. There was something pulling at his head—no, pushing it from the inside. It made the trees fly around him. Hughes put a hand to his forehead and felt the warmth of sweat and fever.

"Who are you?"

The voice seemed far away and angry. It was British, a faint accent. Hughes turned around and found himself looking up at a huge figure. The man was a good six inches taller than he, and he stared down at Hughes with no expression. Then Hughes noticed the cape and remembered what Janice Lors had said. He pulled out his gun.

But when he finally found the energy to pull the trigger, there was nothing to shoot. The clearing before him was empty.

"Fever," Hughes told himself as he crumbled to the ground.

* * *

There were no lights on in the house when Hughes finally returned to consciousness. He glanced at his watch and cursed out loud when he saw the time. 12:51.

He walked on legs that barely seemed there, wishing to God he hadn't been out cold for two hours. He had looked right at the guy. He almost had him!

17

It had been a quiet week. Melanie was thinking that as she hung the last of the balloons she had bought to decorate the playroom for Gina's birthday party. A few things had happened, such as toys and books disappearing. Melanie had combed the entire house (except the attic) to find the diary—to no avail. She had been able to spend several peaceful hours a day in her studio. They had enjoyed a nice Thanksgiving, with Gary's parents as their guests. Melanie had almost expected them to say the house felt strange to them, the thing people usually said about haunted houses. But Mr. and Mrs. VanBuren had only good things to say. And it was fine by Melanie, who wanted to enjoy every minute of this holiday.

"What do you think, Gina?" she asked, stepping down to the floor. She bent her head back to survey the ceiling. The decorations she had put up there had turned it into an array of brilliance. Green, pink, blue, and yellow balloons completely covered the gray paint.

"Oh, it's gorgeous!" Gina gasped, her eyes smiling. "I love it, Mom! I love you!"

She turned around to look at the entire room. Gina was convinced her mother was the best party-giver in the world. Across the back of the room, a long card table had been turned to line the wall under the windows. A pink tablecloth with three-dimensional daisies (Gina's very favorite color and flower) had been laid carefully over it. To its left was a small table that held the stereo, on loan from her father for this special occasion.

Gina went to it and slowly lifted the cover, then knelt down until the needle was at her eye level. She looked down her nose at the tiny chip of diamond. The turntable was a black one that contrasted greatly with her own little plastic portable. Wouldn't her friends be *impressed?*

"I hope Doreen remembers her Billy Joel records," she said, walking over to Melanie.

She gave her a hug, then turned and walked from the room. With her eyes closed, she could have walked the path from the playroom to the living room. She had done so a dozen times since the mail had arrived that morning. There were eight birthday cards from assorted aunts, uncles, and friends and an enormous package, one that contained a stuffed animal, she guessed, from the way its brown wrapper gave with pliable ease when she poked a finger at it. She couldn't wait until her parents would give her the okay to open it.

Finally, needled by her constant requests, Melanie said yes. The gift, from Melanie's parents, who were away on a cruise, was a stuffed mother kangaroo with a baby in her pouch. Gina squealed with delight when she unwrapped it, since she had never had a toy as big as herself. She hugged her mother and father and said, "I'm going to name her Happy, because that's how I feel right now."

"What about the baby?" Kyle asked.

"His name is Joey," Gina said.

"That's appropriate," Gary commented.

At that moment, a crashing noise sounded from upstairs. Conditioned by the events of the past weeks, Gary and Melanie did not hesitate to run to its source. At the top of the stairs, Melanie gasped to see Nancy sprawled head over heels on the floor. She was crying, pointing to the statue. The sphinx was lying on its side, not two feet from her. It had been torn from its mount.

Gary dropped to his knees beside her and helped her to stand up. Melanie had dressed her in her best outfit that day for Gina's party, but now the velveteen dress was crushed and dirty. Gary smoothed it as best he could and checked the little girl for bruises. But, except for a bad scare, nothing seemed to have happened to her.

"Do you hurt anywhere?" he asked.

"Uh-uh," the little girl said.

"Nothing a little ice cream wouldn't fix," Melanie said, lifting her.

"What happened, sweetheart?" Gary asked.

"The lion jumped on me," said Nancy.

"Jumped on you?" Gary echoed. "Honey, it's a statue!"

"It did, Daddy!" Nancy insisted. "It said, 'vissus waif,' and jumped!"

Her tears began to fall again, and Melanie said quickly, "Nancy, I think you mean 'vicious.' So you see, you must have dreamed it. My little girl is sweet, not vicious!"

He threw it at her.

Melanie took her down the stairs with promises of ice cream. In a short while, Gary heard giggling from the kitchen. He turned to the statue, to put it in the closet until he had time to remount it. He tried to lift it and was surprised to find it was solid brass.

His wrist, free of its cast for only a few days, buckled under the weight of it. Gary couldn't understand how anything so small could be so heavy, even if it was solid brass.

The statue suddenly thrust forward into his chest, as if the sphinx had decided he was prey to attack. The blow was so quick that Gary was stunned by it, and he forced his way back from the stairs, terrified he would be pushed down again.

He tried to call out to Melanie, but shock and the incredible pressure of the statue were fighting too hard against him. All he could muster was a faint, long gasp. His face began to turn red as the pressure increased against his lungs.

He was pushed roughly against the grandfather clock, and, under the weight of the statue, he slid down to the floor.

I can't breeeaaattthhhe.

He felt as if he were caught in a vise, wedged between the smooth oak of the clock and the relentlessly pushing statue. But the hands that worked the vise were invisible. And that voice didn't come back to him again. The thought crossed his mind that he was being murdered. And there wasn't a thing he could do to stop it.

He tried, again, to push the statue away. But something (nothing) was holding it fast against him. Gary's hands flew into the air in front of him, feeling that cold. *He* was here!

Must-get-Mela . . .

The sound of laughter reached him, sounding near and far away at the same time. Knowing he was no match for what he couldn't see, Gary tried in vain to scream for help. He heard a faint cracking sound from within his chest cavity. The laughter stopped.

Gary clenched his fist and began to punch at the glass door of the clock behind him. It was awkward, but his fist finally smashed through the panes. The sound of shattering glass brought Melanie running upstairs, and the statue pulled away from him.

Melanie found him hunched over, breathing like a runner at the end of a strenuous marathon. Some two feet away, the sphinx stood silently.

"Gary!" she cried.

When she stooped down to touch him, he looked at her with terror in his eyes. He closed them and tried to breath evenly.

"Where are you hurt?" Melanie demanded.

"I—I think I cracked a few ribs," Gary wheezed.

Melanie was on her feet. "I'm going to call an ambulance."

Gary tried to stand, leaning heavily against Melanie. But the pain forced him back down to the floor again. He tightened his jaw against it, feeling like he wanted to cry. He never knew anything could hurt so much.

"It attacked me," he whispered.

He fell down into blackness.

18

Gina stared through the diamond panes of the living-room window at the ambulance that was carrying her father to the hospital. She was filled with hurt and confusion. Why did this have to happen tonight? Though the young woman in her knew it was only right to forfeit her party and lament over her father's mishap, the child she still was wanted to enjoy the party she had dreamed of for so long.

Her mother hadn't said very much, except that Daddy had fallen while carrying the sphinx. Gina didn't buy a word of the hasty explanation. It was another one of those strange accidents, like the night her and Kyle's bedrooms had caught fire. And like the time she had fallen on the beach, when a voice had called her a name. Gina had forgotten just what it was, and she was glad. She didn't want to think about bad things like that. She had tried to steel herself to the situation, remembering that her mother had said she could spend the night in their room. She had been glad to right after the fire, but she soon moved back into her own redecorated room. She didn't want her parents to think she was a baby, yet she longed to be always in their presence, protected from whatever it was that so frightened her.

She felt a hand on her shoulder. Looking up behind her, she saw the understanding eyes of Mrs. Calder, her friend Beverly's mother. The woman had been the first to bring her daughter to the party—it had been much too late to call it off—and had volunteered to stay with the children until Melanie could get back home again. Melanie, who had met her at PTA meetings several times, was relieved by her offer.

"Your daddy's going to be just fine," Bonnie Calder said. "I'll bet your mom calls any minute now."

"You're wrong," Gina started to say, but she nodded and replied instead, "I guess so."

From outside there came the sound of a car and then the squealing and laughter of a new group of guests. Beverly took Gina by the hand and led her to the front door. It was thrown open, and the girls were welcomed with a halfhearted smile by Gina.

"What's up, Gina?" Lorrie Moulin wanted to know.

Gina shrugged. "My dad had an accident and my mom had to take him to the hospital."

"Wow, really?"

"In an ambulance?"

"Uh-huh," Gina said.

"Gina, what happened?" Doreen Wiley asked.

"My dad hurt himself," Gina explained, "when he was carrying a really heavy statue. He hurt his ribs."

"Yecch," Lorrie said with a grimace.

"One time," Doreen said, "my dad fell off our roof. *He* cracked his collarbone, and he was out of the hospital in a few hours."

"So cheer up, Gina!" Beverly insisted.

Gina's eyes lit up for the first time in an hour. Then her lips parted with a smile, and she said, "So, let's have a party!"

Beverly turned to her mother with her mouth open to speak, but Bonnie didn't have to be told her presence was quite unwelcome among these teenagers. She slipped quietly from the room and went upstairs to check on the other children. She found them in Kyle's room, watching television. Even though he had met her earlier, Kyle's eyes narrowed with suspicion when she walked into his room.

But his friendly personality took over quickly, and he offered her a seat on his bed. Bonnie sat with him, leaning against the back. She asked, "Don't you want to go downstairs to see what's happening?"

"No," Kyle said. "That's my birthday present to Gina. I promised not to bother her or her friends all night."

"That was nice of you," Bonnie praised. She turned to the little girl curled up next to him. "How are you doing, sweetheart?"

"When's my daddy coming home?" Nancy asked, in a voice so tiny that Bonnie grabbed her and hugged her to give her comfort.

"Oh, sweetie, soon," she cooed.

The telephone rang then, and Kyle sprang to his feet to run to it. But when he lifted the receiver, he found to his dismay that Gina had beat him to the extension.

"Hi, birthday girl," he heard his father say.

"H-hello, Daddy," Gina replied, ready to burst into waves of laughter at his voice.

"Enjoying your party?"

"Well, I wish you were here."

"What?" Gary asked. "If I were, you'd want me to hide in a closet. Any boys there yet?"

"Daddy!" Gina cried with a giggle.

"Don't worry, Dad, the boys at school are too smart to—"

"Hiya, Kyle," Gary said. "What's up?"

"Nothing," Kyle replied. "But when are you coming home?"

"I don't know," Gary said. "Not tonight. It's too late to leave here. But tomorrow, I promise."

"Are you okay?" Gina asked carefully.

"Kind of," Gary lied. "I did crack my ribs, but the doctor says I'll be okay soon. I just have a bruise on the outside. But I'm okay. So enjoy that party, will you?"

"Okay, Daddy," Gina said.

Melanie was on the line now. "Gina, honey? Tell Mrs. Calder that I'll be home in a few minutes. I'm bringing a treat for everyone. How many girls are there now?"

"Eight now," Gina said, "and five more are coming."

"Good," Melanie said. "I'll see you later, sweetheart. Bye, Kyle."

"Mom?" Gina asked.

"Yes, Gina?"

"Hug Daddy for me?"

"Me, too!" Kyle put in.

"Sure," Melanie said. "Love ya."

Gina put down the receiver and jumped up and down. The party was saved! Daddy was all right, and so was her birthday! It was great!

It would have done Gary a great deal of good to see how happy his phone call had made Gina. He had fallen against his pillow after he handed the phone to Melanie. He was amazed at how cheerful he could be when every part of him hurt.

"Okay, now," Padraic O'Shean said. "You've saved your little girl's party. Lie down and rest. I'm going to give you something to help you sleep."

Gary watched the needle go into his arm and said, "I don't want those kids alone in that house."

"Gary, I wish—"

"Shh," he said, "we'll talk about it ano . . ."

He was asleep.

"What did you give him?" Melanie demanded.

"Just a sedative," O'Shean replied. "He'll need it. He's going to hurt for a while. May I walk you to the elevator?"

"Please," Melanie said.

Dr. O'Shean got right to the point. "Your husband is rather hapless, isn't he?" he said.

"I don't know," Melanie said. "I can't explain this one off as easily as the last—what should we call it, an accident? This time, there was no way anyone could have attacked him without my knowing it. I was right downstairs!"

"Don't worry," O'Shean said. "If you need help, I'm on duty all night."

"I appreciate that," Melanie said. "Really."

The elevator door slid open.

"Please," she said, "I've got to go home now."

All Gina's guests had arrived when Melanie carried two pizzas into her house and set them on the table. She was happy to see that even Gina was laughing and enjoying herself. And, like the perfect hostess, Gina asked each little girl what she wanted to drink with her pizza. She headed for the kitchen with her mother to fill the order.

"Is Daddy really all right?" Gina asked, as she poured soda into pink-and-white cups.

The question stunned Melanie. When she responded, she didn't look her daughter in the eye, for fear the little girl would know she was stretching the truth. Yes, she said, Daddy was just fine. Dr. O'Shean said so.

"Let's take these out," she said, lifting the tray of cups.

Bonnie Calder declined when offered a piece of pizza. She said goodbye to her daughter and left. Melanie suddenly wanted her to stay, but when she found herself unable to explain why, she kept silent and watched the woman close the front door.

"Let's have a séance!" she heard one of the little girls suggest from the living room.

"Yes!" someone else agreed.

Melanie stepped in the room. "No!"

"Why not, Mom?" Gina asked. "It's just fun."

"It isn't safe," Melanie said. "Who knows . . ."

"It's no big deal," Doreen interrupted. "We do it at my parties all the time."

Melanie looked at the pairs of eyes watching her and realized how ridiculous she sounded to these teenagers. So, although her fears didn't subside, she gave her consent.

"I'll be upstairs," she said. "If you happen to conjure up George Washington, let me know. I want to find out if he ever slept here."

The jokes passed over the girls' heads, and, with a sigh, Melanie left the room. Gina went over to the stereo and turned it off, handling it as if it were a priceless antique.

"I have to go to the living room to find a candle," she said.

"The candle's supposed to be black," Judy Young said when Gina returned.

"It's red," Gina answered. "That's good enough."

The table was emptied and the candle placed in its center. Carefully, Gina lit it and turned off the lights.

"Who should we call?"

"I know," Christine Haynes suggested. "Jimmy Carter!"

"He's not dead," Doreen said with a click of her tongue. "Let's try—umm—Boris Karloff. He's good and creepy."

"Yeah," Gina said. "I watch all his old movies."

"I'll do the chant," Beverly said. "Hold hands."

She breathed deeply. "Booorrrrissssss!"

Lorrie giggled.

"Shut up," Beverly snapped. "Boorrrissss!"

There was a scraping noise along the table, but none of the girls would open her eyes to inspect. A few tittered nervously, and Beverly told Lorrie to keep her hands to herself.

"I didn't touch it," Lorrie said softly.

"I know you did!"

It was Doreen who first opened her eyes to see that the candle had been moved. Then she saw, in almost slow motion, Christine's long, braided hair snake toward the flame. . . .

"Chriiissss!!" she screamed, jumping up.

Whatever happened next could not be recounted by the girls without confusion and contradiction. Gina saw Doreen—or was it Judy?—toss a half cupful of cola at the tiny flame on Christine's hair. She lifted another cup herself, and soon Christine was a sobbing, soaking mess.

Melanie burst into the room and demanded to know what had happened. Christine stared up at her, her dropped lower lip quivering. Her tears, which flowed in abundance from hurt brown eyes, mixed with the orange and brown of the soda and painted her face like a clown's.

"Gina?" Melanie asked. "What happened?"

"I just don't know, Mom," Gina admitted.

Except for the whimpering of Christine Haynes, no sound filled the room. The little girls stared around, not quite knowing what to do now. Finally, Melanie touched Christine's shoulder and led her into the kitchen to clean her up.

"Don't you worry, Christine," she said. "As soon as I get that soda wiped off your face and dress, you'll look fine."

She wasn't certain herself if there was reason for optimism. So he had harmed one of the children. God only knew what he would do later in the night. But Melanie had this little child to take care of right now. She set herself to comforting her, checking to be certain the little girl's skin hadn't been harmed. To her relief, she saw that there was no red mark on Christine's cheek and that her hair had barely been singed.

Christine burst into new tears and fell into Melanie's arms. She didn't understand what had happened to her, and she was terrified.

The kitchen door opened.

"Mrs. VanBuren?" asked Doreen.

"What?"

"I—uh—saw it all happen," Doreen said.

"You did?" Melanie asked, standing. "What did you see?"

"It kind of looked like the *wind* blew her hair at the candle," Doreen said. "I felt a really cold draft right before it happened."

"Sure," said Melanie.

He's after them. He's after them and Gary isn't home tonight. She thought about calling the police. But what could she tell them? They'd write her off as a neurotic housewife.

"Do you want to go home, honey?" she said to Christine, pushing bad thoughts from her mind.

Christine nodded. Melanie took her by the hand and led her to the telephone in the foyer. The other children were waiting in the hallway, and they immediately set about putting Christine at ease. Melanie eyed Gina for a moment, debating whether or not to send the others home. She decided against it. So much had happened to ruin the little girl's birthday that such a thing would be nothing short of cruel. No, the party would go on.

"I'm sorry, Christine," Gina was saying. "I don't get it."

"S'okay," Christine sniffled.

"It'll grow back soon," Gina went on. "I got my hair cut once and it grew back in just a few weeks."

"You only lost a tiny bit of it," Judy put in.

"Yeah," said Beverly. "You look fine."

"I do?"

"Sure," Beverly said. "Heck, you'll look terrific by the time we get to Belle Bay High. Who cares now? There aren't any boys worth impressing at St. Anne's!"

"Yeah," Lorrie said. "When we get to high school next September, you'll probably knock out the seniors!"

"Yeah?" Christine asked. She fingered her hair and began to smile at last. It wasn't so short, after all.

Melanie hung up the phone. She hadn't really heard a word the woman screamed into the phone. Her ears were sharpened for the sound of that familiar British accent.

When Christine had left, and the party started to return to its happier, pre-séance state, Melanie left the girls and headed up the stairs. At the top, she noticed the light spot where the sphinx had been torn from the banister. She placed a hand on it and, looking up to the ceiling, seethed, "Why don't you leave us alone?"

19

Melanie's eyes stayed open late into the night, her ears sharp for any screams or gasps from the group sleeping downstairs. The house was still, so still that when the radiator banged suddenly, Melanie jumped, startled. It was well into the early hours of the morning when she finally found sleep.

She had a dream that night. Not the terrifying nightmare that found her opening doors, but a loving nightmare. For in fact, what Melanie was experiencing as a dream was too real. But she wasn't frightened by it—she was lost in that ecstatic state between sleep and consciousness where everything seems very slow and warm.

She was in the arms of a man, an incredibly handsome man who kissed her with a warmth and passion she had never known. When her conscience tried to remind her of her promised faith to Gary, she ignored it. This was too beautiful, too beautiful—this encounter with a fantasy lover, a lover who hadn't appeared in her dreams since the days before her affair with a man who had turned her affections from Gary. And now he was back, to comfort her when Gary had gone away from her. Where was Gary tonight when she was so, so frightened?

She felt those full lips against hers and pressed her mouth hard to them. Her fingers ran through silken hair and down over a warm, powerfully muscled neck.

He spoke, in the strange whisper she had heard that night when the meeting with Helen Jennings had sent her running through the halls.

"My darling," he said. "It's almost over now. I've almost saved you."

"I love you," Melanie breathed.

"All that remains now are the children," he went on, his voice stiff with determination.

"The children are asleep," Melanie said, as if she were reminding Gary that they wouldn't be interrupted in their lovemaking.

"They shall never again harm you," the voice swore. "I shall destroy them. I shall do it soon."

Destroy? Destroy?

The word jolted Melanie to full consciousness. It was wrong—it didn't belong here in this dream of love. With a long sigh, she tried to steady her heartbeat and calm her jittering nerves. She kept her eyes closed, trying to let all thoughts pass until she felt serene again.

The bed was too hard. She could feel springs pushing through the mattress—in a mattress that had no springs.

Melanie bolted upright. Her mouth dropped open at what she saw. She wasn't in her bedroom at all. This was the attic (oh, my Lord, what am I doing here?) and she was in a small cot, with heavy wool blankets laid over her. At the bottom of the bed was a little dresser with a lit oil lamp on it. Its golden flame made the room seem warmer. It had a strange scent that reached Melanie's nostrils and reminded her that someone must have come to light it.

She threw the covers aside and stood up. So this was it—wasn't it? The *pièce de résistance*. She had been lured up here and taken advantage of in her sleep. She wondered, in a strange way, if he had enjoyed it as much as she. And she *had* enjoyed it. But right now she wanted to erase the memory of that dream forever. It was ugly. She had made love to a man who had tried to kill her husband and children—and she had enjoyed it!

"I'm so sorry," she whispered out loud, in a plea to her family. She started to say "if I had known," but the thought was cut off when she put her arms around herself for comfort.

Her hands felt the smooth coolness of silk. She looked down to find that she was no longer wearing her own flannel nightgown, but was dressed in the silk gown she had found outside her studio door that morning so long ago. The fit was almost perfect. The arms fit tight to the elbow, then belled in rows and rows of lace. The neckline was low, so low it showed a good deal of cleavage. Self-consciously, Melanie covered herself. She wanted to rip the gown off. She wanted to use it to smother the man who had dressed her in it.

"I want out of here," she said aloud, looking around at the chests and crates and old pieces of furniture. Someone had cleaned them up and set them in neat order.

She started to run toward the trap door, but was stopped by a flow of sweet, gentle music. She whirled around and caught sight of the dancing figurines on a small music box.

"I guess my walking set it off," she told herself nervously. Her voice echoed strangely in the empty room.

She went over to the music box and took it in her hands. The tiny porcelain figures were of a man dressed in knickers and a white wig and his lady, her skirts swirling as the sculpture froze them in time at the height of their breathtaking waltz.

When Melanie turned the box upside down, she read an inscription that verified everything she had believed of the haunting of this house. It told her that the existence of Jacob Armand the ghost was as real as Helen Jennings had said. And that he had a strange, fanatical purpose in all that he was doing.

"To our first month together, my Lydia. In love or death I am yours. I shall protect you, forever.

Yours in love,
Jacob Nicolas Armand
April 23, 1797"

Melanie slammed the figurine down. That was it! He was haunting the house because he was keeping this vow to protect her. Hadn't he said to Melanie that he would do so? But why?

"Who do you think I am?" Melanie asked.

She had to go downstairs. She *had* to go now. She pushed boxes and crates out of her way in her haste to get to the children. They shouldn't be alone down there.

The crying in the nursery started up behind her. Melanie was ready to ignore it, thinking it was those little boys again. She didn't want to see them. But she couldn't ignore the strong smell of smoke that was coming from the room.

She picked up a wooden beam from the floor and walked into the room. She should have known it—there was no smoke in the nursery. It was quiet, exactly as she had left it the other night, with its half-burned bed and its dresser drawers pulled out. She started to back out of the room and felt something tug at her gown. She looked down to see the silk fabric around her knees pinched and folded. She tried to wrench away from the unseen hand that clutched it. That was when the child appeared to her.

"Who are you?" she demanded of the small boy who looked up at her, his eyes pleading. "Who are you?"

The tiny boy sniffled, but no tears ran from his eyes. Then, suddenly, there were no eyes. There was no face.

Melanie screamed and bolted from the room. The terror inside tightened her every muscle, slowed down her ability to run. She wanted out of here, now. She wanted Gary. Oh, God, how she wanted Gary!

She stumbled down the last steps into the hall and reached out to steady herself against the wall. She pushed the closet door shut and rolled herself along the wall until she was pressed against it. Upstairs, she could hear the faint music of the sculptured box. It had started up when she slammed the door.

I shall protect you forever. . . .

"But why?" Melanie demanded in a choked whisper. She tasted a sourness in her mouth and swallowed hard.

Protection meant hurting her husband and children. God only knew how far this sick mind would go in that promise of protection. Would he kill? Innocent children? An innocent man?

"What do you want of me?" Melanie asked. "If you love me, please leave my children and husband out of it!"

But there was no one there to respond. Melanie stood against the door like a statue, the only sign of life in her the heaving of her breasts as she breathed deeply for strength. The more time passed, the more she relaxed, until she was ready to declare it all a very bad dream, something that never happened.

But she was still wearing the silk gown. . . .

A thought occurred to her: just how long had she been upstairs? Minutes? Hours? Enough time for something terrible to happen to the . . .

Melanie didn't let the thought continue through the word *children.* Lifting the skirt of the gown (it was much too long), she ran through the hall until she came to Nancy's room. Carefully, she opened the door and walked over to the child's bed.

(Let her be all right, please God. . . .)

The little girl stirred in her sleep and sighed. Melanie bent to kiss her, thankful she was all right.

Kyle was sound asleep, clutching his pillow as if it were a teddy bear. Melanie kissed him, too, and covered him up again. On her way out the door, she stubbed her toe on a toy truck and sent it rolling across the floor. She stared at it, wondering if she would look at it one day and remember Kyle at age eight. But she didn't want to dwell on such morbid thoughts. She wanted to look at Kyle in the future to remember the Kyle of eight. What a beautiful child he is, she thought suddenly. A surge of love made her vow that no one would ever hurt him—or his sisters.

Melanie was on her way downstairs when a scream fractured the stillness of the night. Her walk turned into a run, and she took the steps two at a time. Her arm reached out to the doorknob of the playroom, and she wrenched open the door. It was a deafening sound, like the blast of a hundred rifles.

Inside, the girls were cuddled in terror in each other's arms. Wide eyes fixed themselves on the ceiling, ignoring Melanie. She followed them and saw the source of the noise. The balloons she had used to cover the ceiling were bursting in quick succession, as if an unseen torch were being run under them. A few of the girls covered their ears in terror at the deafening noise. Melanie was frozen to the floor.

Across the room, the cover was knocked from the stereo. Gina and Beverly ducked out of its path as it came flying toward them. Then the turntable switched on and the record was touched by the needle. The volume dial turned until the record was playing at full blast.

When she saw Gina running toward her, Melanie found her voice.

"Stop it!" she demanded, screaming the words. *"Stop!"*

The needle came off the record player with a scratching sound that sent chills through Melanie and the children. The room was quiet once again. Then the sounds of whimpering began. Melanie hugged Gina hard, stroking her brown hair. Her daughter looked up and asked, "What's wrong here, Mommy?"

"I don't really know, sweetheart," Melanie admitted in a strained voice. "I don't know."

She looked at the young faces across the room, some stained with nervous tears, others wearing stunned expressions. She tried to comfort them.

"Strange things happen in a house this old," she began, finding the words difficult. "I—I think the room was too hot, and the radiator made the balloons burst like that. It was just that there were so many that it was so loud."

"What about the stereo?" Doreen wanted to know.

"Maybe," Melanie suggested hopefully, "someone fell against it and it started up."

Some of the girls nodded at the possibility. But others, including Gina, knew they hadn't seen anyone near the stereo at all.

But it was so much easier to accept Melanie's words.

"No one's hurt?" she asked. When the response was negative, she offered to make hot chocolate for them. But no one wanted it.

"I'll be upstairs if you need me," she said finally. "You can stay awake and talk if you want—it's already four-thirty."

Halfway up the stairs, Melanie heard the sound of her daughter's voice. She leaned over the banister and acknowledged the call. Gina looked up at her with worried doe's eyes.

"Mom," she asked, "you do know what happened, don't you?"

Without answering, Melanie shook her head and stared hard at her daughter. She knew, she thought she knew. But she didn't understand.

20

July 27, 1941

Toby Langston toddled across the grass in his back yard after the tall man. Toby had often seen him, but the child hadn't yet learned the words to tell his older brothers about it. All he could explain was that he had seen a man, but they shook their heads at him in wonder, knowing there were no men living here.

They were in the house, helping with chores. On occasion, one would look out the back door to be certain Toby wasn't into any mischief. They saw him skipping around the barn, calling to someone they couldn't see. Poor Toby! they thought. He doesn't understand that Father is gone now.

Toby walked into the barn, looking for the man. He wanted to play with him, but the man ignored him. Toby peered into the darkness and hesitated to step further inside.

"Where you go?" he demanded in a three-year-old's squeak.

Herbie, his ten-year-old brother, appeared at the barn door. Limping on a weak ankle that had been, until yesterday, encased in a plaster cast, he walked over to Toby and took him by the arm.

"Toby Langston," he said. "What are you doing in here? If Mama saw you, she'd skin you alive!"

But Toby wanted to play. He threw himself on

the ground and began to kick the air, screaming all the louder when Herbie insisted he be quiet. Exasperated, Herbie pulled him to his feet and swatted him hard.

"Want man!" Toby insisted, crying from the pain of Herbie's blow.

"You be quiet or I'll use a belt on you," Herbie snapped. Since his father had died, he had assumed the role of authority, and it was wearing him down. Ten years old was much too young to bear a weight like this.

Audrey Langston looked up from the basket of laundry she had set on the kitchen table. Her eyes had no expression, and her voice was dull when she asked, "Why is Toby crying like that?"

"Oh," Herbie sighed, "he's mad because I took him out of the barn. He keeps talking about some man out there—but I didn't see anyone!"

The blank expression on Audrey's face changed momentarily, and her eyes became wide. But she quickly erased the look and sent Herbie out of the kitchen. She shoved a cookie into Toby's hand, and for a while his crying stopped.

So Toby was seeing it, too. She thought she had seen someone walking through their back yard the day Justin died, a wide smile across his dark face. But when she ran out to have him help her—to tell him Justin had fallen from a window—she found the back yard empty. There were no footprints on the soft dirt.

She passed it off as imagination, until one night she felt a strong hand on her shoulder and heard a voice say, "Fear not, for I shall not let them hurt you again."

She remembered now that she had been too terrified to cry out.

Half a year had passed since that day when she had heard Justin's scream. Audrey had tried to be both mother and father to her four sons, and the burden was taking its toll. Though she tried to be cheerful and patient, exhaustion chipped away at her nerves, making her stern and distant toward her sons. But more than that, her growing, irrational fear of the dark frayed her sanity. Each night, as she lay in bed, she wondered if she would feel that strong hand and hear that voice again.

"Toby have 'nother cookie?"

"No," Audrey said, snapping out of her day-dream. "Mama's going to fix our dinner now."

When Toby started to cry, she pushed him roughly out the door and sent him to play with his brother Frank. Toby walked into the playroom, where he found his favorite brother coloring. Frank handed him a crayon and the little boy set about scribbling on the piece of old newspaper Frank gave him.

He held the crayon in his fist and began to scratch circles and lines. Finally, he pushed it toward his brother and said, "Man looks like that?"

"What man, Toby?" Frank asked, leaning closer to study the picture. He clicked his tongue. "That's not a man! He's got a pony tail! Men have short hair like you and me."

"My man has a pony tail," Toby insisted.

"Well, okay," Frank consented. "If you want him to. Say, Tobe—why don't you draw a picture for Mommy?"

With a smile, Toby tackled another sheet of newspaper and drew a lopsided flower. Frank wrote his name across the bottom and told his little brother to put it on Mama's plate at dinner.

"It will make her smile," he explained.

And it did. Audrey picked up the drawing and grinned broadly, then leaned over and kissed Toby on his jelly-stained cheek. He giggled. Soon his brothers joined in, and Audrey, who couldn't be sad when her children acted this way, started to laugh merrily.

She even read to them before they went to bed that night. She kissed them gently, hugging each little body to her. Even Justin Jr., who hated to be coddled, did not protest when she leaned toward him with a goodnight kiss.

For several hours, the boys slept quietly, filled with content. But later in the night, that content was broken, and Audrey woke to the sound of her children's screams. She ran from the room, not stopping to put on a robe or slippers. To her horror, she saw that smoke was gushing out of the linen closet.

She yanked the fire extinguisher from its holder and started to climb the stairs, squinting against the stinging smoke. But her feet would not make contact with the steps.

She moved her hands through the space in front of her and felt nothing. When she thrust her hands out sideways, her fingers touched the ragged edges of what had once been a set of shelves cut like stairs to lead up into the attic. They had been smashed to bits.

The screams went on upstairs, tearing at her. A thick curl of smoke seeped into the closet, grabbing her by the throat. Without wasting a moment, Audrey ran out of the closet to go to the cellar for a ladder. Even down there, in the remotest part of the house, she could hear the screams of terror.

She tore the wooden ladder from the pegs that held it up, keeping her eyes on what was straight ahead of her. She was too afraid to turn around—there might be something waiting for her in the darkness of the basement.

If the ladder was heavy, Audrey was too intent on getting to her children to notice. She slammed the ladder against the shelves and, tearing the extinguisher from its holder, climbed to the top.

"Oh, my Lord," she prayed, "let me get to my boys—please, oh God, just do this for me!"

The smoke was so thick that she could barely make out the door to the boys' room. The horror of this moment made her remember the argument she and her husband had had when he chose this location for the nursery.

She had argued that it was unsafe for four little boys to sleep up here. And now her fears had come to pass, and her husband was not there to make things right.

A prayer began to run through her mind: *Now and at the hour of our death, now and at the hour . . .*

She groped toward the door. Just a few feet away from it (she could see the tiny faces now), her foot caught on a beam that had fallen across the floor, and she stumbled to the ground. Her head smashed against the wooden floor, cutting off her senses.

Herbie caught sight of the extinguisher, rolling out of her hand, and braved the flames to get to it. The sound of his sobs increased as he ran from the room, beating at the flames on his pajamas. He had never used an extinguisher before, but that fact didn't stop him. He aimed it at the fire and shot the white foam, trying not to look at Justin Jr. Why was he staring like that?

Something pushed hard against his back, sending him stomach-first onto the blazing mattress. The extinguisher flew from his hands, its hose spurting wildly.

The very last thing he saw was a man, dressed in a strange costume, lifting his mother in his arms. The man fell to his knees and threw back his head with a loud, triumphal laugh.

"She is saved!" he screamed insanely. "She is saved!"

* * *

He kept her in her room for days, undisturbed by calling neighbors. Since school was closed for summer vacation, no one called to find out where the boys were. And few people contacted Audrey Langston, a quiet, shy woman who kept to herself.

She woke once, and he touched a glass of wine to her lips. She drank, sucking in the liquid as if it were a life-giving nectar. Nothing mattered to her. Nothing.

He lay in the bed next to her, in his most human form, and held her in his arms, stroking her hair. To Jacob Armand, this was the moment he had pined for over the past two hundred years. He had his beloved again. He kissed her and caressed her, and in her delirium Audrey found his body warm and comforting. She didn't care about Justin any more. She had found another man to love.

But one morning, her mind came back to her.

She awoke, alone. The sun was beating through the windows and the air was already humid. Audrey lay there for a few moments, lost in a limbo where nothing could reach her—from either side of her mind.

Then she was fully awake, feeling as if she had slept on and off through a rough night. She thought she had to get up and fix breakfast for the boys, who must be bickering with each other over the morning paper by now. Audrey rolled out of bed, not aware that she had been lying there for days.

He came up from behind her and put a strong arm around her shoulders. He bent to kiss her neck, whispering of his love. But Audrey was no longer his love. She swung around, abruptly putting up her arms to defend herself. She stared into the handsome face and gasped.

"Who are you?" she demanded, her voice shrill.

"Fear not, my love . . ." he started to say, moving to pull her into the folds of his cape.

Audrey struggled to get free and ran from the kitchen. Her boys! Why weren't they down here? She ran up the stairs, crying out for them. But the only answer was silence.

Audrey pulled open the door to the linen closet, and at the moment she saw its interior, her mouth dropped in a soundless scream. As her eyes took in the broken shelves and the soot-covered towels that had fallen to the floor, it all came back to her—every moment of that terrifying night.

She fell forward against the splintered shelves and held fast to them, a long scream thrusting from her lungs.

"Oh my Gooooooddddddd!!"

She ran from the house in her robe and slippers, screaming and ranting. She had to get to the Jennings' house. . . .

21

Melanie sat before a microfilm projector at the library, carefully turning forward the filmstrips of Belle Bay's newspaper. To her left, she had stacked up a pile of reels that had proved worthless, evidence of her hours of sitting here. Since eight-thirty, when Janice had opened early for her, she had been studying these pages.

She set this spool aside, then wound another, and another—until her wrist stopped suddenly to freeze an image that had come up on the screen. She looked at the headline, then down at the picture beneath it—a photograph of four little boys. Calling to Kyle to send for Janice, she sat mesmerized.

"Melanie, what's up?" Janice asked, following Kyle into the reference room.

"I've found something," Melanie said, pointing to the screen. "I've had a recurring—" she paused for the right word—"nightmare, where I see little boys dying in a fire up in our attic. I'm sure that's a picture of the same children."

"It couldn't be!" Janice said, bending to take a closer look.

"Read the headline, Janice."

"Four Boys Die in Mystery Fire," Janice read. She advanced the film and went on. "A mysterious fire took the lives of four young boys here in Belle Bay some time earlier this week. Due to an extreme case of shock, Mrs. Justin Langston, mother of the children, could not be reached for comment. The Langston children, who lived at Starbine Court Road,"—Janice looked at Melanie with wide eyes—"ranged in age from three to ten. Terence, nicknamed Toby, Francis, Herbert, and Justin Jr. shared an attic bedroom. An anonymous source reported that Mrs. Langston's husband died from a fall this past winter."

"You don't have to go on," Melanie said. She wiped her fingers over her eyes. "I've known for a long time there was something evil in that house. Janice, how could I have imagined those boys when I had no idea until today that they even existed?"

"I don't really know," Janice admitted. "What do you think this means?"

"It has something to do with the first owner of our house," Melanie said thoughtfully. "With Jacob Armand. I think I've come in contact with him a few times."

"I read you, Melanie," Janice said. "Are you saying the place is haunted? What fun!"

Melanie's startled look was almost a glare.

"Well, it isn't fun," Janice said quickly, realizing her mistake. "But it is interesting. I usually don't go for those things, but if you look at all the weird things going on in your house, well . . ."

"I want to tell Gary about those boys," Melanie said. "Will you come over tonight and back me up?"

"Do you think he'll be willing to listen to all this just after he's out of the hospital again?"

"The sooner the better," was Melanie's reply. "And I'm going to tell him something else—that no matter what goes on in that place, I'm going to fight it. It's our house and I want to keep it!"

"Bravo, Melanie," Janice said, giving one quick clap of her hands. "I'm glad to see you're not giving in to the pressure. Sure, I'll come over tonight."

Kyle was tugging at Melanie's sleeve.

"It's time to go get Dad," he reminded her. He was already in his coat.

A few minutes later, Melanie walked out the glass doors with her two youngest children. They picked

Gina up at a friend's house, then drove in silence to meet Gary at the hospital. Even talkative Kyle, reading his mother's solemn mood, kept quiet.

The checkout was quick, all papers were scribble-signed, and Gary leaned lightly on Melanie to walk out the door. She noticed his hands rubbing where his chest had been bruised. Her eyes told him it was all right to talk about his pain, but he said nothing. When they had driven some five minutes, he pointed to a small store and said:

"Pull over there, Melanie. I want to get the paper."

He slid out of the car, turning his head so that Melanie couldn't see his grimace, ignoring her offer to get it for him. "It" turned out to be one copy of every paper in the store. He tossed them onto the seat and climbed into the car.

"Gary?" Melanie asked.

"We're moving," was the simple reply. "I'm sick and tired of that place. I'm going to spend the next week looking for another house."

"But I like our house!" Kyle cried.

"Shhh," Melanie said, pulling up the driveway. "The decision is between your father and me."

Inside, Gary carried the papers into the house and spread them out over a table in the library. His finger ran up and down columns in a smooth motion, until it stopped and tapped one small box.

"Here," he said. "6 rms, bath, ¼ acre. It's in Garden City."

"Six rooms!" Melanie cried. "Why don't we just move back to the city? No way am I going to live in six rooms with three kids! Gary, we're going to give this a fight. We have to! It's our home—not his! And don't argue with me about that. I've got proof something is strange about this place."

"So do I," Gary said. "And it's all I need to want out."

"But Gary," Melanie pressed, "I'm beginning to understand things now. I think I know what we're fighting."

"Melanie . . ."

"No, Gary," she said quietly.

He looked up from the paper, surprised. So the roles were reversed. He was ready to run scared, and Melanie had stopped running. He could tell by the look in her eyes that she loved this house and that it would take hell to move her from it.

"I was down at the library today," she said. "Looking through microfilms of the town paper. Do you remember those little boys in the attic that I saw a few weeks ago—when you thought I was dreaming? They existed, Gary. I saw a picture of them. They died in a fire up there forty-odd years ago."

"It's just those things that make me want to get out of here damned fast," Gary said. "After the things I've seen in these past weeks, I don't need to hear that my children may be murdered."

"Not if I read my ghosts right," Melanie said. "I don't quite know what I mean by this, but I think Jacob Armand has some strange feeling of love for me. I think he might be jealous of you and the kids, and that's why he's trying to drive you out. But if I can communicate with him, I think I can end it. Gary, I'll say it again: this is *our* house, and I'm going to fight to keep it!"

Gary knew there was no use fighting her. She was steadfast in her belief, and damn it all, she was right. The best he could do was cooperate, to make sure nothing else went wrong. But he did not know that there would be no time to make plans and dream up a line of defense against the evil in his home.

22

The snow was falling lightly when Janice drove up the hill to the VanBuren house. The silence of this late November night was somehow calming, easing the tension she felt. There was something eerie and chilling about going to a man's house to testify that a ghost existed there, when she herself hardly believed it.

She could see flecks of snow falling into the beams of her headlights. A dark form blocked the whiteness with its massive shape, and Janice leaned on her horn. The figure didn't quicken its pace—but turned for a brief moment to look in her direction. Janice gasped when she caught a glimpse of the face she had seen the night Tony DiMagi was murdered.

"It's him," she whispered.

He moved out of the headlight beam and into the darkness of the woods. Janice brought the car to a full stop and climbed out, all the while telling herself she should really speed up to the front door and scream like crazy. But Janice was too excited by this moment of terror to run away from it.

The man was no longer on the road, but she guessed his footprints would be some distance ahead. If she hurried, she could find them before they were covered. She ducked her head against the snow and walked forward, looking for tracks. There were none.

"How do you like that?" Janice said aloud. Her

breath formed tiny clouds, and her body gave one hard shudder.

A gathering of clouds moved in front of the moon, and the roadway was suddenly very dark. Janice had left the headlights on, and she moved quickly in their direction. Behind her, a dead branch fell from a tree, and she turned on her heels with a gasp. In the shadows, the limb was twisted in a shape that grotesquely resembled a human form. She quickened her pace to the car.

She put her fingers around the handle and pulled at it, swinging the door just far enough to let her slide inside. But as she stooped to get in, something pulled her away, and she fell clumsily into the snow. The car door slammed shut, and Janice saw her automobile slowly lose its traction.

"Hey!" she cried, jumping to her feet as it quickened its pace down the hill.

There was no use running after it. She looked around, half expecting to see that tall man again. She moved a step forward, and then another . . .

. . . and then she was running wildly toward the house. Why did it seem so damned far away? If she cried out, would anyone hear her?

She wheezed as she ran, years of smoking taking its toll. But Janice was too frightened to pay attention to the pain in her chest. A shadow blocked her vision suddenly, and she veered into the woods just in time to avoid the outstretched hands.

She didn't turn when she heard the sound of her car as it crashed at the bottom of the hill. She ran back toward the road, knowing it was the safest and quickest way to make her escape. Up ahead, a light suddenly came on in the upstairs. They had heard the crash! They would be out in a second or two to check it out!

But there was little time for relief. Janice felt something tug at the fur of her jacket. She turned, her arm raised to strike, and in the bright light of the moon she saw his face for the first time. She dropped her arm and gasped in awe. He was the handsomest man she had ever seen in her life.

"Oh . . ."

There was something in those eyes that began to drain whatever will power she possessed. They were so solemn, filled with centuries of pain. Janice could feel something happening to her under their spell, yet she could not make a move to run away. His fingers moved to encircle her neck. Even through her thick scarf, she could feel their iciness. Something was happening. . . .

He drew her up close to him, his cape falling around her. She breathed deeply and closed her eyes, lost in a hellish ecstasy. He pulled her close, still clinging to her neck, and moved to kiss her. She did not protest. But before his lips touched hers, he pulled abruptly away and tightened his fingers.

"You're not my Lydia."

When he said this, Janice snapped out of her spell. She was immediately struck with the realization that she was about to become a victim like Tony, and she had to think quickly to get out of it. If she knew his name . . . it was a biblical one, she remembered. Something very romantic. Jason—Joshua—Jae—Jae . . .

"JaCOB!" she cried out suddenly.

The grip around her neck loosened. His hands fell to her arms and he held her fast, staring at her with those sad eyes.

"Jacob," Janice said again, softly.

The eyes fixed themselves on her in that draining way. She felt herself being drawn inside him, being pulled with such a force that she couldn't fight against it. She was losing herself in that passion again, overcome by his mysterious sensuality. She no longer felt his cold.

"Jacob Armand," she breathed, hearing a voice that sounded far away. "I want to help you."

* * *

Gina leaned closer to her mirror and studied the freckled face that stared back at her. So this was what it was like to be thirteen? She certainly didn't feel any different. For all the change in her, she might as well still be twelve. She studied her childish figure, wishing she had Doreen's build. Lucky kid, Gina thought. She isn't flat like I am.

She stood up and walked over to her desk, where she turned on her radio to the sound of Christmas carols. Christmas! Gina threw herself on her bed and thought of the holiday. Just then, a crashing noise reached her bedroom from somewhere outside. But she ignored it, too wrapped in her thoughts.

A while later, her thoughts were again interrupted, this time by the sound of tapping at her window. Was it the tree outside, swaying? Or perhaps the snow had turned to sleet. She watched the glass and saw a handful of pebbles come flying at it. She went to the window to investigate.

At first she saw nothing, then she looked down to see Janice standing in the snow, signaling for her to open the window. Gina twisted the latch and gave the window a hard push. As it scraped over the sill, a fluff of snow fell to the ground.

"Hi, Janice!" Gina cried, leaning out.

"Shh!" Janice hissed, bringing a finger up to her lips. Gina noticed she wasn't wearing gloves.

"What's up?" she asked.

"Uhm," Janice said, taking a step backward in the snow. She looked uncomfortable. "I brought a welcome-home gift for your father!"

"Should I get Mom?"

"No!" Janice cried, in an almost frantic tone. "No, don't do that. It's a surprise for her, too. Can you come down and help me carry it inside?"

"Sure," Gina said. "Be right there!"

She pulled the window back in place and clicked the lock shut. Then she sneaked downstairs to the kitchen, where she pulled on her coat. No one saw her leave the house. She slipped out the back door and felt the snow crunch under her feet. It was covered by a thin layer of ice.

Gina walked to where Janice had been, but no one was there. Of course, Janice had already gone to her car! Her footprints were in the snow. Gina put her feet down next to them, measuring her stride to match Janice's.

She had taken three steps like this when someone grabbed her from behind. She felt a heavy arm around her, and struggled to turn around. She stared up into a face she had never seen before, a hard, cruel face. Her thoughts screamed for her.

DDDDAAAAADDDDDDEEEEEE! ! ! !

The man, his eyes cold, flung his cape around her and pulled her close to his body. Gina felt her legs give way and was barely conscious when he lifted her into his arms and headed into the woods.

23

The kids were giggling about something. The sound of their laughter had waked Gary, and he sat on the edge of his bed with his head in his hands. He looked through the weave of his fingers at the clock and jumped to his feet. He had been sleeping for *hours*.

His ears sharpened to the sounds coming from downstairs. He heard the dishwasher starting up, then Melanie calling to the children to settle down. Kyle's cheerful voice announced they were playing "Wild Kingdom" with Gina's new kangaroo. It was nice to hear them laughing. It made him think Melanie was really right about staying in this house.

He walked out of the room to head downstairs for a late dinner. When he reached the stairs, he instinctively reached out his hand to pat the sphinx. His hand touched the air, and he remembered what had happened to the statue.

He was halfway down when he heard the doorbell ring, then the sound of Melanie greeting Janice. With a shake of his head, he went back upstairs to watch TV in Kyle's room. He was in no mood to socialize. He even turned up the volume when he found he could hear Janice's voice.

Downstairs, Melanie was listening with amazement as Janice told of her car's mishap. The two walked into the living room and sat across from each other. Melanie tried to remember when she had seen her friend look like this. She was positively *forlorn*. That gorgeous blonde hair, usually swishing cleanly over her shoulders, had been drawn up sloppily in a knit hat and wet strands hung around her face. When Janice raised her hands to brush them away, Melanie looked with dismay at the lobster-red skin.

"You lost your gloves," she said.

"Yes," Janice said. "Guess I dropped them when I was running after my car."

She leaned against the back of the chair. "I thought I saw one of your kids walking up the hill, so I stopped the car and got out to offer her a ride."

"It wasn't one of ours," Melanie said. "They aren't allowed out after dark."

"Well," Janice said with a laugh, "it really wasn't anybody. My eyes were playing tricks on me. Some trick! Next thing I knew, my car was rolling down the hill!"

"Funny," Melanie commented. "I didn't hear any crash."

"I did, for sure," Janice said with a frown. "It's in a heap in front of a telephone pole."

They sat in silence for a few moments. Melanie brought her legs up and tucked them under her, feeling uneasy in Janice's presence. No matter how cheerfully Janice spoke, there was something in those eyes that was out of character—something very frightening. Melanie started to ask her about it.

"Janice . . ."

"Melanie," Janice said distantly. "I saw him tonight."

"Who?"

"I understand him now, as you would if you had listened to him. I know everything now."

"Janice, I don't understand," Melanie said softly, though the rapid beating of her heart told her exactly what Janice meant.

"He tried to recapture what he had lost that day," Janice went on. "And every time, he failed. But he won't fail again, for I have given myself to his service."

"Janice, who are you talking about?" Melanie demanded.

"Jacob Armand."

The reply was a scream. Janice was on her feet and moving toward the couch where Melanie sat. Melanie brought her legs closer to her body, like an armadillo wrapping itself for protection. Janice came over and sat beside her. Melanie didn't move, except to pull a throw pillow to her chest.

"In 1797," Janice said, "Jacob witnessed the execution of the only woman he had ever loved."

"Lydia?" Melanie asked, recalling the music box.

"Lydia Browning," Janice said. "She had been married to a merchant, and she had two little daughters. Jacob told me that her husband was a cruel man."

She spoke of Jacob as if he were a longtime friend. As if he were still alive. Melanie felt her skin creep.

"He met her in the market one day," Janice continued. "There was an ugly bruise under her eye, where her husband had hit her. Jacob offered to take her home to give her a salve for it, and she accepted."

"Then they fell in love?" Melanie asked.

"Yes," Janice replied. She closed her eyes in thought. "For weeks they met secretly at his house, at *this* house. He even had a room made for her."

"The room with the four-poster bed," Melanie put in.

"Then her husband heard of their meetings," Janice went on, ignoring Melanie. "He deeply hated the British, and when he heard of his wife's lover's nationality, his anger at her sharpened to a hateful edge. He had her brought to trial for adultery and threw in a charge of witchcraft. Do you know what that beast did? He made the two daughters testify against Lydia!"

"But what about Jacob?" Melanie asked. "Wasn't he brought to trial?"

"He wishes he had been," Janice said. "But he brought a good deal of money into the town when he decided to live there, and the people were more ready to forgive him than to give up having him as a patron for their shops.

"He did *try* to save her," she went on in a low voice, "by bribing the jury. But they took his money and found her guilty anyway. He had been tricked, and there was nothing he could do about it."

Janice's eyes were slits now, and her cold hand reached out to latch onto Melanie's leg. She heaved her shoulders once and clenched her teeth with bitterness. She was feeling for Jacob Armand.

"They found her guilty," she said again. "They put a rope around her and dragged her along the streets. He was there—he saw it all. And he couldn't stop it! Do you know what it's like to see someone you love dragged like a dog along a dirt road? Can you imagine what it's like to see the mouth you had once so lovingly kissed fill with dirt and pebbles? She had nearly choked to death before they propped her against the stake."

"Oh!"

"She screamed for mercy," Janice said, "but they turned a deaf ear to her. They were in the mood for a good execution that day—the burning of a witch adulteress. Jacob told me they had trouble starting the fire because of the mist rolling in from the bay."

"It happened on the beach?" Melanie asked.

"Yes," Janice answered. "The salt water sprayed them as the flames went up around her. It took only a few minutes. Jacob stayed after the crowd had gone home. He broke off a piece of her fingerbone to keep it with him, always."

"That explains why our ghost is so unhappy," Melanie said. Janice's hands, still clinging to her leg, had begun to turn frostbite gray. "But I still don't see what it has to do with us. I mean, that happened so long ago!"

"Do you think a memory dies when a body dies?" Janice demanded. "When Jacob died, his heart was loaded with guilt. He couldn't live with the memory of what had happened to Lydia, something he couldn't—didn't—prevent. He's carried that burden for nearly two hundred years."

"But we weren't there when it happened," Melanie protested. "Why should he take out his problems on us?"

The graying hands tightened. "Don't you understand, Melanie? In you he sees Lydia Browning. In

Gary, her husband. And in your children, hers. He needs to defend you against Gary and the children, because he thinks they're out to send you to the same fate as Lydia's!"

"That's just ridiculous," Melanie insisted.

"Is it?" Janice asked, her voice husky. "Can you really say that after everything that's happened in this house? *You* are the cause of his anger. Each family that ever lived here experienced the same things. Each time a woman moved in, he saw his Lydia, and the obsession to save her drives him to want to destroy her family."

"But can't anyone make him understand what he's doing is wrong?"

"It isn't wrong," Janice snapped. "It's very right. He loves with a great passion. He loves you!"

"He loves what he thinks I am!" Melanie cried.

The women were standing now, staring at each other. Melanie was unable to understand why Jacob tormented her family. Why didn't he take out his revenge on those who really killed his Lydia?

"The children in the attic," she said then.

"Bastards," Janice spat. "They've been trying to warn you. He set their nursery on fire to save another Lydia—the Audrey Langston we read about on the microfilm. He almost had what he wanted then. He had her in his arms. Do you know ghosts can cry? I swear there were tears in his eyes when he spoke of her. They carted her off in a straitjacket. She had gone crazy when she found her son's bodies."

"He killed her little boys," Melanie said, shaking her head. "And he says he loved her?"

"Burned them," Janice reminded her. Her head cocked to one side, and she smiled sweetly. "Children burn sooo easily. He's going to kill yours tonight."

Melanie's fear was suddenly overcome by anger. This was insanity! Before her stood the personification of evil in her home. She threw herself at Janice with a growl, lashing her hand out, catching tiny bits of flesh in her fingernails.

She picked up an ashtray and swung it forward, with an animal-like cry. Janice fell to the floor, throwing up her arms in defense. Melanie struck her again and again, her anger making her blind to the blood that flowed from the temple of the girl she had once called her best friend.

"No! No! No!" she screamed with each blow. "I won't let him have my children."

24

Something was tugging at her arm. Melanie stood staring at Janice's unconscious form, the ashtray dangling from her fingers. The tugging became more firm, and a voice reached her mind from very far away. She dropped to her knees and touched Janice's forehead, feeling the stickiness of blood on the blue, swelling skin.

That voice was persistent. Melanie looked toward it and saw a child. A little boy—the little boy she had seen in the attic? He was screaming at her, his blue eyes moist. She didn't want him here. She pushed . . .

"Mommy!" Kyle cried, sprawling backward. He steadied himself and went back to her.

"Please, Mommy!" he yelled, wondering if she could hear him. "You hafta come upstairs!"

"Oh, Janice," Melanie whispered. "I don't know why I did that!"

"Mommy," Kyle pressed, "Daddy's acting funny!"

He was so confused. Why had Mommy knocked Janice down? Why wouldn't she talk to him? Worst of all, he couldn't comprehend the strange scene he and his younger sister had just left upstairs. It had looked as if their father was fighting something—but there was nothing there. Kyle needed his mother to help, but she was in a daze.

Nancy started to wail and joined Kyle in pulling at their mother. At last, Melanie snapped out of it and stared in confusion at the two. Then she touched her swimming head and said softly, "Kyle, honey, don't look. Nancy, don't look at this."

"Come upstairs, Mommy," Nancy said. "Daddy's doing funny things."

(Funny things—mime? comical? clown?)

The two children took each of her hands and led her up the stairs. Melanie heard the crashing noises now, coming from her studio, and the sounds of two angry male voices. When the three reached the studio, Melanie gasped to see Gary go flying against the portrait of Nancy and Gina, breaking its wooden frame in half with his weight. She let go of the children and ran to him.

"Leave him alone!" she screamed at someone the children couldn't see.

Gary looked at her with eyes that spoke of fright and pain. He opened his mouth to cry out to her, revealing blood-stained teeth. His lower lip had swollen to twice its size.

"Dear God," Melanie whispered, choking on her tears. "Please help him! Please make Jacob Armand stop!"

But Jacob Armand would not stop. Suddenly, Gary let out a gurgling scream that spattered blood from his mouth and sprawled backward with a violence that sent him crashing through the window. Melanie caught her breath, watching the diamond-shaped pieces of glass fly, hearing the sound of metal reverberating as her husband hit the trash cans on the ground below.

But there was no time to stand here in shock. She turned quickly and grabbed the children, leading them from the room.

"Where's Gina?" she demanded.

"I don't know, Mommy," Kyle said tearfully, tightening his grip on her hand.

Melanie ran down the hallway to the child's room, but found it empty. She screamed her daughter's name through the halls, hearing nothing in reply. Did he have her already? Was Gina dead? *Oh God, oh God.*

It's happening to us, she thought frantically. He's destroying my family and I can't stop him! Just like the Langstons . . .

"GIIINNNAAAA! ! ! !"

Nancy reacted to her mother's frenzy and buried her face in the folds of her skirt. Melanie was frantic. The child wasn't up here. Where should she look next in this enormous house? She had to get to Gary. She had to find Gina soon, before Gary . . .

(Don't think of that!)

She knelt down to Kyle and kissed him on the forehead.

"My baby," she said. "I want you to do something for me. Can you run outside *really* fast and see if Daddy needs help?"

Kyle nodded. "I'm scared, Mom."

Melanie pulled him close and hugged him, kissing his curled hair.

"Please, Kyle," she said. "I'm going to try to find Gina downstairs."

Kyle mumbled something about the "crazy night" they were having and ran from the room. His mother called out that he shouldn't speak to anyone out there. If he saw someone, he was to come back inside, *immediately.* In the kitchen, Kyle pulled on his coat and boots and, without bothering to buckle them, went out the door.

An iciness shot through him as he walked toward the trash cans. His daddy was lying there, twisted strangely, one arm hung over a metal can. A leg was so misshapen it seemed not to be part of Gary's body. It bent over his back and touched a toe against his neck.

"Dad?" Kyle whispered cautiously. His father didn't look—*real.*

He had seen firemen on his favorite TV show lift a man's arm when they wanted to see if he was alive. Kyle did the same, but it told him nothing.

He bolted to his feet and ran away from his father, stooping over to vomit in the snow. He was crying now, tasting the bitter bile that had gushed over his tongue. He was frightened, but he had to look again. He had to see if his father was all right.

He looked down at the snow, at his footprints that covered the ground. And at another set. He stepped inside them, finding his feet were only an inch smaller. He knew at once to whom they belonged and started to run toward the house. Gina had been out here!

He stumbled into the kitchen, falling down on the newly waxed floor in his haste. As he pulled himself to his feet, he heard someone come into the room, and looked up to see Janice Lors, leaning heavily against the door jamb. Her long blonde hair hung in strings around her face, spotted and streaked with blood that dripped from her forehead. Kyle backed away from her, his childish instinct telling him she wasn't to be trusted.

"Kyle," Janice said, licking her lips. She laughed —a drunken laugh that chilled the little boy. "Kyle, let me help you."

"Go away!" he cried. *"Mommy!"*

"Aww, c'mon Kylie," Janice drawled. "You know I'm a nice lady. I've got someone I want you to meet. He's a *real* nice man. . . ."

"Mommy!"

"He just *loves* little boys like you."

For every step she took, Kyle took one away from her, until he was against the sink. Carefully, his arm sought the utensil drawer. His fingers grabbed at it, and he pulled it open. Even as Janice watched him, moving closer, his hand pulled out a knife and pointed a gleaming blade straight at her.

"Mommy!" he screamed again.

"Don't you cry for your mommy!" Janice snapped. "She's crazy! She hurt me, see?"

She was getting too close. Kyle didn't want to hurt her, he was afraid of the knife, but he had to defend himself. She looked as if she meant to kill him with those outstretched hands.

"Coooommme oooonnnn, you naughty boy," Janice singsonged. "Give Auntie Janice the nasty widdle knife."

"Go away!" Kyle warned.

Then she was so close he could feel her breath. Without thinking, he lashed out at her. The tip of the blade caught her just above her right breast. Janice looked down at the two tiny droplets of blood on her blouse and let out a monstrous scream. She gnashed her teeth and knocked the knife from the boy's hand. Her hands grabbed his upper arms, and she pulled him up close to her face.

"You vile beast!" she hissed. "You've been spoiled too long. I'm going to bring you to that man. Jacob will see that you don't turn your mother in to the authorities again. He'll see that she's saved this time!"

Kyle kicked her hard. "Let go of me! *Mommy!*"

"Calling your mother," Janice said, in a disbelieving tone, "so you can turn against her again, so you can call her witch? No, my dear brat!"

Kyle struggled and spit in her face. Hissing in anger, Janice grabbed his arm and dragged him to a chair. She sat down and threw him over her lap.

"You need to be taught a lesson," she said hoarsely. Her voice was deep, not her own. "Yes, to tame you once and for all!

"Jacob, I am helping to save her!" she screamed. "You deserve worse punishment than this, piglet. You deserve to die as your mother did!"

Kyle tried to get up, but Janice's hand was too firm against his back. He wasn't afraid of being hit, but he was afraid she might do something worse. Her hand raised high in the air . . .

. . . but stayed there. Janice felt something cold and round against the back of her neck. She didn't move.

"I have a gun on you," she heard Melanie say. "If you lay one finger on him, I'll kill you."

"You don't understand," Janice insisted. "The children want to have you executed!"

"You're out of your mind, Janice," Melanie said. "He's got you under some kind of power. Can't you see that?"

"No power," Janice insisted. "I do this on my own. Let him destroy the children and save you. Let him love you Melanie. Mela-melydia. Lydia! Lydia!"

Kyle felt a momentary lull in her grip and jumped off her lap.

"I saw Gina's footprints in the snow," he said.

"She's out there somewhere. I don't know if Daddy's . . ."

"Shh," Melanie whispered. She still held the gun to Janice's head. "Where's my child, Janice?"

"It's too late now, Lydia," Janice replied, the insane giggle spitting from her lips again. "He's taken her down to the beach. She should be honored. He's going to kill her on the very spot where they executed you that first time. Oh, yes, Lydia, the child should be honored."

Janice suddenly jumped at Melanie. In a reflex reaction, Melanie swung the gun out and struck her, hard enough to knock the life from her. Janice's body sagged to the floor, catching the chair.

Melanie was trembling. It wasn't fear—it was fierce determination. She was suddenly filled with the instinct common to so many animals, the need to protect her young. There was no time for fear and crying now.

Quickly, she handed Nancy a coat and pulled on her own. She helped the little girl buckle her boots, but when the three ran from the house, her own feet wore nothing but house slippers.

They weren't alone, Melanie knew. He was watching from somewhere. But she also knew that as long as the children were in her sight, they were safe. She took one look at her husband and felt a cry choke her.

No, don't do that! If there's any hope to save Gina . . .

But she couldn't resist a short prayer.

"Oh, Lord, please help her! Please help my Gary, too!"

Then she turned and walked quickly into the woods. The trees loomed above them, some naked, some with pine needles covering them. Their branches looked like arms ready to grab.

It seemed as if time were endless. The walk was long, longer than it had seemed the day they had gone down to the beach for a picnic. She scooped Nancy up into her arms and started to walk-run. When they reached the beach at last, the three of them were breathless.

The snowy, icy sand clicked under their feet. The bay was silent, stretching black and forever. Against its horizon, Melanie caught sight of her daughter, several hundred feet away. She was leaning against a pole. But when Melanie got closer, she saw that Gina wasn't standing at all. She was tied to the pole!

And around her feet was a pile of dried wood chips.

25

"Can you believe this, Tony? Two inches of snow on the ground and it's only Novem—"

Jack Hughes sank about three inches into his car seat. Damn, he thought, cringing, he'd done it again. That made the fifth time this week. He'd have to face facts: Tony was *dead*. And no amount of hoping would ever bring back his talkative, smiling partner.

But Jack Hughes still hoped. He thought: if I turn right now, Tony will be sitting next to me. And he'll have his hat pushed back like always. And he'll be . . .

"Are you going crazy, Jack?" he asked himself. "Are you so damned obsessed with Tony that you think he's still alive?"

He'd have to stop talking to someone who wasn't there. And he'd have to stop going to the VanBuren house every chance he got. Lord only knew what Davis would do if he found out he'd been here.

"Just once more," he vowed. "Just tonight, and if I don't find anything, I'll give up."

He started to sing "White Christmas," hating the silence. Some Christmas it would be, without Tony.

He turned off the main road and drove slowly toward Starbine Court Road. The clusters of people shopping for Christmas thinned out, until he was alone. In this section of town, where the VanBurens lived, there were few people and no stores.

Up the hill, he could see that magnificent white house—and the grounds that had kept his mind in their power for days on end. The VanBurens obviously had money, he thought.

Tony had once made a comment that he'd love to be so rich he could buy the place. But nobody really wanted to live there. Everyone would gasp about how beautiful it was, but even the ones who could afford it refused to live there. There was some story behind the place. He had heard it once when he was much, much younger, when he had first come to this town. Something about the place being haunted. But Jack Hughes just thought it was a bunch of bull. Give anyone an enormous old house and he'll write the spook story of the decade.

But Tony had still been charmed by the place. Hughes remembered how his younger partner saw the good in everything. He had even said one day, "Wouldn't it be nice, Jack, to live and die in a place like that?"

It was ironic, Hughes thought, but Tony had gotten his wish, in part. He had never lived there, but dying there was easy. Hughes bit his lip. He was crying again.

He turned off his lights as he approached the house. The moon was behind a cloud now, and just about the only things visible were the house and snow, both stark white against the total darkness. He stopped the car some hundred yards away and got out, ready with his flashlight.

It was cold. The quilted blue jacket he wore did its best to keep him warm, but its best wasn't good enough. Hughes sneezed, still feeling the aftereffects of his flu.

He heard a metallic noise from the side of the house. Trash cans, he told himself, rolling in the wind. But when he moved closer, he found it wasn't the trash cans at all. It was the back door, opening and slamming in the wind.

He hesitated, wondering if someone would catch him sneaking about these premises when he was specifically warned not to do so, then pushed the back door tightly closed. With the cessation of the noise from the slamming, the night was suddenly very still. Still enough for Hughes to pick up the sound of an animal whining. Making terrible noises.

A picture of the putrefied cat suddenly came up too clearly in Hughes' mind. He shook his head to clear it, then took a few steps toward the sound. He saw an arm flung over a trash can, hugging it as if it were a capsized boat. His fingers moved to touch his gun.

"My God," he whispered when he saw Gary. "Can you hear me?"

Gary's eyes fluttered. "Uuuhhh."

"Okay, take it easy," Hughes said quickly. "Just don't move, and I'll get an ambulance."

Hughes took off his jacket and tucked it around Gary's shivering body. He could see the bare hands and the feet going gray with frostbite.

"Mel . . ."

"I'll find Melanie," Hughes said, thinking he understood.

"Nnnnoo!"

Gary's cry stopped Hughes midway up the stairs to the kitchen door. He turned and saw the man trying to struggle to his feet, finding his feet quite unwilling. Hughes ran down to him and wrestled him back to the ground.

"Just stay put," he said firmly. "You might be hurt worse than you think. Don't make it worse!"

"Mel-a-nie . . ."

"I'll get Melanie!" Hughes promised.

Gary settled again. Hughes looked down to see that he had fainted. He got to his feet again and went into the kitchen, wondering out loud where in the heck Melanie was and why she hadn't found her husband. How long had he been out there?

The kitchen light was on. Hughes took in the opened utensil drawer, the knife (blood on the tip, he noted) on the floor.

And a lump on the floor like a woman's body.

Hughes walked over to it, his breath caught. He expected to see Melanie lying there, the leg of an overturned chair pulling up the back of her sweater.

Had something finally come of his obsession, he wondered? Had the bastard who killed Tony come back again to finish off witnesses?

He stooped down and carefully touched the mat of bloodied blonde hair at the back of the woman's neck. He was on his feet in a flash when he saw the ashen face of Janice Lors. He walked into the hallway in search of a phone and found one at the bottom of the stairs. Something made him recall what Janice had said the day after Tony was killed—that the phones had been dead in here. He let out a sigh of relief when he heard the dial tone.

"Captain Davis?" he said when his officer answered. "Hughes here. Look, I'm down at the VanBuren house. I *know* I wasn't supposed to be here! But I am, sir. There's been some bad trouble. I'll need backup and an ambulance. I found Mr. VanBuren outside—looks like he fell out a window. And the Lors woman, too. I can't find the wife and kids—I'll need a search party."

When he hung up, he started to call out names. But there was no one in the house to hear him. Where in the hell were Melanie and the children, he thought? Were they hiding somewhere?

He found the bloodied ashtray in the living room, where Melanie had dropped it on the rug. A cushion that had been pulled from the couch sat too near the fire, still burning, and Hughes moved it as carefully as he could, without changing the actual scene in the room. He had a feeling there was much more here than he could see.

He heard the ambulance coming up the road and went out to meet Davis. Once his captain had heard the story, he set about assigning people their duties. Two young paramedics tended to Gary, moving with an efficiency that Hughes could only admire. Of the three remaining officers, two were sent out into the woods and one accompanied Jack Hughes and Bryan Davis into the kitchen.

"You didn't see Melanie and the children anywhere?" Davis asked, crouching down to get a better look at Janice.

"No, sir," Hughes told him. "The house seems undisturbed, except for the living room. There's evidence of a struggle in there. I found an ashtray with blood on it—I think it might have been used to hit her. I haven't been upstairs yet."

"Get on it, Towers," Davis said to the younger cop who had come inside with them.

"Tear the place apart!" Davis yelled after Towers. "They may be hiding somewhere, scared to death! And keep near your gun; we might have some nut on our hands!"

He and Hughes walked back outside and examined the grounds. When a slight wind brought the smell of Kyle's sickness to them, neither man grimaced. They had experienced worse. And they were too interested in the strange footprints they found in the snow.

"I would guess these belong to Melanie and the kids," Hughes said, pointing to the sets of prints, two small and one large. "But I don't know what happened to the third one."

"If she's in the house," Davis said, "Towers will find her."

Hughes walked further around the house, keeping his eyes to the ground. Then he called to Davis, seeing a row of a dozen or so footprints that stopped—*just stopped*—dead in the middle of the snow.

"The other child," Davis said knowingly. "It looks as if she were picked up about here. See the way the snow is fluttered—as if it'd been kicked?"

"But where's the footprints of whoever did the picking up?" Hughes asked. Davis shook his head.

"Chief," Hughes said, after a long silence, "I think we ought to get another team out here. It might take us all night to find them."

26

If they had turned at that moment, they would have seen a bright flash of light shoot up from the mile-away beach. It was a flame that had leaped to devour the stake Gina had been tied to only seconds earlier. Now, the little girl was being squeezed tightly in Melanie's arms. Melanie closed her eyes and sighed with relief, rocking the semiconscious child.

Thank God, thank God . . .

The knot had been tied carefully, but Melanie had worked quickly and patiently as the flames began to crackle at her feet and a bodiless voice roared at her. By the time the knot gave way, her freezing fingers were bleeding. But she had gotten her daughter safely in her arms before any harm at all was done. For the time being, Gina was safe.

She watched the flames now, trying to push from her mind the thought that if she had been a few seconds late . . .

In one hand she held the gun, but she knew it would do little to help her tonight. She debated throwing it away, but decided to keep it. It would be her security blanket. When she heard the cries again, her finger moved to the trigger. Still holding Gina, and feeling Kyle and Nancy clutching at her, she began to cry out in anger.

"Just leave my kids alone, you son of a bitch! Just because you screwed up your life you have to take it out on innocent people? You couldn't make things right when your Lydia died, so you have to hurt little children? You *coward!*"

His cries became louder, sounding as if he were standing very near to her. When she felt his touch, she shrugged it off roughly and tightened her grip on the children.

"You *bastard!*"

"Nnnnnoooooooo ! ! !"

"You didn't like that, did you?" she asked, smiling. "Did you, coward?"

"Nnnnnooooo! !"

"COWARD!"

"Lydia, my love—what lies have they told you?"

"I am not your Lydia!"

"Why do you turn against me now?" he whimpered. Though Melanie could not see him, she could imagine the look on his face—pouting, ugly.

"Leave us alone," Melanie said darkly.

"Know you not the danger?" he asked, appearing to her in a hazy form that did not reveal his features.

Melanie spat at him, and he roared, dropping to his knees. He began to howl, rocking back and forth. He slammed a massless fist against the snow. Then he was gone again.

There was dead silence. Melanie didn't dare move from her place, watching the beach in front of her. Where was he now? And now? He could easily move anywhere he wanted within seconds, couldn't he? Couldn't ghosts do that, she asked herself?

Without warning, Gina was tugged away from her. The shock brought her daughter to complete consciousness, and the little girl began to scream in terror, not understanding why she was being jerked back and forth by nothing.

"I shan't let them hurt you again, my Lydia!" he cried. "I-shan't-let-them-my-Lydia!"

"Can't I make you understand?" Melanie cried, rushing desperately toward her daughter. "I am *not* your Lydia! Lydia is dead! She's *dead!*"

But Jacob Armand wouldn't understand. He thought his Lydia was under the spell of these three children. Angered that he couldn't persuade her, he threw the child he held across the sand. Her head struck a piece of driftwood that jutted like a broken bone through the sand and snow. There! The daughter was gone, and the father. The younger two would be easiest. *Samantha and Sarah Browning. Two evil-wench children. Sarah so dirty she looked like a little boy . . .*

"Mommy, I want to go home!"

Nancy's pitiful cry snapped Melanie from her staring spell. Was that Gina—her beautiful Gina—all crumpled on the snow? Was she alive? Was she alive?

"Oh, God," Melanie whimpered. "Oh, God—my baby!"

But Nancy and Kyle needed her now. Melanie lifted her little daughter in her arms and started to run up the beach. If she had lost her husband and her oldest child, she still had to protect her youngest. The shock of the insanity of this night was cushioning her mind against the terror of realizing what really had happened to Gary and Gina.

(Let it be a mistake. . . .)

"Just try to get them from me," she snarled as she ran along the sand and snow. "Just try, you bastard!"

He was standing in front of her in his most solid form. Melanie did not hesitate to look him straight in the eyes, challenging him to dare to pull the children from her arms. Though he was grimacing in anger, his features were still breathtaking, but Melanie was so filled with hatred that she wasn't taken in as Janice had been. He stepped toward her, his eyes reflecting his purpose. He said firmly, "You mustn't trust them, my Lydia. Come with me now!"

"Stop calling me that!" Melanie snapped.

She turned from him and stumbled up into the woods. She couldn't hear him behind her, and it frightened her. She couldn't fight what she couldn't see. And Nancy was so heavy!

"Kyle," she said breathlessly. "Run as fast as you can. *Hide* somewhere! Mommy's right behind you!"

The little boy picked up his speed and shot forward. Still grasping Nancy, Melanie followed as closely as she could, until she lost traction in the snow. She fell backward, Nancy on top of her. The little girl rolled off and the two helped each other up. But when they were standing again, Kyle was gone. Completely.

"Kyle?" Melanie cried.

No answer came.

"Kyle, answer me! ! !"

But the night was silent. Had her child already reached the house? But it was a half mile away! On a straight path! Kyle couldn't have run that fast!

"Kyle, where are you?"

"Hey!"

The voice that answered her was masculine, but not young. It wasn't Kyle, but it wasn't Jacob Armand either. Gary? Could it be Gary? *Oh, please, God, let him be unhurt!*

"Hey!" the voice called again, closer now. It was Jack Hughes. Melanie didn't stop to ask him where he came from.

"Did you see my little boy?" she asked.

Hughes shook his head. "What's going on here?"

"Please find him," Melanie implored, ignoring the man's question. "That maniac's killed my husband and my dau-dau—"

She fell to her knees, the terror of the night finally reaching her. As Nancy hugged her neck, her body shook with great sobs. Nancy cried with her.

"Mrs. VanBuren," Hughes said gently. "Your husband is alive."

Melanie looked up.

"Please, did you see the man who hurt him?" Hughes asked.

Melanie nodded.

"Was he armed?"

"He's a ghost," she said quickly.

Hughes looked at her strangely, then pulled his walkie-talkie out. The captain was summoned, and in minutes he arrived with Towers. When he heard what had happened, he told the younger cop to take Nancy back up to the house and to find Kyle. Two other policemen arrived in a few moments and were sent to join the search for the little boy. And if they spotted the suspect, they were to take him alive.

"I want to have the pleasure of seeing him suffer," he explained. "As much as you, Jack."

"I was right about this," Hughes said softly. Before Davis could agree, he said, "The woman is hysterical, sir. She says he's a ghost."

"That would explain his knack for disappearing, wouldn't it?" Davis replied, not meaning it as a joke. "Let's get a move on here. We'll find him tonight."

"I hope I get him, sir," Hughes said, anger in his voice.

They heard a shot fired some distance ahead and were running to it before it had time to echo. Frank Croyens was pointing to a clearing in the woods with his gun. He had just seen a tall, caped figure run through the trees. Hughes caught Davis' eyes, and the story Janice Lors had reported was brought back to them.

"It's him," Hughes said softly.

Melanie, who had followed them here, suddenly broke into a run, heading toward the beach. The policemen followed, their guns drawn. But Melanie was as confused by her action as they were. She had no idea what made her suddenly rush toward the bay, but when she arrived, she saw her daughter standing up. Gina was rubbing the bump on her head, crying. Croyens rushed to the little girl's aid. But before he reached her, something struck him from behind and he hit the sand in a dead faint. Stunned, Hughes and Davis looked around for the assailant.

"Nnnnooooo! ! !"

The cry was a horrid, dragging sound. Jacob Armand was here again, Melanie knew. But Hughes and Davis saw nothing. They watched Gina running to her mother, then saw her stop in midflight, as if someone had grabbed her. They watched, unmoving, as she screamed and flailed her arms through the icy, empty air.

Davis shot his pistol in the air, but the child's unseen tormentor did not let go. Gina began to gasp, her face bloating like an overripe tomato. Hughes rushed forward and grabbed her, pulling with all his might. She fell, limp in his arms, and he laid her on the sand. He began mouth-to-mouth resuscitation.

"She must die!"

Someone was trying to tear him away. But he fought, hard, to save this little girl's life. Somehow, Hughes felt that saving one life would make up for the loss of Tony DiMagi. He wouldn't let the bastard who had killed his partner have a child too.

Something like a foot connected with his head, and Davis saw a string of blood trickle from Hughes' head. Down the beach, Croyens had picked himself up, and he limped to his captain.

"Who hit me?" he asked.

"I don't know, damn it," Davis admitted. "You okay? Get up to the house and help Towers find the little boy."

Jacob Armand had stopped his fighting for only an instant to study this situation. Why wasn't the girl dead? What was this man doing to her, and why didn't he fear what he couldn't see?

"Aaaaaahhhhhhh!"

Davis looked around. Hughes kept working with Gina, pressing his mouth to hers, listening for her breath. Davis clicked on his walkie-talkie.

"Towers?"

The airwaves crackled.

"Do you know what that was?"

"Negative, sir," Towers answered. "It came from down there."

Jacob was desperate now. He hadn't believed the children could possibly deceive him again, as they had done every time he had tried to save his Lydia. These were the men who would see her burn! He had to stop them!

He grabbed at the back of Hughes' jacket and pulled with an unnatural strength. The little girl beneath them opened her eyes and blinked a few times at the men standing over her. Two men. Three . . .

Both Hughes and Davis tried to pull him away but suddenly found themselves grabbing at empty air. The man who had been there only a split second earlier had completely vanished. Gina kicked up at nothing, her cries mixed with her efforts to breathe. He was strangling her.

At that moment, another voice cried out. It was Melanie, who had stood watching the scene in terrified silence. She walked toward her struggling child, an angry look set on her face.

"Stop it, Jacob Armand," she insisted.

"No!" the bodiless voice shot back. "She must die so that you may live!"

"Stop it now!" Melanie screamed.

"She must die! She must die, my Lydia! ! ! !"

"I! AM! NOT! YOUR! LYDIA! ! !"

He started to screech viciously. And then, hell came to the night. . . .

27

It began with the sound of faraway voices, a muffled noise that Melanie had, so many weeks ago, blamed on a hissing radiator. No one had noticed it at first, so occupied with Jacob Armand were they. But now the beach was so quiet that the sounds could be plainly heard.

It was like the sounds at a crowded party—definitely voices, but unintelligible because each utterance masked another. Here and there, one would hit a loud intonation, and a full word or phrase could be understood.

"Armand!" a woman's voice cried.

"To hell with Armand!" bellowed an unseen man.

"Revenge! Revenge!"

Mumbling. Then more voices. Davis and Hughes moved carefully forward, alert to spot anyone who might come leaping from behind one of the large rocks on the beach. Melanie had taken the now-conscious Gina in her arms. She bit her lip to steady its quivering.

"Who's out there?" Davis called. "Come out—the game's over!"

He shot his pistol once into the air, but the voices did not cease. Instead, they grew ever louder and closer. Davis and Hughes looked at each other and knew the thoughts in each other's minds. There was something very wrong here—more wrong than anything either man had encountered in all their years as cops. It was something they couldn't deal with, and they began to empathize with each other's helplessness.

Jacob Armand had started screaming again. But they were no longer the cries of anger and determination. This time, he screamed for help. It seemed as if he were in terrible trouble.

"Help me! Don't let them hurt me! Oooohhhh please!"

"Who was that?" Davis cried. "Come out where we can see you!"

But he already knew no one was hiding from him.

"To hell!"

It was a child's voice this time! Shadows appeared to the living humans. A flash here, a man with his fist raised—then a cluster, so much like a group of children. Faces in the ghostly crowd became visible for fleeting moments. Melanie gasped to see Helen Jennings among them. The woman looked over to her and smiled with an eerie sweetness.

She saw the four boys, the massless forms shifting from wholeness to the hideous state of their deaths. A man was with them—the father? His head lolled from side to side on a deformed neck. His opened mouth roared the name of Jacob Armand.

They were all visible now, moving straight forward on feet that left no marks in the snow. There were some fifteen of them—almost half were children. Jesse Prentice was there, with her infant son in her arms. The child's head was still wreathed in the seaweed that had caught him at the bottom of the bay.

"We shall send him back to hell!" a man cried.

"To hell! To hell! To hell! To—!"

The cries took on such fervor that they soon became one massive noise. The crowd moved ahead.

Jacob appeared again, no longer standing tall and proud, but hunched over and pleading mercy. He knew he was finished. His victims had at last arisen to send him back to the hell he had avoided for nearly two hundred years. He tried to find safety with Melanie.

He threw himself to his knees and buried his face in Melanie's coat. Startled, Melanie did not attempt to pull away from him. But her grip around her daughter tightened.

"Don't let them hurt me, my Lydia!" he moaned. "I only wanted to save you!"

"But I'm not your Lydia," Melanie said again, softly now. "Nor was Audrey Langston, or any of the other women here. The people you killed were innocent victims of your need for revenge."

The words Melanie spoke set the crowd into a new fervor, and the chant was taken up again:

"To hell! To hell! To hell!"

"Stop it!"

The scream came from Melanie's lips. The crowd turned their glazed eyes to her. Feeling a trembling starting inside her, Melanie took in a deep breath and tried to reason with them.

"I can't stop you from doing what you feel is necessary," she said. "But I don't believe you're doing the right thing. Jacob Armand is guilty—*yes*—but only of being insane. He's mad! But what does it make you if you destroy him? Doesn't it reduce you to his evil level?"

"We must have revenge!" a little girl cried.

"And I want this finished!" Melanie cried angrily. "I'm sick of the things that have happened to my family! I want to be guaranteed they won't ever happen again! Who will promise me Jacob Armand won't find his way out of hell to come back and hurt us again? My God—look at my daughter! She's just a child! I don't want her to suffer like this!"

"We *shall* end it, my dear," Helen insisted. "Now move away from him. Let us have him, and it will be over!"

"To hell! To hell!"

Helen stepped closer. A few yards away, Hughes grabbed his captain's arm and pointed to Tony DiMagi. The cop turned around at the sound of their astonished calls and smiled a deadly smile.

But Helen wasn't smiling. She moved closer to Melanie, until her cold hand touched the young woman's face. Melanie was in a state of shock now, not understanding the words she had just spoken, but not afraid. She didn't back away when Helen stroked her cheek.

"My dear girl," she cooed, "there is only one way to deal with him. He must be sent to hell, to the punishment he deserves. Now, dear, we don't want to hurt you—you've done nothing to us. But don't try to stop us."

"Save me, my Lydia, oooohhh!" Jacob whined. "I don't want to be hurt by them!"

The crowd had had enough. Jacob was wrenched from Melanie's side and dragged down the beach. He was beaten—his massless body struck again and again by equally massless fists. Bloodless veins gushed red. Shapeless mouths screamed.

They disappeared, but the cries were still full on the wind. Jacob Armand pleading his innocence. That terrible chant: "To hell! To hell!"

Hughes and Davis ran to Melanie.

"She's in shock, sir," Hughes said, snapping his fingers in front of her eyes. They did not blink.

"I'm near to it myself," Davis admitted. "Come on, let's get these two back up to the house."

"What about them?" Hughes asked, looking down at the now-empty beach.

"It isn't for us to handle," Davis said. He lifted Melanie into his arms.

She was dead weight, in spite of her small frame. Her arms hungs limply, her eyes still staring. If not for the slight rise and fall of her chest, Davis would have thought she was dead.

Then her eyes blinked once. Melanie's arm shot backward, striking Davis so hard that he was forced to drop her. Before she could be stopped, she was running down to the beach.

The two policemen blinked in disbelief. As Melanie ran screaming down to the bay, her clothes seemed to vary from a dress to a gown, at times so briefly that they seemed to blend. Her hair went from blonde to dark, dark to blonde.

"What the hell is this?" Hughes whispered, holding Gina tightly.

Melanie was no longer there. In her place stood

a young girl. Melanie VanBuren had become one with Lydia Browning.

Jacob Armand's lover had waited these years, as the women of her day had waited for their men to return from the sea. She did not understand his cruel deeds, but she did not question them. He was a man—and she had been taught not to question men.

But he needed her now, and she could not let her prudish upbringing keep her from him. She cried out his name and ran to him, toward a crowd that was once again visible. Jacob straightened himself at the sound of her voice and turned swiftly to face her, his great height knocking down the two men who held him. The two lovers ran and embraced each other. Their whimpering over the joy of finding each other was like the sounds of animals. For the moment, the crowd left them alone.

Jacob closed his eyes and ran his fingers through Lydia's curls. He buried his face in their softness, shaking his head. Lydia threw back her head and let out a cry.

"You were so different these times," Jacob whispered.

"No, my darling Jacob," Lydia said. "I have always been the same. I have always waited for you."

Jacob bent to press his lips of nothing to hers. But the ghostly kiss was brief, for Jacob was suddenly ripped from her arms. Two brawny men held him fast and started to drag him away again. A little child began to chant (to hell! to hell!) and Toby Langston giggled in evil delight as the crowd pushed forward. Jesse Prentice's baby screeched.

"You cannot have her now!" Helen said.

"Yes," Justin Langston agreed. "This child is not for hell."

Jacob struggled.

"Please, oh please!" Lydia begged. She moved toward them in a motion so smooth it seemed she was made of liquid. Her arms, Melanie's arms, reached out.

"I only did it to save you, my Lydia," Jacob whimpered.

"Then *I* am the cause of this!" Lydia insisted.

"You must punish *me,* not my Jacob! Oh, mercy, not my Jacob!"

Helen Jennings smiled at her. She knew what this woman wanted. And if it meant getting it, Lydia Browning was willing to burn in hell with her lover. That they would do, she thought. That they would do.

"Stay with him then, child," Helen said. "Not for his sake, but for yours."

"Why should he win his prize after his deeds?" a man wanted to know.

"I feel it is best," Helen insisted.

"Silence, woman," the man shot back. "Only a man could know what is best!"

Helen let out a wail. "I lived longer than any of you!" she cried. "And I was the most recent to die! You must understand me—if Jacob is kept from his Lydia, he will come back! He'll destroy more like us!"

"Lydia!" Jacob moaned.

The young woman threw herself at Jacob. And as she did so, her spirit passed from Melanie's body, giving back its form. Melanie watched the scene in a daze, seeing, not seeing. Helen Jennings reached out and stroked her cheek with a cold hand.

"He shall not bother you again, my darling," she promised. "It is in our hands now."

Melanie was suddenly alone, staring down at the water at her feet.

Hughes snapped from a disbelieving stupor to see Davis running down to Melanie. He caught her just before she collapsed.

"I was dreaming," she whispered.

"Yes," Davis said. He took her gently by the arm and led her to the others. "Jack, get that little girl up to the ambulance."

"I want to stay with my mother," Gina said.

"We'll go up together," Hughes said.

"Where's Kyle?" Melanie demanded. "Did you find him?"

"Right here, ma'am," someone behind her said. She turned to see Kyle, his face streaked with tears, in the arms of one of the policemen.

"Where were you, my baby?" she asked, pulling him close to her.

"I hid up a tree," Kyle answered, a choke in his voice. "I was so scared when I looked back and couldn't see you any more! I just closed my eyes and got so scared!"

"I heard him crying up there," Towers said.

It was Melanie's turn to cry now—an insane sobbing mixed with wild laughter, muffled into the plush of Kyle's jacket. She had talked to a ghost, ha! ha! She had talked to a lot of ghosts!

"Gary?" her face went straight again.

"He's already at the hospital," Davis said. "We'll take you to him now. Towers, take them up to the house."

Hughes was staring down the beach, thinking hard. He had solved his mystery, and he knew Tony lived forever. He would no longer weep for him.

Towers escorted Melanie and Gina back up to the house. Hughes and Davis stood on the beach, not speaking, not knowing what to say. At last, Davis leaned his head back and let out a long sigh.

"When I get home," he said, "I'm going to drown myself in Bud."

"Ditto," Jack Hughes promised himself.

"I might even retire," Davis said thoughtfully.

"You're kidding?"

"Of course," Davis answered.

Hughes shifted on his feet. "How're we going to write this up?"

"We aren't," Davis said. Catching the surprised look in Hughes' eyes, he said, "Look, Jack, if we did, everyone in Belle Bay would treat us like madmen. This town would go crazy! Be realistic, Jack—who would believe a story like this?"

"Then what about Janice Lors?" Hughes demanded. "Who killed her?"

"Janice Lors," Davis said carefully. "Janice Lors was killed by a man who later set himself on fire down at that pole. It's charred, see? That's proof enough. And there'll be a promotion for every man here tonight who can remember that."

"But, sir," Hughes pressed. "When they make the investigation, they won't find any human ashes!"

"Of course not," Davis said, reaching out a hand to catch the bits of snow that were falling. "That's a damned strong wind blowing out to the bay, isn't it?"

Epilogue

Gary would walk again, with a bad limp. The children were just fine—by some miracle, there was no sign of frostbite. Their natural resiliency would heal the trauma of the night before. Melanie, knowing it was over and that her family was safe again, would adjust to a normal life in a short time.

"I hope I'm not in here too long," Gary said, feeling cheerful in spite of his body cast. "How can I train a dog in this getup?"

"We don't have a dog," Melanie said, thinking her husband was delirious.

"We'll get one," Gary said, winking at his oldest daughter, who sat with her brother and sister at the foot of his bed. "I promised Gina, didn't I?"

"A puppy!" Gina squealed. Nancy and Kyle began to bounce up and down, laughing with delight.

Soon they were all laughing. They laughed because they were certain life in their new home would be as it should always have been. But there would only be a short time for that laughter. Their lives would just be settling down to normal when the evil of the house would rise again—in the hateful, disturbed form of Janice Lors.

A Special Preview of
the opening pages of
the chilling sequel to GHOST HOUSE . . .

GHOST HOUSE REVENGE

by

Clare McNally

coming soon from
Corgi Books

PROLOGUE
Summer, 1975

The little girl clung to her father's hand, feeling a warmth that made her happy and secure. It was a beautiful afternoon to be seven years old, and Alicen Miller was very happy. Her father smiled down at her, seeing the anticipation in her brown eyes. She was such a cheerful little girl!

They were standing on a corner, a block away from their apartment building, watching the cars that sped down the highway. Alicen and Derek were looking for one car in particular, a blue sedan that belonged to Alicen's mother, Elaine. She had spent the last week in Maryland attending the funeral of her only relative, Alicen's great-aunt. Both Derek and Alicen missed her terribly.

"Now, listen," Derek said. "Mommy might still be very sad, losing her aunt like that. After all, your great-aunt practically raised her. Now all she has are you and me."

"I'll be extra-special nice to her," the little girl said in a singsong tone.

Just then, they spotted Elaine's car. Alicen jumped up and

down, waving excitedly. Derek raised his arm to wave, too, but he never completed the gesture.

There was another car behind Elaine's, about thirty yards away. It was weaving erratically across the highway and coming up on Elaine's car—fast, too fast.

Desperately, Derek tried to signal her off the road. Reading his gesture, Elaine looked up into her rear-view mirror and saw the car behind her. Quickly she tried to turn out of its path, but it was too late. There was a loud crash, a screech of tires, and a scream.

Elaine's car flew over a road divider, tumbling down a deep embankment. Derek felt his legs pull him forward. His arms stretched out as if he could grab his wife and save her.

"*Elaine!*"

This couldn't really be happening. . . .

Derek's legs gave way from under him as Elaine's car went up in flames, and he fell to the sidewalk. His mouth dropped open, and his palms pressed hard against the warm sidewalk as he gazed at the inferno. He vaguely heard sirens, barely registered the sight of fire trucks and water-gushing hoses. He was too busy watching the fire and praying.

Please let it be a mistake. Please don't let it be Elaine.

He pulled himself up onto his feet, his legs as heavy as tree trunks. Derek hardly felt the sidewalk underneath him as he walked toward the car. He heard humming in his ears—was it the whispers of the curious bystanders or the shouts of the paramedics? Or maybe it was the hacksaw they were using to get Elaine's door open.

That's not my wife, he thought.

Two hoses at last managed to still the flames enough for firemen to get inside the car and pull out Elaine. Or what was left of her. What had once been a beautiful woman was now a blackened mass. Not a woman. Not his Elaine.

Then he noticed the blackened hand. On one finger was a diamond ring—the ring Derek had given Elaine the day he had asked her to marry him.

He threw back his head and screamed. And then he felt a small, cool hand in his. He looked down and to his horror saw his little daughter standing at his side, staring at the flame-engulfed car.

"Oh, my God," he whispered.

He grabbed Alicen into his arms and turned her away from the sight, hugging her tightly as if to protect her. If only someone would protect him . . .

He heard laughter. Sweet, childish laughter that rose above the sirens and screams. It was Alicen's laughter.
"Oh, daddy," she said, "I made a mistake. Mommy isn't coming home today at all. She's coming home later on."
She's in shock, Derek thought. Thank God she's being spared from all this. Thank God we both don't have to suffer.
"Mommy will come home when she's ready," Alicen said. "When she wants to see me again, mommy will come for me."

1

When the noon sun struck the mansion at the top of Starbine Court Road, its whiteness seemed to glow like a holy vestment, and anyone seeing it might have thought: "There is a good, beautiful old house." And on this April Saturday, it seemed everything *was* good about the 185-year-old structure. Nothing set it apart from dozens of other Long Island mansions. Its large front porch faced the town of Belle Bay. Magenta azalea bushes ran from either side of the wooden steps to the rounded towers at its sides. These towers, added over a hundred years after the original Colonial mansion was built, made the house all the more breathtaking.
But those who had the powers to see beyond pretty flowers and inviting front porches would have known the house harbored a terrifying evil and that those who lived within its walls faced unspeakable dangers.
For now, though, all was well. Behind the house, two children were working on a corner of the back yard, which stretched for an acre to the thick woodlands that surrounded the house on three sides. Kyle and Gina VanBuren tugged hard at weeds and dug up rocks in preparation for a spring garden. Kyle found a fat grub and dangled it in front of his sister's nose.
"Daddy, make him stop!" Gina cried, her mouth turning down in a grimace.

Their father looked up from the legal papers he was reading. Kyle was giggling, but he had put the worm down again. Gary smiled at him.

"You're a rip, Kyle," he said. "Be nice to your sister."

Gina decided the incident had been funny after all and started to laugh. Both children rolled around merrily on the newly cut grass. Gary grinned at them, forgetting his work long enough to watch them play. He felt a surge of love for his two oldest children and decided that in the long run it had been a good idea to move from the city into his house. They would have to put last year out of their minds. It was over, and now it was time to enjoy their new home.

Gary looked up at the house. Although the front was somewhat gingerbready, the back was more true to the original Colonial style. His eyes roamed proudly across the back of the house. Suddenly they stopped at one particular window, which stood out because of its modern construction. The odd window brought Jack memories that made Gary shudder, and he forced them out of his mind. He quickly raised his eyes higher.

The weather vane at the peak of the roof needed straightening, he thought. Someone would have to come and fix the whole roof. The shingles were all curling up at the edges. Gary sighed to think that less than a year ago, he could have been the one to climb up there and do the job. But that was impossible now. He couldn't even climb stairs.

Gary looked down at his legs, muscular after so many painful hours of exercise, and yet useless. His fingers wrapped around the arms of his wheelchair. He'd been confined to it for four torturous months, ever since an—*intruder*—had pushed him out of that hated upstairs window. That November night, when he had become a cripple, had been so horrible that he and his family never talked of it.

He shivered, then pushed the accident from his mind and went back to his paper work. Gary refused to let the wheelchair hinder him. Maybe he couldn't go to his office in the city, but he wasn't about to give up on the law practice he had had for fifteen years. He had arranged with his partner to have all paper work sent to the house. Clients were handled over the phone and were invited to the house to discuss divorce settlements in his upstairs office. But he still longed to get back to his Manhattan office.

Well, Gary thought, sighing, that was impossible right now. As part of his rehabilitation program, he had to go to physical therapy sessions four days a week at a distant medical center.

Gary worked himself hard and amazed the doctors by his progress. His bones were mended by now, and they said he would soon be able to walk on crutches. Nothing would make him happier.

''Daddy,'' Gina said, interrupting his thoughts, ''would you hold the bag open for us?''

''Sure,'' Gary said.

He closed his briefcase. Lad, the Weimaraner puppy at his feet, jumped up from his nap, and Gray patted the puppy's smooth, silver-brown head, then unlatched the brake of his chair. He wheeled himself toward the children. ''When's Mom coming home, anyway?'' Kyle asked, obviously hungry for lunch.

''In a while,'' Gary said, looking at his watch. ''It's just noon now.''

Gina had something else on her mind as she filled the plastic bag with debris. ''Daddy, the school glee club is singing next Wednesday afternoon,'' she said. ''Can you come?''

''Oh, honey, I'm sorry,'' Gary said. ''I have therapy that day. I can't miss it.''

''It's okay,'' Gina mumbled, though it was clear she was disappointed. A moment later she looked up and asked, ''Do you mind going to the hospital so much?''

''I'd much rather jog on the beach,'' Gary said, playfully flicking the long dark braid that hung down his thirteen-year-old's back. ''But therapy helps me, and the sooner I get out of this wheelchair the better.''

Having finished cleaning up the debris, Kyle put a twist tie on the bag and carried it to the barn. Gary couldn't help smiling to see the grim expression on his son's face. Though he was barely nine, Kyle was already a go-getter who considered no job too big. God bless my kids, Gary thought. They make it so much easier.

As Kyle turned back to the house, he saw someone move past the bay window of the dining room. She stopped, and through the lace curtains Kyle made out her blond hair. He waved. She did not wave back.

''Mom's home!'' he cried, racing toward the house. Lad ran after him, barking and wagging his tail.

Gary, wondering why he hadn't heard his wife's car, wheeled himself around the side of the house. The driveway was empty. For a few moments he stared in confusion at the strip of gravel.

''Hi, honey!'' someone cried.

Gary jumped a little when an arm wrapped around him from behind and a kiss landed on top of his head. He turned so abruptly that his wife, Melanie, backed away from him.

"I'm sorry," she said. "I didn't mean to startle you."

"It's okay," Gary said. "I was lost in thought. Where's the car?"

"You wouldn't believe the trouble it's been giving me. It stalled three times this morning, and then it died completely down on Houseton Street. Nancy and I had to walk up the hill."

"I'm glad you were close to home," Gary said.

"Well," Melanie said, shrugging it off, "the station wagon's an old car. It was bound to start giving us trouble some time."

"We'll have the garage check her over," Gary said. "Tell them to do a complete overhaul. I don't want my wife driving a dangerous car."

With that, he reached out and slid his hand around Melanie's small waist, pulling her onto his lap. Before she could protest, his fingers weaved through her hair and squeezed the back of her neck. He brought her face to his and kissed her warmly.

"Love you," he said.

"I love you, Gary," Melanie replied. "Now, let me up. I'm much too heavy for you."

Gary snarled playfully but let her go. He wouldn't admit that under the weight of her body pain had shot through his legs. No less a man because of his wheelchair, Gary winked up at his wife.

"Never mind, Romeo," Melanie said, turning him around. She pushed the chair toward the ramp. "I know that look in your eyes, but I've got three hungry kids in the house and a car full of groceries down the road."

In the kitchen Melanie poured Gary a glass of beer, then steered Kyle and Gina out to help fetch the abandoned groceries. Gary grinned at his five year old, Nancy, who sat on the floor playing imaginary games with a stuffed yellow rabbit. "You've got a mustache, daddy," she said, pointing a chubby finger.

Gary erased the offending stripe of foam with the back of his hand. Then he opened his arms, and Nancy ran to him.

"I want a ride!" she squealed, wriggling onto his lap.

Gary laughed, kissing her golden curls. He wheeled the chair toward the kitchen door, into the dining room and down the hallway. Nancy laughed with delight, trying to touch each brass doorknob as they raced past. Neither Gray nor his daughter knew that were being watched by a pair of malevolent eyes. A beautiful young woman stared at them, her heart almost set aflame with desire to destroy their happiness and their lives.

On Monday Melanie dropped Nancy off at kindergarten, then headed toward the medical center with Gary. She hummed softly as she drove, enjoying the scenery.

"Long Island is so beautiful in the spring," she commented. "I'm so glad we moved here from the city."

Gary mumbled a reply, staring out the window. He was thinking how much he hated these long drives. In truth, he hated them less than the fact that he himself was not doing the driving. Melanie recognized his frustration and tried to cheer him up.

"Dr. Norton says you're doing remarkably well," she said. "Pretty soon, you'll be able to stop coming here."

"Nothing would make me happier," Gary said.

At the clinic Gary was greeted by his doctor, a middle-aged woman with a perpetually sunny disposition.

"My colleagues and I had a meeting about you this morning," she said. "We're all very impressed by the progress you've made. Looks like you'll be out of this wheelchair in a few weeks, Gary. And there isn't anything you're doing here that couldn't be done at home, under the care of a private therapist."

Gary smiled broadly and said excitedly, "When do I start?"

Dr. Norton laughed. "Next week, possibly. I know a fine therapist who is available. His name is Derek Miller, and I recommend him highly."

"Then he's the one," Gary said. "Uh, what sort of setup will it be? Does he live near Belle Bay?"

"He's from New Jersey," Dr. Norton said. "I'm sure he could find an apartment near your house."

"When we've got lots of extra bedrooms? He'd be welcome to stay with us."

"I haven't finished telling you about him," she cautioned.

"Why would I have any objections?"

"Because Derek hasn't done private work in three years," Dr. Norton said. "You see, he's a widower with a teen-age daughter. If you were to board Derek, you'd have to take in Alicen, too."

"That's okay," Gary said. "There's nothing wrong with the kid, is there?"

"No, nothing really. She's rather shy. She wouldn't be any trouble."

"I'm sure," Gary said. "Listen, I want to discuss this with Melanie before I give my final answer. But I can't see any problems."

The entire family was sitting around the dinner table that night when Gary announced his news. The children were delighted. Now their father would be able to spend more time at home. They asked dozens of questions about the therapist and his daughter. Melanie, however, remained silent. Gary looked at her, not understanding the worry in her eyes. But he decided it was best to discuss her objection in private.

Later that night, as they lay in bed, their arms entwined, Melanie told Gary of her fears. "I just don't think it's safe to bring people into this house," she confessed.

"Why not?" Gary asked. "We certainly have enough room. And if the extra housework is too much for you, we'll hire a maid."

"I can get along fine without a maid," Melanie said. "Gary, you know what I'm talking about. You know what happened last year! What if it happened again? What if . . ."

"That is over, darling." Gary said. "We promised not to talk about it, remember?"

"Perhaps we *should* talk about it," Melanie said. "Let's get the statement out in the open, Gary. Our house was haunted. And not by nice harmless ghosts flitting around in white sheets. What's our guarantee that the ghost won't come back again?"

"I just don't think it will," Gary said firmly. "You know, lightning doesn't strike the same place twice."

"Yes, it does," Melanie protested.

"What do you expect me to tell the man?" he demanded. "'You're taking this job at your own risk, Miller. We once had a ghost in our house who may come back again'?"

"Stop making fun of me," Melanie said. "I think my fears are justified."

Gary's expression softened as he bent to kiss his wife. "I'm sorry," he said. "But don't you see how much this means to me? I *hate* going to that medical center. It would be easier for me—and for you. Just look at all the time you take out of your painting just to drive me."

"That never bothered me," Melanie said.

"Look, Melanie," Gary said. "Nothing is going to happen. I want this so badly and I'll go ahead and do it in spite of your objections. But please say it's all right with you!"

His eyes were so like a little boy's that Melanie felt herself melting. She nodded slowly.

"All right," she said. "All right, do what you want. I'm just being ridiculous."

"No, you're not," Gary said. "But don't worry. Everything's going to be fine."

2

"Are they here yet?" Gary asked as he wheeled himself into the living room.

"Not yet," Melanie said. She was standing near the bay window, her slender hands resting on the back of an antique chair. Gary came up beside her.

"Are you still worried?" he asked.

"No, I've gotten used to the idea of house guests," Melanie said.

"They'll turn out fine," Gary insisted. "You'll see."

"From the looks of that rain," Melanie said, "they may not make it here today."

But just then, through the heavy downpour, they heard the sound of an engine. A few minutes later, a green Volvo came over the top of the hill and stopped in the driveway. Melanie and Gary watched as Derek Miller got out. He was wearing a raincoat with an upturned collar, which hid his face. He opened his daughter's door, and the two shared an umbrella up to the porch.

Derek was shaking the rain from his umbrella when Melanie opened the door. He looked up and smiled.

"I'm Derek Miller," he said.

"I know," Melanie answered. "Come in out of that rain, will you?"

Derek immediately introduced his daughter, then bent down to shake Gary's hand. Doctor Norton had told him about his patient, and Derek was impressed by the firmness of Gary's grip. Gary, in turn, was scrutinizing his therapist. After Derek removed his coat, Gary saw he was a well-built man of about thirty-five. The muscle lines under his cardigan told Gary he was a man who cared as much for his own body as those of his patients.

"Can I get you some coffee?" Melanie asked. "Or hot chocolate?"

"Not for me," Derek said. "Thanks."

Alicen declined with a shake of her head. Melanie folded their coats over her arm, thinking how handsome Derek was with his boyish features and dark, wavy hair. Unfortunately, none of his good looks had been passed on to his daughter. Alicen was the sorriest-looking child Melanie had ever seen with a chubby body and stringy black hair. Melanie noticed she was staring at the mirror backplate of an elaborate wall lamp that hung in the hallway.

"That's called a girandole," she said. "It's an eighteenth century antique. Isn't it lovely?"

Alicen nodded but said nothing. Gary led the group into the living room and indicated seats for everyone. Derek sat on the overstuffed burgundy-colored couch. Alicen kept her distance, choosing a huge slat-back rocking chair near the fireplace.

"You collect antiques, Mrs. VanBuren?" Derek asked.

"Oh, no," Melanie said. "Gary does. He decorated this entire house."

"Some of the furniture came with it," Gary said. "That table there, for instance. It was built around 1795, the same year as this house."

Abruptly Gary changed the subject. "How was your trip?"

"Not bad," Derek said. "It's only two hours from Englewood."

He stood up and went to the fireplace, looking at the portraits that hung over it. There was one of a blond boy and another depicting two little girls looking out a window.

"Dr. Norton said you had three children?" he asked.

"Kyle, Gina, and Nancy." Gary said, pointing to each in turn. "They're in school right now."

"Gina's your age," Melanie said to Alicen.

The little girl mumbled, "I know."

"I guess that's one reason you let me bring Alicen," Derek

said. He picked up a pewter vase and fingered its smooth rim. "Most people think she'd be in the way, even before they meet her."

"But you seem like a well-behaved girl, Alicen," Melanie said, smiling at her. Alicen had left her rocking chair and was now sitting on the window seat, watching the rain pummel the azaleas. She said nothing.

"She's a teen-ager, though," Derek said, "and that bothers people. They think she'd bring drugs into their houses or something. It's idiotic. I prefer private work, but it's impossible to get it with a kid in tow. I've been stuck in a clinic for three years."

"We like children," Melanie said, thinking it was very rude of Derek to speak that way in front of his daughter.

"Well, your call was a godsend, Mr. VanBuren," Derek said, ignoring the glare in Melanie's eyes.

"It's Gary," was the reply, "Mr. VanBuren is for clients and children. I'm hoping we'll be friends."

"After a few days of therapy with me," Derek said, laughing, "you may not want to be friends."

Alicen suddenly spoke up, in a clear voice that surprised Melanie.

"Who lives in that house down the road?" she asked, still staring out the window.

"It's empty," Melanie said. "The owner—the owner died last year."

As if to indicate she didn't wish to discuss it, Melanie stood up abruptly. "Well! How about letting me show you your rooms?"

"Sounds good," Derek said.

Gary had rigged a lift along the stairs so that he could get up and down them easily, and was quite adept at sliding himself into it. Melanie started to push the wheelchair up, as she usually did, but Derek took the handles from her.

"You're too pretty for work like this," he said, putting his suitcases on the seat.

"I've been doing it for months," Melanie said. "I'm not a weakling."

Derek agreed, but still held fast to the chair. They ascended the stairs slowly, so that Gary could keep up with them. As they walked down the hall, Derek stopped to look at the paintings that lined the walls. He saw Melanie's name on a few of them and complimented her. When he saw that the others depicted naval scenes, he asked if they had an interest in that field.

Melanie and Gary e[illegible]ces, and after a moment's hesitation, Gary said, "T[illegible] of this house was a captain in the eighteenth-ce[illegible]meday I'll tell you about him."

When they came to the last door, [illegible] it and led Derek inside. The room was [illegible] only a bed and dresser.

"We can bring other pieces down from th[illegible]" [illegible] said. "I thought it would be best to ask wha[illegible] first."

"This is just fine," Derek answered.

"Now, Alicen," Melanie said, "come across the hall an[illegible] your room."

Thinking the original furnishings had been too plain for a young girl, Melanie had added pretty yellow curtains and a white desk. There was a big bouquet of flowers on the window seat. Alicen looked around, then sat down on the bed, which was covered with a yellow and white quilt.

"Well, how do you like it, Alicen?" Melanie asked.

"It's nice," Alicen said in a soft tone.

Derek shook his head in a gesture of eternal patience, then left the room. Out in the hall he turned to Melanie and said, "You'll have to forgive my daughter's lack of enthusiasm. She's been withdrawn like that since my wife died. It's been six years, but . . ."

"Don't make excuses," Melanie said. "I promise, Alicen will get along just fine here. My children are very friendly."

Indeed, Gina lost no time in making Alicen feel at home. After dinner, she showed the girl her collection of records and stuffed animals. They sat on Gina's bed in their robes, Gina's frilly quilted one a sharp contrast to Alicen's flannel robe.

"Do you like Billy Joel?" Gina asked.

"I—I don't know any boys yet," Alicen faltered.

"I mean Billy Joel the singer!" Gina cried. Seeing the confused look on Alicen's face, she said, "Never mind. I'll play some of his records for you later. Don't you listen to the radio?"

"I like to read," Alicen replied. Thinking Gina might ridicule her for being a bookworm, she climbed from the bed and busied herself with a stuffed kangaroo.

"We have lots of books," Gina said, coming up next to her, "Come on downstairs and I'll show you our library."

"You have a library?" Alicen asked incredulously as she

... "It's got hundreds of books, ... special shelf."

... became very round when she and Gina ... Arched bookshelves decorated with carved ... ads lined three of the walls, while a fourth held ... stands for maps and atlases.

"It's beautiful," Alicen whispered.

"This is our shelf," Gina said. She stood on her tiptoes and pulled a book down. It was so huge that she had to use both hands to carry it to the brown Chesterfield sofa. She laid it down on the long table before her, and Alicen saw the title: *Collected Works of Charles Dickens*.

"Grandpa said the pictures were painted by hand," Gina said. "See the date? 1850!"

"It's just beautiful," Alicen said again.

"My favorite story is *A Christmas Carol*," Gina said. "See this picture of Scrooge? There's this guy named Mr. Percy at school who looks just like him. And he's just as mean."

"Will I get him?" Alicen asked, worried.

"I hope not," Gina said. "You'll probably be in my class. We live together, don't we?"

"Are the kids in your class nice?"

"Real nice," Gina said. "How come you look so worried?"

"I hate school," Alicen said. "All the teachers I've ever had have been mean to me."

"My teacher is nice," Gina said. "So stop worrying."

A knock on the door interrupted their conversation. Melanie poked her head in and said, "Do you know it's almost eleven? Come on up to bed."

"Let me put this book away first," Gina said.

"Well, Alicen," Melanie said, "how do you like our fancy library?"

"Oh, I love it," Alicen said, with more enthusiasm than Melanie had witnessed all day.

"You're welcome to use it any time you like," Melanie said. "If you don't find what you want, I can drive you to the library in town."

"Thanks," Alicen said.

Melanie leaned against the door as the two girls filed out of the room. She hadn't been near the public library since—well, since Gary's accident. Libraries depressed her. They reminded her of a librarian friend she'd had. But that friend had died last year, violently. And though it wasn't her fault that Janice was dead, she still felt guilt twisting at her stomach whenever she thought of her. Why? Why so much guilt?

Stop that, Melanie told herself. *It's the past. It's over!*

With memories of Janice still heavy on her mind, she went to Alicen's room. The girl was surprised to see her and jumped under covers as if ashamed of the pretty gown that hung over her fat body.

"How do you like it here so far?" Melanie asked.

"It's nice," Alicen said softly.

"I'm glad you like it," Melanie said, wanting to put her arms around the girl. But something in her manner held her back, and she simply said good night.

Alicen settled back against her pillow, all the while thinking how nice everything seemed to be. She hoped Gina would become her friend. Then, exhausted after a long day, she fell asleep immediately. Her dreams, of her mother, were sweet. Alicen was completely unaware of the woman standing over her, considering her as a pawn in a diabolical scheme.

THE LONG-AWAITED SEQUEL TO THE CLASSIC THRILLER THAT STARTED IT ALL!

PSYCHO II
by Robert Bloch

For the last 20 years, Norman Bates has been in a state hospital for the criminally insane. With the help of his psychiatrist, Norman appears to have been cured of his mother fixation, and now decides that he wants OUT. His opportunity arises when he is visited by a nun. He kills her, uses her habit as a disguise . and escapes. The psycho murders are about to start again . . .

0 552 12186 X £1.50

THE GIFT
by Madeena S. Nolan

Heidi's own childhood had been haunted by a strange power . . . to her horror, her small daughter has inherited –

THE GIFT

It began at the social club for some of the young wives of the neighbourhood – a get together for tennis and coffee.

Against her will, Heidi was persuaded to join the club. But sensing immense danger and evil, she found she could no longer hide her legacy of power – or stop the terrifying consequences of

THE GIFT

0 552 12005 7 £1.50